GENEVIEVE MORRISSEY

MARRIAGE AND HANGING

A NOVEL

PREFACE

Marriage and Hanging was inspired by, and very loosely based upon, the 1832 murder of Maria Cornell near Fall River, Massachusetts—a crime resulting in what was referred to in the popular press of the day as "the trial of the century." Sixty years later, the title was passed to the prosecution of the axe-murders of Lizzie Borden's father and stepmother, also committed in Fall River, Massachusetts.

MILLTOWN, 1832

Marriage and hanging go by destiny; matches are made in heaven.

— Robert Burton, *The Anatomy of Melancholy*

The mill for which the town had been named was a small New England sawmill, its great heavy wheel constructed on the spot by men who celebrated the first log cut there with a toast to King George, far away in England. The site was a good one for the purpose: the wooded hills all around provided the lumber, and the river that powered the wheel flowed briskly toward a fall a mile downstream and was not prone to flooding. The sawmill's owner prospered, and soon other sawmills were built nearby. When the sawmills had sawn enough of the trees, farms were established in the clearings with a small town amidst them, its straggling street of houses and shops built of boards locally cut.

The proudest work of the sawmills was a small fortress erected at the crest of a low hill overlooking the road running north of the town. Built in haste, it was intended as a deterrent to any British army that might otherwise have considered passing that way. A different

1

George—General Washington this time—was the toast of the fort's proud and weary builders, and when they had finished the work, they laid down their tools, took up their muskets, and manned it. As the fort had no cannon, when a British army did try to pass a few months later, its defenders found it more convenient to confront their enemy on the road itself. Nevertheless, when after three day's contention the British withdrew, the citizen-soldiers were proud enough of their redoubt to debate for some days whether the town should not be renamed "Fort Independence" in its honor. Eventually the idea was dropped, and the place remained simply, Milltown.

The question of a name-change was raised again early in the next century, when reference to mills began to seem an anachronism. Although the town had (modestly) prospered, it was now largely a farming village. The native forests had by then been cleared, and the crumbling remains of the last sawmill were swept away by the river when the water rose in the spring of 1799.

But the place was still a good one for a wheel, and the boats which loaded the farmers' wheat and corn at the dock at the end of the town's main street could as easily carry other cargo. In 1815, a new kind of mill was built in Milltown—one for spinning cotton thread. The farmers stayed on, of course, but with increasing irrelevance to the town's economy and by 1825, Milltown was no longer a village.

In 1832 there were six mills in Milltown, all making cotton thread or cotton cloth. When a shift at Number Four Mill let out on a frosty day in January, a hundred young ladies streamed forth, heading to the row of boardinghouses nearby, where, if they had no family in town, they were required to live. The women were as young as fifteen years old, and few were more than thirty. Their ambition was to acquire in the mills a little money, clothes, and experience of the world before returning to the farms from which, overwhelmingly, they had come. Most would afterwards marry a young man from a neighboring farm who had probably spent a few years at sea for the same purpose.

Among the young ladies who had a shift at Number Four this day was a small, dark-haired girl whose pleasantly rounded form was at a variance with her thin, sharp-chinned face. Not many passers-by would have had a chance to see that face, for she wore a calash bonnet pulled well forward, but her tidy little figure, cloak pulled tight around it, as well as the bird-like grace with which she darted through the crowds in the street attracted a few admiring glances. The girl was evidently used to such attentions, and paid them no heed.

Though sawmills no longer lined the river's edge, there was still a woodyard in Milltown, with a sawpit enclosed in a shed where some lumber for the town's immediate needs was still produced. It was to this place the young lady was heading, and she walked quickly because the woodyard was more than a mile from Number Four mill and night was falling fast. Her name was Mary Hale, and she had no need of lumber. She was going to the woodyard because, when the men who worked there had gone for the day, it was a secluded place where people could meet and talk who did not necessarily wish to be seen together. The only thing overlooking the woodyard, in fact, was Battle Hill, where the Revolutionary War fort had once stood, but the fort, like the sawmills, had largely crumbled away, and few people bothered to climb the hill now.

One who did was Josiah Woodley. He climbed because he was proud his grandfather had fought at the fort, long ago, and also because it was a lonely spot, which suited his present mood.

Josiah was the youngest and least tried of the three ministers who saw to the spiritual needs of the congregation of the largest church in

Milltown. There were those who questioned his fitness for the position. The Reverend Woodley's previous experience consisted of a single year pastoring at a small country church. But the church deacons assured doubters that, though generally quiet, Josiah was well-spoken, well-educated, and doctrinally sound, and therefore certain to do well once he had acquired a more confident air. The deacons were quick to add that furthermore, as the Woodleys were mourning the death of a baby daughter the year before, to offer them a change of scene was an act of simple Christian charity.

What the deacons did *not* mention—though everybody knew it—was that though the mill girls were required by the terms of their employment contracts to attend church regularly, the denomination in which Josiah had been ordained was losing its younger members to the Methodists and Baptists at an alarming rate. In fact, in what the deacons felt was a most un-Christian spirit of rivalry, the Methodists and Baptists offered a livelier sort of Sunday service on purpose to attract them. The deacons had some hope a younger face—handsome, but not dangerously so—and new ideas in the pulpit might counteract to some extent the enticements of Young People's Picnics, and competitive "Bible Bees."

From the hill, Josiah saw Mary Hale as she slipped in at the woodyard gate, but he gave the event little thought. His mind was on his marriage, in which something had somehow gone terribly wrong, and he had no interest in what business a mill girl had going into a deserted woodyard at such an hour.

Josiah's wife, Rachel, was at home, of course—the only fit place for a woman to be. Her company there was the "help," a farmer's daughter called Kitty, whose single qualification for a position as maid-of-all-work was that, since her father did not want her to go into the mill, she was willing to take the job. Rachel would rather have had no help at all. She was a competent cook and housekeeper, and there were—sadly—only herself and Josiah to look after. But it would have been unsuitable for her to have been alone all day and having Kitty in the house forestalled gossip. This evening, when Rachel had seen to it the preparation of supper was progressing smoothly, she sat in the gloomy front parlor, silently knitting a stocking while the last rays of day faded from the room.

Josiah had no idea how he and his wife had grown so apart from one another, but Rachel knew. She knew it was simply and completely that he had failed her, both as a husband and as a minister of God. Their baby girl, born in pain as babies are, lived only long enough to learn what it was to suffer, and her death had left Josiah as broken as Rachel, and at a loss for fit words to strengthen and reassure her. There were a great many comforts Rachel needed to hear—as that little Lucy was safe in the bosom of her God, where they would all one day be happily reunited; and perhaps—putting God aside for a moment—that time was a better medicine for a heart broken as hers was than any the doctor could bring in his bag. Josiah might have been stern and warned her God was assaying their faith, and it must not be found wanting, even in the face of so crushing a blow as they had suffered. All these were things which, though Rachel knew them already, she needed to be reminded of again and again.

But instead, when she cried, he had cried with her, as hurt and lost as she was, and scarcely able to murmur so much as, "Thy will be done, O Lord" by way of a prayer. Instead of reminding her of her duty, as the weaker vessel of Grace, to submit humbly to the inscrutable ordinances of heaven, he seemed to wonder at them himself.

Even when the room was completely dark, Rachel sat on in the parlor, needles clicking softly, lips moving faintly as she counted her stitches, struggling against acknowledging a secret wish that instead of her husband, someone very *like* Josiah, only strong and confident in himself and with strong and confident comforts to offer her, would come in at the door wanting supper.

Someone like the Reverend Dr. Conrad, perhaps.

Dr. Conrad, the oldest of the three ministers of the Milltown church, was reading to his wife. He had intended to go out for a walk, but when Mrs. Conrad, seeing him putting on his coat, expressed a wish that he read her letters for her instead, he had immediately put aside all other considerations and done so. He was devoted to his wife, who was an invalid.

Sophronia Conrad's health had been ruined in the bearing and rearing of six children, two of whom died before they learned to walk. The four remaining children grew up with the idea their frail mother might at any time be taken from them, but Sophronia, though a humble and patient sufferer, was a determined woman. She had lived in spite of all, and three of her children were now well started in life. Even her last son was nearly grown and, to her joy, spoke of entering at the seminary where his father had once studied. Sophronia was devout and never questioned God's will, but had she done so, Rachel was certain Dr. Conrad would have, lovingly but firmly, applied the necessary correction.

An hour passed, and whomever Mary Hale had gone to the woodyard to meet had failed her. It was dark when she left there, walking back toward the mills and her boarding house, where she was sure of a scolding for staying out late. Though she had been in Milltown for nearly six months, she had no friends yet upon whom she could depend to cover for her. She showed less haste going back than she had in coming, and pushed back her bonnet as if to tell the world she did not care who saw her now.

Josiah, meanwhile, had also started home. The church where he preached lay on his way, and he stopped by his study there to add a few lines that had come to him for the sermon on which he had been working in the afternoon. As he came down the church steps, Mary Hale passed by. He did not connect her with the dark figure at the woodyard, but he knew who she was, and started at recognizing her. When he saw she knew him as well, he flushed and turned away, and rather than falling in with her, started off in another direction.

Avoiding Mary made him late for supper, but Rachel did not ask for any explanation. The two of them spoke pleasantly to each other over the meal, and Josiah was particularly pleased at one point to make his wife laugh. Except for the hurt look in Rachel's eyes, grown habitual over the preceding months, anyone might have imagined all was well between them.

Sophronia Conrad kept early hours, and by the time the letters were read and talked over, it was time for her supper to be brought on a tray so she could be put to bed. It was also too late for Dr. Conrad to go out, as he acknowledged to himself after a discreet check of his watch. Instead, he sat reading until the clock struck ten, and then, after writing a few brief notes and tucking them into his coat pocket, he went to his own room, which was far enough from his wife's that he need not fear to disturb her.

By eleven o'clock, the town was quiet. All the farmers and most of the town's citizens were asleep. The few workers at Number Four in the late hours were not girls, but men, whose job it was to see that the machinery was serviced and ready to go again in the morning. Number Four mill was still powered by a vertical shaft rather than, as in the most up-to-date mills, having belt-driven machinery, and as the gears could not be precisely made, they wore quickly and needed almost daily maintenance. The mill girls themselves were clever at repairing their spinning machines on the fly—they were paid by the number of spindles of thread they produced, and a broken spinner brought them nothing at all—but the mechanics saw to it as many as possible were serviceable when the first shift arrived in the early morning.

Mary Hale, in the bed she shared at her boardinghouse, lay awake, staring blindly into the dark, surrounded by the deep and peaceful breathing of girls who worked hard and slept well.

The Woodleys lay as far apart as their narrow bed permitted, with Rachel turned on her side, her back to her husband. Josiah made tentative overtures to his wife, shyly suggesting if she were cold, she could lie nearer him and be warmed, but Rachel responded that she didn't feel cold, and suggested an extra blanket for him if he did. Then she waited for him to say—half-hoped he would say—that the situation was one in which, as duly married persons, he had a right and she had a Duty.

When he did not, however, she decided that it was better so. She wanted no more little Lucys to break her heart again. Both Woodleys then lay still, pretending to be asleep, until they were asleep in fact.

CHAPTER ONE

"I believe there is nothing in the world so quickly undone as a woman's work," Mrs. Tudge murmured, breaking in on Rachel's thoughts next evening. "You probably spent half the day ordering the parlor and arranging the tea tray, and within five minutes the men have pulled the chairs about, slopped the cloth, smeared the cups and spoons, and left nothing of all your bread and butter but greasy crumbs, which they will now proceed to tread into the carpet. I dread these Sunday teas, don't you?"

Rachel managed a smile, although she did not like the suggestion her parlor required half a day's labor before it was fit for guests to see. "Preaching is hungry work, I suppose," she answered instead, with false cheer. "The men must be fed somehow. But if you dislike this way so much, we could find another, I suppose."

Replied Mrs. Tudge quickly, "Oh, no. How could we? Tea before evening service has been the custom here since—*forever*, I think. And men are like children and hate for anything to change, particularly with regard to their food. Just look at them! The reverend gentlemen have their *spiritual* eyes fixed on heaven, of course; but their fleshly ones have fastened on that cake."

Mrs. Tudge's tendency to disparage all males was one of the things

Rachel liked least about her. She found it difficult enough to keep it continually in mind that even a man like the Reverend Mr. Tudge was her spiritual better without being continually reminded by his wife that he was also selfish and a bore.

"How are your little boys, Mrs. Tudge?" she asked politely.

Mrs. Tudge was not ready to change the topic. "You baked it yourself, didn't you? The cake, I mean," she continued, eying the tea-board in a way that seemed to imply it looked wrong. "I'm sure that gawky girl in the kitchen can't be trusted so far. I know her family, you know. They take their meat on their knives—yes, they do!—and think cake is effete. It's always pie with them—morn, midday, and night. Buy cake of the baker's instead. It's nearly as cheap, and men don't care what they eat so long as it's plenty."

"Kitty is coming along well," Rachel said. "I did make the cake, but I think another time I would trust Kitty to do it."

"Oh, as you have no children to look after, I suppose you have plenty of time to bake. Oh, I'm terribly sorry! How very thoughtless of me to say that! We are all so very sorry for your loss."

Rachel could not immediately answer. After a minute, she asked again, "Your boys are well, I hope?"

"Oh, perfectly; thank you for asking. And you'll soon have a little Comforter sent you, God willing, for them to play with."

Rachel cast about for something else to say, lest silence tempt Mrs. Tudge to offer further consolation.

"Cake, Deacon Birdwell?" she offered—and then had to look away to avoid seeing Mrs. Tudge's arch smile when the men all surged at once toward the table.

Through talking with Mrs. Tudge and loading the gentlemen's plates (Mrs. Tudge did not take cake), Rachel missed some of the

men's conversation, but had no trouble picking up the thread of it
again. Since the Reverend Mr. Tudge was holding forth on a topic
about which he felt deeply enough to make his pronouncements in his
ringing "pulpit voice," she could easily guess the subject was either the
Frailty of Women, or the Methodists, both of which notably annoyed
Mr. Tudge.

"Perhaps the Methodists are sent by God as a spur to our efforts,"
Dr. Conrad said smiling, "lest we become flabby in His service, and
make a poor sermon one Sunday."

Rachel was pleased that Josiah laughed at this sally.

Mr. Tudge, on the other hand, frowned. "Any man who would
flag in his efforts though every last citizen of this Republic were in
his proper pew on every Sabbath of the year ought to be a farmer,
instead," he declared. "We stand, every one of us, AT THE EDGE OF
THE ABYSS. HELL yawns before us, and if I can frame a sermon to
make a sinner see that sitting in church is not enough, but he must put
out his hand and seize the LIFELINE OF GRACE and be drawn back
from the brink, I must do it."

"It's interesting to hear you put it like that," Dr. Conrad replied,
after brief consideration. "I believe you were with me last July when
Mr. Henry said much the same thing."

Mr. Henry was one of the Methodist clergy. Rachel stifled a smile.

"Did he?" Mr. Tudge asked, eyes wide. "I don't recall it. After two
hours of listening to that mush of bad grammar and doctrinal error I
put my thoughts elsewhere. I'm surprised you could stomach it."

"What is this?" Josiah cried, interest piqued. "Am I to understand
you go on reconnaissance behind Methodist lines, Mr. Tudge?"

"One of their camp meetings," the Reverend Tudge said, his upper
lip curling. "I let Dr. Conrad persuade me once to go, but never again,

I promise you! Sleep half the day, if one can; preach half the night, if the torch-smoke doesn't choke one; and every meal a squalid affair termed a Love-Feast, at which (since all provisions are placed on the tables in common—an unspeakable practice—) one is privileged to watch as the nicest bits make their way round and round the gaping maw of the dirty fellow opposite. Meanwhile, one tries to wash down enough of something which may or may not be wheat bread—sour, and half cinders—with dirty river water to keep up one's strength sufficient to last the next round of sleeping, preaching, and 'feasting.' Mrs. Tudge sent me off with a nice roast chicken for my part, and I didn't get a taste of it."

His wife allowed Rachel to observe the meaning smile she hid behind her hand.

"I've never seen a camp meeting. Are they common here?" Josiah asked. Dr. Conrad would clearly have little trouble persuading him, if he next invited Josiah to go.

"Once a year," Dr. Conrad told him. "There's a place across the river where they're usually held, not too near any town. They frequently draw very large crowds—five or six thousand or more. Mr. Tudge doesn't approve, but we don't discourage members of our congregation from attending, if anyone wants to go. Grace is occasionally stumbled upon in unlikely places."

"Grace is the thing you are least likely to meet with at a camp meeting," said Mr. Tudge. "But if you are looking for the Tempter and all his SORDID HOST, you need only walk five steps beyond the fire's light where the Jezebels of six towns keep up a regular trade, and you will surely find him there."

Mrs. Tudge asked sharply, "Did *you* meet the Tempter, Mr. Tudge? You didn't mention it."

"I did not, Mrs. Tudge," he assured her.

"Then that's a pity," Dr. Conrad said cheerfully. "For God has said, 'Blessed is the man that endureth temptation: For when he is tried, he shall receive the crown of life.' But you may go again next summer, if you like, and hope to get your crown then."

Mr. Tudge stared as though he did not entirely understand the remarks, before proceeding to share at length his thoughts on the subject of the Crown of Life.

Dr. Conrad frequently found, or made, opportunities to speak aside to Rachel, a habit that touched her heart, since she would otherwise have no one to speak to but Mrs. Tudge. Now he took the opportunity to say quietly, "You and Mr. Woodley seem to have settled in well. You have made this room quite comfortable. How long have you been here? Let's see... This is January. It must be three or four months now, mustn't it?"

"Three months, yes."

"And are you quite recovered?" He must have seen Rachel hesitate, for he explained gently, "I was referring to your bodily health. It will take longer for your heart to mend, I know."

The state of Rachel's heart was expressed in her dress of unrelieved black. Black did not suit her russet hair or pale complexion, but Rachel would wear nothing else. "My health is good," she said. "And Josiah has gotten past being uncomfortable at preaching to so large a congregation and enjoys the variety of life here."

"Do you?"

As he said this, Dr. Conrad laid his hand gently upon Rachel's.

Rachel experienced no urge to reject the comforting touch. "I don't see so much of it, I suppose. There's more to buy here, certainly. But home matters are the same, and though I see more faces on the streets,

I don't think my circle of acquaintance here is any larger than it was in New Seabury. I think where we live doesn't make as much difference to me as it does to Josiah."

"That's what it is to be a woman," Mrs. Tudge put in, nodding vigorously. "For us, life in the biggest city is only to be distinguished from life on the most isolated farm by the availability of stylish bonnets." After a moment's reflection, she added, "Although on a farm, one doesn't really need a stylish bonnet anyway."

"Your wife is better, I hope, Doctor?" Rachel asked, finally withdrawing her hand from under Dr. Conrad's.

"My wife is much the same," he answered gravely. "And we are thankful she is no worse."

At that moment, the Reverend Mr. Tudge's remarks reached a climax.

"Let them go in their DOZENS. Let them go in their HUNDREDS," he cried, rocking up on his toes. "If they will only attend at a church that will preach a LAX CREED, I, for one, can endure that they shall not attend at mine. We know 'strait is the gate and narrow the way that leadeth unto life.' It is only my DUTY TO GOD to say so plainly."

The men's conversation had evidently swung round to the Methodists again.

Dr. Conrad explained to Rachel, "Mr. Tudge doesn't like to say it, but his soul is troubled that our fellow toilers in the vineyard have made conversions amongst our people."

"Mill workers," Mr. Tudge put in. "Looking for Sunday Schools and 'fellowship' instead of salvation. And hymns set to dance tunes. The dancing itself will be instituted next, no doubt."

"I think fellowship a reasonable thing to expect to find at church," Deacon Birdwell blurted, and then looked startled and ashamed to hear his own voice. The attending deacons customarily formed an admiring audience to the minister's conversation and were not expected to participate.

The Reverend Mr. Tudge eyed the embarrassed deacon scornfully. Turning coolly away, he continued, "The trouble with young people today is they want nothing to do with the *hard* truths of faith. They simply will not hear of sacrifice, or of works, or of the fire that is to come. 'God is love' is the only text they like. They don't want to be told they should eschew sin, only that their sins will be forgiven them. And if the Methodists are more willing to give them what they want than we are, then"—he abruptly resumed his pulpit inflection—"TO THE METHODISTS THEY WILL GO."

"But 'God is love' is not false doctrine, is it?" Josiah asked quietly. "The mill girls, most of them, are so very young. It's natural they would find the fearful truths of religion less attractive than the Lord's gentler words. Perhaps it was for them that He spoke those words."

Mr. Tudge drew back as though astonished; then affected a smile.

"I can see you have a tender heart, Mr. Woodley," he said. "But the difficulty with a tender heart is that the heart is not the organ with which one reasons, but the one that circulates the blood. If you let it be too tender, it may not send the blood to the brain in quantities sufficient to stimulate clear thought."

Rachel went hot with fury at the remark—and even more so at her husband's not taking offense at it. Was he so blind as not to detect he had been addressed disrespectfully? Or was he simply not man enough to defend himself?

Josiah replied calmly, "Rather than lose them in a body, I think it would be consistent with duty to provide Sunday Schools."

"Oh, for the ones who can't read, perhaps," Mr. Tudge replied—offhand, as though upon reflection he cared little about the matter one way or the other. "Although I think when a mill girl shall have learned to recognize the words 'Blessed are the *meek,*' her education may be held to be sufficiently advanced. They're a saucy lot, most of them."

Dr. Conrad may have observed that Mrs. Woodley's supply of meekness was being badly taxed. "As there are three of us," he said quickly, "you may preach the strait gate, Tudge, and Woodley and I will make soft Methodisty sermons for the mill girls. What is your text for tonight, by the way?"

Mr. Tudge allowed himself to be distracted.

*

As if in continuation of the earlier discussion, the Reverend Tudge's sermon that evening, though it began hopefully enough with "Rebuke me not in Thy wrath," dilated much thereafter upon the pains of hell. Rachel, of course, had noticed a certain fixation upon "the hard truths of faith" in Mr. Tudge's preaching before, but since teatime the propensity had become excessive.

Struggling, as she and Josiah walked home from church, to find words to both express and yet also conceal the extent of her irritation, she cautiously ventured, "I didn't quite like the way Mr. Tudge spoke to you this evening at tea, Josiah. I think you were right in what you said about the mill girls and by what sort of doctrine they could be won. If Mr. Tudge feels called to preach another way, then he must do so, I suppose; but I don't think he ought to judge you for your way." Hastily, she added, "Though I may be wrong to say so, of course."

"Why wrong?" Josiah asked. "You're entitled to your opinion." Taking his wife's hand, he drew it through his arm. "I took no offense at Mr. Tudge."

Rachel pulled away. "You *never* take offense."

To her frustration, Josiah replied to this thrust with, "Thank you."

"I think you might properly have said something in your own defense," she cried, "and not left it to Dr. Conrad to change the topic! Though it was kind of him to do it."

"Very kind."

"I think at least at evening service," Rachel went on, "Mr. Tudge might speak more reassuringly. I know he only means to warn the young people away from sin, but it isn't the young people who come in the evenings. It's the old folks, mostly, and they're wanting to be helped to make their peace with God, not be frightened with hell fire. They're past the age of much sinning."

Josiah said grimly, "You'd be surprised."

Rachel blushed for her sudden, keen desire to hear more on this interesting topic.

"Tudge is a Godly man, of course, and a fine scholar," continued her husband, "but I'm afraid his anxiety after his eternal home and the company of God's elect make him impatient with us poor sinners. Unless"—he smiled down at Rachel—"you think it's his digestion that's at fault. My father used to say sweet words couldn't be expected from a man with a sour stomach."

Refusing to be drawn in by this—or any—attempt at humor, Rachel didn't reply.

"Do you remember Mary Hale?" Josiah asked abruptly, as they turned the last corner toward home. "From Seabury church?"

"Hale? No. I don't remember any family of that name."

"Not a family, just the one young lady. Her people were at Bristol."

Something registered in Rachel's mind. "The one who'd been read out of Bristol congregation for—for *lewdness*? Goodness! What made you think of *her*?"

Josiah flushed. "I saw her on the street Friday, and heard today she's living here now. She's got work in one of the mills."

"There are enough of her kind here already," Rachel retorted crossly. "Mr. Tudge will have to preach harder than ever to counteract the likes of Miss Hale."

"Yes. Although I don't like to speak too unkindly of her. The young man in the case wasn't read out of the congregation, though he was as guilty as she. And anyway, it was never proved against either of them that they did more than take a buggy ride. It was foolish and unseemly, but I'm not sure it was really a sin."

"A buggy ride *alone*, with a stop on the road at a tavern, where they were seen taking wine!" scoffed Rachel. "At what point *does* one call it sin, then?"

"Oh, no, you're right, of course," Josiah hastily conceded. "But, on the other hand, having been read out of the congregation at Bristol and then made unwelcome at Seabury, Miss Hale's joined the Methodists here, it seems. That's one defection our Reverend Mr. Tudge can't blame on the devil. We as much as sent her to them."

"Unwelcome?" Rachel repeated, her jaw tightening. "Why, of course we welcomed her at Seabury! Or, some did, anyway," she amended. "Anyway, if Miss Hale had been truly repentant, wouldn't she have borne more patiently with reproof? I think the Methodists ought to be warned about her."

"About her character, do you mean?"

"Yes. I think you ought to warn them. You got to know her well in Seabury, didn't you?"

"No, not well," said Josiah uncomfortably. The Woodleys were at their own door by now, which Josiah opened, standing aside to let Rachel enter first. "She came by my study now and then with a question. Relating to doctrine, I mean. I thought Miss Hale...light-minded, perhaps, but sincere in her religion." He helped his wife off with her cloak. "Come and warm yourself in the kitchen before we go up."

Rachel understood this was an invitation to closeness and more conversation. Uncertain of her feelings, she temporized. "Oh, the fire's long out."

"Come and see," urged Josiah.

Rachel allowed herself to be persuaded.

Unfortunately, once in the kitchen, the two found that Kitty had apparently forgotten she had been instructed to leave a brick in the oven on cold Sunday nights, or that the ashes in the firebox must, *without fail*, be shaken down. Not only was there no hot brick waiting to warm the cold bed upstairs, but ash blew over Josiah's good clothes when he opened the oven door to look for one.

The day had neither been fine, nor spent in congenial company, and had ended with a sermon not calculated to remind Rachel of her duty to deal with her fellows in a spirit of loving kindness. Her mood was unforgiving. Shivering, she pronounced (in a style somewhat recalling Mr. Tudge), "I think the Methodists ought to be warned they have a viper in their bosoms."

Her husband looked away. "Viper" must have seemed too strong a term for a tiny woman like Mary Hale. "Maybe she means to make a clean breast of things and stay out of trouble here."

"Maybe she does. But if you only warn them and she behaves herself, what harm to anybody? Whereas if you say nothing—! But— do as you think best, of course."

"I'll speak to Mr. Henry," Josiah agreed.

CHAPTER TWO

Here and there, in shaded spots, patches of white remained on the hills, but though it was January, the ground for the most part lay bare of snow, though last summer's grass, long since trampled flat, was hard frozen. The booted feet of the men coming early to the woodyard to work left no track behind them.

The first man to arrive on a Friday in mid-January had his head down and his hat pulled low against the cold. He reported afterward that, intent on getting into the shed to light the stove, he noticed nothing out of place in the yard. His two young assistants came in shortly after, flushed and laughing. They had met on the road coming up and raced each other the last hundred yards to the saw pit, their breaths white before them. Having reached it together, they continued their horseplay for a few moments, chasing each other around the pit and shouting, until called to order by the woodyard's owner stepping in at the door.

"What are you about, boys? What is this you've done?" this gentleman asked irritably—or words to that effect (no one could recall them exactly after). It took a moment of everyone answering at cross purposes to establish it was not the running and capering to which he referred.

The four of them, the young men still panting from their games, all crowded at the shed door to look where the woodyard owner pointed out the thing which had caught his eye.

Silhouetted against the rising sun, a shape like a sack hung from an upper log of the higher of the two piles of undressed logs in the yard. As the men looked, squinting against the light, a breath of wind caught the shape, which moved and turned slightly. Something like a feather appeared to be stuck in the top.

"Looks almost like—" one of the young men began, and then stopped. His eye caught the eye of his friend, whose open mouth suddenly closed into a grim line, and they both looked again at the sack.

The woodyard's owner was nearsighted.

"Well, whatever it is, take it down at once," he said firmly, turning away and hastening toward the welcoming stove.

None was quite willing to go alone, but after nervous glances between them—but nothing said aloud—all three of the young men moved together toward the log pile.

The body of a young woman hung there, her back to the yard and her face to Battle Hill.

Though her face, set and white, was somewhat distorted, the men all thought her a pretty little thing; slight; with thin cheeks, and a delicately pointed chin. Her eyes, almost closed, were encircled by long lashes, and where her calash had fallen back, its jaunty feather jutting skyward, it revealed untidy dark curls over her forehead. Under her brown cloak, one arm was drawn up toward her bosom while the other hung limply at her side. She wore no gloves. The men's eyes were drawn to a lady's pocketbook laying on a log protruding from the pile at about the level of the woman's knees, which were slightly bent. The toes of her boots rested lightly on the frozen ground.

Although he must have known in his heart she was dead, the bravest of the three men pulled off a mitten and laid the back of his hand against her cheek. After a further hesitation, he tried gently to lift her chin with one finger, to get a better look at the rope around her neck, but as all three of the men reported after, the girl's whole body moved as he did so, being quite stiff. The young man looked up to where the rope was looped over the projecting log, reaching out his hand to grasp it as he did so.

His friend caught his arm and pulled him away. "Best not," he murmured.

The three went back to the shed then to give their news, and dispersed soon after. One went to the sheriff and another for a doctor, while the woodlot owner went home to fetch his wife and any other women of character and mature years who could be persuaded to come. The matter was not something he felt could decently be dealt with by men. The fourth man stayed behind to warn away intruders. He stationed himself near the woodyard gate and occasionally glanced nervously over his shoulder at the slight, still form that, from time to time, moved gently with the breeze.

The sheriff was first to arrive, in company with the boy sent to fetch him.

Before going to the body, he stopped to question the man at the gate as to what he had observed of the scene—which was very little. He was a nervous fellow—and had a look around the yard himself to see whether any evidence of someone arriving with a girl and leaving without her could be discovered. The only tracks discernable on the frozen ground were those of the woodyard workers, which were faint, and he concluded a step as light as a woman's would never be seen there. Behind the shed a narrow cart was kept that the workers customarily used to move lumber about, and the sheriff directed the boy who had brought him to bring it around to the wood stack. As that moment, the young man who had been sent for the doctor returned with the news that this gentleman would come as soon as he could. The boy pushed the cart to the place the sheriff directed as the two other woodyard workers withdrew a short distance, and, heads together, discussed the situation in muted tones.

Over the next half hour, they were joined where they stood by a dozen other townsfolk who had somehow gotten wind of the news, and having nothing better to do with their time, came straggling in to see for themselves. One of them thought he recognized the calash and cloak and offered a name.

Hearing it, the sheriff called out, "You know this girl? Come and have a look at her face and tell me if you can say for sure."

Perceiving the fellow's reluctance, the sheriff grimaced and became impatient. "Come on then, you," he said, gesturing sharply to the boy who had brought up the cart. "Bring that wagon up close."

The sheriff bent and put his arms around the girl's waist and lifted the body while the woodyard boy, stepping gingerly up on a convenient log, slipped the rope from where it was tied above her, and then the two men together laid her as gently as they could on the cart. The head lolled weirdly as they did so, and the young worker turned away at the sight, looking sick. Seeing him, the sheriff scraped together a handful of straw from the cart bed and thrust it beneath the broken neck for support.

Once the girl had been laid in the cart, the man who had ventured a name for her came to the cart's side, though he could hardly bring himself to do more than glance at the dead face. "It's Mary Hale," he said, turning quickly away. "She's been at the Sunday School with me."

A vigorous but rather elderly woman came up then, several other women trailing behind.

The sheriff turned back the youngest. To the older women he growled, "I reckon you know what to do. Take her into the shed there. Doctor'll be right along." As the women—refusing male assistance—rolled the cart away, he gestured impatiently in the direction of the gawking bystanders.

"This is an *inquest*, not a show," he informed them. "Unless you got evidence to give, get along home."

Not a man moved toward the gate in response to this suggestion, to the sheriff's visible disgust.

The doctor arrived some moments later, puffing with exertion. His profession notwithstanding, he had difficulty persuading the women in the shed to let him in.

"Madam, I am the *coroner!*" he was heard pleading—to no avail. The women had already done all they considered necessary in the case, having smoothed the dead girl's clothes and hair, closed her eyes, and, with their fingers, gently composed her features into an approximation of peaceful sleep. Almost incidentally, they had also determined there were no marks of violence on Mary Hale's body, and that she was between four and five months pregnant.

All of this had been accomplished without outraging the girl's modesty to the extent of removing even a single item of her clothing, and it soon became clear that the worthy matrons' greatest fear was that the doctor would not be so considerate. It required the sheriff's direct intervention to get the medical man admitted to the shed.

Townspeople, alerted by the young woman the sheriff had turned away, continued to gather. They joined the woodyard men, who had not yet been given leave to go, and importuned them for information. Though the sheriff, with mounting annoyance, repeatedly urged them to move on, the curious bystanders served some purpose in the end. One knew Mary Hale well enough to know she worked at Number Four mill. Glad to get rid of one idle gawker, at least, the sheriff sent him to find her boarding house, if he could.

"And bring up her effects," he ordered.

CHAPTER THREE

I t seemed to Rachel the only one of Kitty's duties for which the girl demonstrated any zeal was that of carrying the basket when they went marketing. She dawdled through any sort of housework, only hurrying when sounds in the street outside suggested there might be visitors. Kitty was lonely, Rachel supposed. She came from a large farm family with a wide acquaintance. The Woodley house was too quiet for her.

Rachel could not, of course, befriend her maid, however lonely the girl—or herself. But for Kitty's sake, Rachel was careful not to buy everything she needed at one time, so that marketing was a chore which recurred throughout the week. Kitty often met with a friend or two along the way, and though Rachel told herself she personally did not care for idle tattle, she felt it was no sin for her to feign five minutes' interest in some item if Kitty's friends had gossip to share.

Mrs. Tudge was too refined a lady for gossip as well, of course. Luckily for her, the sad fate of Mary Hale—with which Agnes Tudge was bursting—fell into the category of *news*. It was not news for young ears, however. When she met Rachel a few hours after the sheriff's inquest concluded, Mrs. Tudge made sure to pull her out of Kitty's earshot before beginning her remarks on the topic, prefacing them with, "Mrs. Woodley, you know I *never* gossip. I abhor gossip. But have you heard the *dreadful* thing that has happened?"

Rachel had heard nothing, which pleased Mrs. Tudge immensely.

"The *most* dreadful thing," she said, rolling her eyes expressively. "A young girl, a mill hand, was found hanged from a log at the woodyard this morning! Have you ever heard the *like* of it? Not anyone *we're* likely to know, of course, but dreadful, nonetheless. I had it from a man who saw the whole thing himself. He went up for a bit of plank to mend a door, he says, and was there all morning, for the sheriff held the inquest upon the spot. It was a clear case of self-murder, it seems, for she was five months gone." This last news came in a whisper, after a quick look around to where Kitty and Mrs. Tudge's housekeeper were chatting together.

Rachel expressed appropriate horror and pity, to which Mrs. Tudge nodded vigorous agreement.

"'Tis a crime *I* should not like to have to answer for at the Judgment Seat," she said. "And to have damned the child, as well! These girls are beyond anything in the way they go on, aren't they? There's hardly a year goes by that one, at least, doesn't break her contract and go home—or go *somewhere*—in a great hurry. And now this! Some of these girls are beyond the reach of a mere Sunday sermon, you know. What *they* require is a complete reformation—under compulsion, if necessary."

Kitty, meanwhile, was inquiring in a low tone of her friend, "So who was the fellow, then? Does anyone know?"

Mrs. Tudge's housekeeper shook her head. "Keep smiling, dear," she advised. "Your missus is looking this way. No, nobody knows who he was. At least, not now they don't. But her bandbox was brought up and looked at, and there was letters in it that'll likely tell the story. She was five months along, or so I heard."

"Poor little thing. And are her people far away?"

"Bristol. She was a Bristol girl."

"Will they come and take the body home then, do you think? If it was me, I don't think I'd like to be laid among strangers."

The housekeeper shook her head. "Oh no, dear; they won't be allowed. It's a crime for the girl to have hung herself, the same as if she'd hung somebody else. She had to be buried on the spot where she done it, once the doctor was finished with her. Well anyway, not exactly on the spot, because the man who owns the woodyard wouldn't have it. He made a great fuss, and in the end she was put just outside the fence. As if a rail fence could keep out a spirit, if it meant to haunt the place where it passed over! From now on, don't expect to find *me* anywhere around the woodyard after dark!"

Kitty nodded her agreement with this resolve. Neither of them was likely to have business at the woodyard in any case.

Continued the housekeeper, "The sheriff made the men who was idling about watching dig the grave, and the ground was froze so hard they all had to take turns to get it done."

"Well, let's hope she's gone on to a better place now, poor thing," sighed Kitty.

The housekeeper replied with feeling, "A better place than Number Four? I think *that* likely, no matter which way she went!"

Mrs. Tudge said to Rachel, "I suppose the whole ugly story *will* get around, though I'm sorry for it. But people do so love to gossip. I *abhor* gossip. It's iniquitous. But I thought you should hear the news. It's better to *know* what's true than to rely on rumors and rumormongers for one's information."

29

"Yes. Thank you. I'm sorry for it too, but I'm certain you're right it's likely to be much talked of. Good day to you, then."

"And a good day to you. The girl was a Methodist, by the way. *That* tells a story, doesn't it? Next we'll probably discover the young *man* in the case was a Sunday School fellow."

"Oh, I hope not. Good day to you."

Mrs. Tudge relentlessly continued. "It's Dr. Conrad's turn to preach next Sunday. I wonder what text he'll choose? 'Woe to her that is filthy and polluted,' perhaps. Something of that nature. 'Woe to her...' I think that would be *very* suitable, don't you? I think I shall ask Mr. Tudge to suggest it."

Rachel's face began to burn. "I'm sure Dr. Conrad has encountered such situations before," she said faintly. "He'll know what to say. Good day to you, Mrs. Tudge."

"Good day, good day. I wonder if he will tell Mrs. Conrad the news? It might be too much for her... Oh, here is Mrs. Birdwell! I wonder whether she has heard? Mrs. Birdwell, good day to you."

While Rachel completed her business, she heard Mrs. Tudge explaining in a low tone to Deacon Birdwell's wife how she abhorred gossip.

The shopkeeper weighed in with a sigh, "Poor little Mary. I hope it wasn't one of our Milltown boys was to blame. Like I teach my girls, 'men are ever false deceivers.'"

"You knew the young lady, then?" Rachel asked, gathering her purchases awkwardly in her arms, for Kitty, still deep in conversation with Mrs. Tudge's housekeeper, had the basket.

The shopkeeper nodded. "Mary Hale," she said.

Rachel's breath left her in a rush.

"A nice girl, I thought," the shopkeeper continued. "Quiet. Mind you, there were stories about her—but I won't say anything of that now. Like I teach my girls, 'Speak no ill of the dead.' Even the dead who might have had a bit of a loose character, if you understand me."

Rachel blinked, dumbstruck until Kitty touched her arm.

"I'll take them things, ma'am," offered Kitty, her tone solicitous. She was pleased to see Rachel troubled over the fate of a poor mill girl. But for her father's prejudices against the work, Kitty might have been a mill girl herself.

*

To Rachel's relief, Josiah came home early, at an hour when Kitty was busy with supper in the kitchen. By meeting her husband at the door, she had time for a private word with him.

"You've heard the news, I suppose," she said immediately, scanning his face. "I can see you have. So shocking! Or yet, perhaps not—to those of us who knew her. Was it the boy in Bristol, do you think? No, it couldn't have been, could it? It's been some time since she lived at Bristol."

Josiah looked tired.

"I assume you mean the news that Mary Hale was found hanged at the woodyard this morning," he said as he put his coat on its accustomed peg. "That's as much as I know. I have had a letter from my sister, Rachel. I think I shall have to go to her."

Rachel was taken aback by the abrupt change of topic. "Is something the matter with her? This is very sudden."

From an inner pocket, Josiah produced what was clearly a letter but did not offer it to her. "Yes, it is sudden. I'm sorry. She writes that her husband is very ill, and she wants me to come to them. She fears William may not survive."

Rachel considered for a moment. "I suppose if you are wanted, you must go," she reluctantly conceded. "Poor Anne! It's not your week to preach, so the church can spare you. Tomorrow is Saturday… Is there a coach on Saturday? Or will you wait for Monday?"

"I can't wait for the stagecoach at all," Josiah said. "I'll take the ferry across tonight, hire a horse and ride to Providence. I shall have to travel on a Sunday, but it can't be helped. I can be at the farm by Monday, I think, if I leave now."

"Now?" Rachel asked, her voice rising. "But you need your supper."

"No, I'm not hungry," Josiah said positively. "I'll go up and get a few things together and then be off. I've just time to make the ferry if I hurry."

He started for the stairs, leaving Rachel gaping.

"Josiah, wait," she said, starting after him.

He stopped.

"May I see the letter?"

She thought he hesitated before handing it to her.

As she read, Josiah's quick footsteps sounded in the chamber above. He was certainly in a hurry to oblige his sister. He was down before she finished reading.

"I don't understand." Refolding the paper and laying it on Josiah's outstretched hand she said, "Anne only writes they would like your prayers. She says nothing of you coming to them."

Josiah had brought down a small traveling bag and a worn old cloak, which he proceeded to pull on. Rachel was struck again by how weary he looked. His eyes were circled with shadow.

"Not in so many words, perhaps," he agreed. "But I know Anne wants me there. It's implied. I won't be gone long." He moved toward the door. "I'm sorry to give you so little warning."

"Oh, if you must, go, then. My love to Anne. Tell her they have my prayers as well."

"Of course. Goodbye. God be with you."

Helplessly, Rachel said, "I think you might at least eat something before you go, Josiah!"

"I've no time. I'll send you word from my sister's. I'm sorry." He stood silently for a moment, staring at the floor. "It's on my conscience, Rachel," he finally said.

At the last it occurred to Rachel to offer her cheek, at least, to be kissed.

As the door closed behind him, Kitty came into the hall and found Rachel there alone.

"Should I wait supper then?" she asked, with evident surprise. "I come out because I thought I heard Mr. Woodley in the house, but I guess he isn't come yet after all."

Rachel replied stiffly, "Yes, he's come. He's been in and gone back out, in fact. Mr. Woodley has been called away for a few days."

"Oh," said Kitty blankly. It took the girl a few moments to digest this unexpected turn of events. "Shall I... Shall I take his plate away, then, Mrs. Woodley? Reverend Woodley's plate, I mean."

Rachel's eyes widened as it came to her that she had never before in her life eaten a meal alone.

"Yes," she said, swallowing. "Do."

CHAPTER FOUR

In the preceding months, Rachel had unexpectedly caught herself thinking from time to time her life might be…easier, perhaps more pleasant, even…if Josiah were not so continually present in it. Not that she did not, she always hastily added to herself, *cherish* her husband as a wife ought. And Josiah was not obtrusive. Still, there he always was. Rachel felt would rather, sometimes, be alone.

Her solitary supper made her reconsider. Josiah's conversation, though characterized by a relentless, unfeeling cheer, was better than a meal silent as a deathwatch, with nothing but the loudly ticking clock for company. Nevertheless, she stayed at the table as long as she decently could, then lingered over washing up the supper things for dread of the moment when she would have to climb a staircase grown strangely longer and darker since the night before to the empty bedchamber above. When the time came, she bid a sleepy Kitty tremulous goodnight, and, once upstairs, knelt at her bedside to recite her evening prayers between furtive, darting glances into the room's shadowy corners.

Even with a hot brick to warm her, the bed was cold. Toward morning Rachel rolled unconsciously onto Josiah's place, where the chill of his untouched sheets and pillow shocked her instantly awake. Blankly, she looked for her husband, and then, recalling he was gone, lay back down. For the previous several months Rachel had been nursing a growing irritation that in no matter what position she began the night, by morning her husband was often spooned intimately against her back. Now, as she hugged her knees to her chest for warmth, it suddenly came to her that the posture *might* have sometimes resulted from an inadvertent, heat-seeking attempt of her own rather than some devious machination on Josiah's part. Unable to fall asleep again, Rachel got up wearily and remade the bed with the extra blanket she had previously recommended to her husband.

It was still so early that breakfast was not near being ready. In fact, Kitty—still in her nightdress—was only beginning to lay the fire. To pass the time until the kettle boiled, Rachel wrote a letter to Josiah's sister Anne, but all the consolations she could think to offer took only three-quarters of an hour to compose, and then she had nothing to do but sit with her hands folded and wait for tea to appear.

The morning seemed interminable, but thankfully in the afternoon visitors appeared. In the parlor, Rachel received deacons' wives, who sipped tea, inquired politely as to the state of her health, and angled to discover Josiah's whereabouts. Each caller sat out the customary quarter hour, and when they found they could get no information, moved on. Kitty had a visitor in the kitchen, a former neighbor, who stayed so long Rachel was still catching snatches of the two girls' stifled laughter and conversation as she ate her solitary supper. Between bites, Rachel wondered whether, rather than a grave lowering of her standards, it could possibly be regarded as an act of charity on her part if she were to go straight into the kitchen—*her* kitchen, she reminded herself—and engage the young people in kindly discourse. Kitty and her friend were, after all, at a time of life when they might gain a great deal of benefit by exposure to a good example and Godly advice.

But a lady did not make a friend of a servant, so—sighing—Rachel resisted this impulse to sociability.

She resisted several further impulses of the same kind the next day as well, through an afternoon which dragged on interminably, and yet somehow still brought suppertime too soon.

"It'll be the end of the beef tonight, Mrs. Woodley," Kitty announced, to the relief of Rachel, who had just been wondering how she had escaped noticing before that she loathed cold beef. Without Josiah at home to eat up a man's share, a single beef roast seemed to supply as abundantly as the basket of Loaves and Fishes. "I thought I might as well cut it all. It don't look like keeping another day."

Rachel, loitering at the dining room threshold, steeling herself to enter the room, didn't answer this. Kitty, misinterpreting Rachel's silence, was nervously attempting to fill it with some remark about the mustard pot when Rachel blurted, "Oh, don't bother about the dining table for tonight!"

Seizing the plate—the lonely, solitary plate—that Kitty had just laid for her, Rachel made for the kitchen door.

"It's ridiculous for you to sit alone on that side of the door and me on this," she said over her shoulder. "And if I join you in the kitchen, it'll save a candle, as well. You won't mind me, I hope?"

Kitty, astonished, scrambled after her mistress.

"Oh, no, I don't mind you at all, Mrs. Woodley," she gasped. "Only…" With a guilty look, Kitty hurried to snatch up the tablecloth, and throwing open the back door, leaned out to shake it vigorously over the wood pile, letting in a blast of cold air that perceptibly chilled the room.

Returning, she said quickly, "Just let me make it nice, now," and attempted to arrange the supper things in such a way as to make the dishes cover the worst of the spots on the cloth. "I won't be a minute about it," she babbled. "It's only that I don't usually bother with china plates and all when it's only me here."

It was Rachel's turned to be astonished. "But if not from a plate, how do you eat, then?"

"Oh, from the pot's good enough if it's only me in here," Kitty replied. "And it saves on washing, after."

Rachel felt she ought to be distressed by the admission, but found she was amused instead. "Let me set the table, then, and you see to the broth. You aren't in the habit of dispensing with spoons and forks and lapping the sauce from the pan like a greedy dog, are you? When it's 'only you here'?"

"Oh, no, I'd never do that, Mrs. Woodley," said Kitty, scandalized. "I'd burn my tongue!"

Once the two had sat down, an awkward silence ensued. Rachel, feeling the weight of her responsibility as initiator of the extraordinary state of affairs, cast about in her mind for something to break it. "Are you—are you lonely here, when you eat alone, Kitty?" she finally managed.

"Oh, I was at first," Kitty replied, helping herself to mashed turnip. "I never ate a whole meal alone before I was here—nor slept alone in a bed. I couldn't sleep at first. I kept waking up, all night long."

As recently as the day before, Rachel might not have understood this.

"Before I was married," she admitted, "I always slept with my sister. She cried on my wedding morn, and said the bed would seem empty without me." With a prick of guilt, she added, "I wasn't very sympathetic, I'm afraid."

"Oh, she likely got used to it quick enough," Kitty replied comfortingly. "Like I'm used to it now."

As she spoke, Kitty half-raised her knife to her lips, a chunk of meat speared on its tip. Catching Rachel's eye, she flushed guiltily, and gently replaced the bite on her plate.

"What was the news from your friend today, Kitty?" Rachel asked quickly, looking away. "I couldn't help but hear Mary Hale's name mentioned."

Kitty stared for a moment at her plate. "Oh," she faltered, "it's just…you know. It's just people do talk so. Some of the millworkers are wanting the sheriff to hold another inquest is all."

"Another inquest?"

"They say they don't think she done it to herself. Hung herself. They think someone else done it."

Rachel considered how direct a question she could decently ask a young girl.

"Had she…reason to despond?" she ventured. "To be so unhappy as to want to end her life? What I mean is, was she in any sort of trouble, do you think?"

"Oh, nothing but only that she'd a baby on the way," Kitty said, beginning to eat again, this time with her fork. "And no husband. Poor little thing can't be let rest, I guess. They dug her up again today."

Apparently, less circumlocution would be necessary in discussing the matter with Kitty than Rachel had imagined. "Exhumed her body? Whatever for?"

"It's the millworkers who wanted it," Kitty repeated. "So's it could be proved she didn't hang herself. She's stone dead either way, but if somebody hung her instead of she hung herself, she can be put in the churchyard, maybe."

Rachel had not previously considered this aspect of Mary's case. Even someone hanged for a serious crime might be permitted Christian burial afterward, provided he had convincingly repented of his deed, but since no one could know whether self-murderers had, in their last seconds, repented or not, their unmarked graves were dug in unhallowed ground.

"I understand the concern of her friends, then," she said.

Supper, endless alone, was quickly over with company; the dishes washed, and the kitchen set in order. Kitty, it turned out, worked quickly when she had a companion, her tongue keeping pace with her hands.

A glance at the clock still showed at least an hour to fill before Rachel could decently go to bed.

Knotted buttons were a recent fashion, and Rachel had heard Kitty admiring a friend's. Desperate for some time filler that was neither praying nor knitting, Rachel asked, "Would you like to learn to knot buttons?"

Kitty's face lit up. "Oh, wouldn't I just! Do you know how? I never would have guessed you did!"

How many other things about her would Kitty "never have guessed," Rachel wondered? She had once been accounted a fine dancer.

The two talked as they worked, Rachel about knotting buttons, and Kitty about the life histories and personal affairs of several of the town's leading citizens. Like Mrs. Tudge, Rachel abhorred gossip, and if she allowed Kitty to continue several of her tales past the point they could be called anything else, Rachel told herself it was only for the sake of humoring the girl. Seeing what close attention her mistress paid to her stories soon put Kitty so much at ease that both women were astonished to hear the clock strike ten.

"My, where did the evening go?" Kitty exclaimed, jumping up. "Did you want a brick, Mrs. Woodley? I forgot all about it until now." The stove had been out for hours. Rachel knew she had no chance whatever at a hot brick tonight. "I don't think I need one," she said, not wanting to embarrass the hapless Kitty. "It doesn't seem so cold tonight."

*

The knock at the door was not loud, but seemed insistent. Rachel, stopped halfway up the staircase by the sound, absentmindedly almost called aloud for Josiah. It was not unheard of for someone to call in the night wanting Josiah to come and pray with the dying, but since she was alone in the house—or nearly alone—would it be enough merely to say through the door that the minister was not available, or must she open to whoever was outside?

The second knock was much more urgent, and Rachel started nervously back down. As she reached for the knob, it occurred to her the door was, in fact, unlocked. Josiah had seen to the locking up every night of their married life, and with him gone, she had not thought to do it herself. She quivered—then told herself her visitor must be well-intentioned, since he hadn't tried the door himself.

"Who is there, please?" she called, annoyed that her voice shook. She was relieved to be informed her caller was the sheriff. Though Rachel did not know him, she reassured herself that surely a sheriff would be an honest man, if anybody was. She opened the door, half hiding herself behind it.

With the sheriff were two other men, and before she could speak, all three crowded into the hall without waiting to be invited. The sheriff addressed her politely, asking for Josiah. The other two, Rachel observed with distaste, peered past her into the darkness and even up the stairs in what she regarded as an insolent manner.

"I'm sorry," she said, disconcerted but determined to be polite. "Mr. Woodley is not here. He was called away suddenly by an illness in his family."

One of the men moved past Rachel to the door of the front parlor. "You don't mind if I look for myself?" he asked. Before Rachel had time to retort that she *did* mind—very much—he did look.

The sheriff spoke up. "I'm sorry to bother you, but it's important we find your husband, Mrs. Woodley. You positive he's not here?"

"Why should you doubt me?" Rachel asked, stiffening. "If you are in need of— of— spiritual assistance, I think Mr. Tudge or Dr. Conrad—"

The sheriff cut her off. "It's another kind of assistance I require, ma'am. I got some questions I want to put to your husband as to what he knows about the murder of Miss Mary Hale, late of Bristol."

Murder? Rachel raised her candle higher and looked from one man's face to another. Her heart began to beat hard. "Was it not self-murder? Miss Hale hanged herself."

Her surprise must have seemed genuine to the men, for the faces of all three softened at her tone. "It was self-murder," she repeated.

In the sheriff's grave face, Rachel believed she read an accusation, and the candle suddenly wobbled in her grasp.

Taking the candlestick from her, the sheriff abruptly seized Rachel's arm and firmly steered her to the front sitting room sofa, where he gestured to her to sit. The other two men lingered by the door, turning their hats uncertainly in their hands.

"What did your husband tell you about the Hale girl?" the sheriff asked. "Your husband, now. Not the town gossips. What did he say?"

Rachel shook her head. "Nothing. Or, almost nothing. Only that she had been found hanged at the woodlot. He said only that much before showing me a letter he had from his sister asking him to come to her. And then he went."

"To his—sister?"

The sheriff's faint hesitation before he pronounced the word "sister" infuriated Rachel. Nostrils flaring, she affirmed coldly, "Yes." She added, with a noticeable edge of contempt, "I don't believe either of us spoke further of *Miss Hale*. Why should we?"

The sheriff, meanwhile, continued to study her, even moving the candle closer to see her face more clearly. Rachel turned away uncomfortably, fearing he might detect the fact that she had not really felt at the time that Anne's letter constituted a summons.

"Have you got that letter?"

"No. I read it, and then gave it back to Jo—to my husband."

"Tell me where he's gone," the sheriff demanded. "No, don't bother to write it." (Rachel had started for her writing box.) "Just tell me the place."

Rachel did, and the men took their leave. One muttered apologies for the lateness of the hour.

On trembling legs, Rachel started up the stairs again, telling herself as she did so that—the sheriff's wicked insinuations notwithstanding— her faith in her husband was absolute.

Halfway up, she recalled Josiah saying, "It's on my conscience," and stopped, confused.

He could not have been speaking of Mary Hale's death, she told herself quickly. Why should Josiah's conscience trouble him on Mary Hale's behalf? The girl was nothing to him. He'd never seen her in his life save from the safe distance of the pulpit.

From the pulpit—and when Miss Hale had visited his office at the Seabury church.

She'd come to him several times with questions. Josiah had admitted as much himself. Rachel frowned, suddenly wondering exactly how long (and private) a visit was necessary for her husband to answer a query about faith or doctrine. Preoccupied first with her pregnancy and then with her loss, she hadn't kept close track of her husband's comings and goings in New Seabury. Josiah went to his office every day. How much of his time there was spent writing sermons, and how much in giving…counsel? And to whom?

Once in bed, Rachel lay awake for hours, trembling with cold—and fear.

*

Since she heard nothing further from the sheriff for two days, Rachel was half able to convince herself she had no genuine reason to think her husband was in difficulty. The men who'd come in the night had asked nothing more than to speak to him, and the likeliest reason for anyone to want to speak with Josiah about Mary Hale was because he'd been acquainted with the girl in Seabury in his professional capacity, and therefore might have information relating to her earlier life, or people. While the sun shone, Rachel could think of several plausible reasons for the sheriff to have come to Josiah for information at an hour when her husband could reasonably have been expected to be peaceably abed.

But nights were another matter, and as soon as Rachel lay down, her mind raced.

On the third morning, a stranger brought a brief note from the sheriff informing her that her husband, having been intercepted "on his way," had agreed to return to Milltown. The sheriff did not specify where he thought Josiah had been on his way *to* when apprehended, which Rachel read as a slur on her honesty. The note further indicated that Josiah was presently lodged "near Town Hall," a periphrasis intended, Rachel supposed, as a palliative. The jail was "near Town Hall."

The note ended with a terse sentence telling her to stay home.

Left to herself, Rachel would have gone to the jail at once. However, she was not in the habit of disobeying direct commands from men of legitimate authority, so instead she paced the parlor, mentally debating what *other* man of authority—a man whose advice might be more to her liking—she could consult as to the proper course of action in the circumstances.

A clatter from the kitchen startled her from her musing. Kitty was beginning to make the midday dinner. The people of Milltown had regular habits. In another hour, all the men whose counsel she might seek would be sitting down to dinners of their own. Her opportunity was now, or two hours from now, Rachel thought—and she did not see how she could survive another two hours passively waiting.

Instantly, she started toward the hallstand. Her hand already extended toward her long, black cloak, she called, "Stop what you're doing and put on your bonnet, Kitty. We are going to the church this minute!"

CHAPTER FIVE

"**M**adam, do you want to help your husband?" Mr. Tudge demanded—rhetorically, surely, Rachel thought, for she had already said at least ten times she did.

Her gaze humbly lowered and resisting an urge to scream, Rachel nodded. She had not merely hoped, but actually prayed all the way to the church that it be Dr. Conrad and not the Reverend Mr. Tudge whom she found there, but God ordered otherwise. Apparently, He also ordered she be reminded of her duty to submit to the will of heaven, for Mr. Tudge, inferring what had brought her, began lecturing her on the subject as soon as she crossed the threshold of his office. After a quarter of an hour, he gave no signs he would be concluding his remarks on the topic anytime soon. Mr. Tudge was extremely positive in his manner, a characteristic Rachel usually found reassuring but now for the first time in her life believed could be carried to excess.

"YOUR PLACE, Mrs. Woodley," Mr. Tudge summed up— eventually—"is at home. At home, and upon your knees. A woman's sphere is the home. Go to the earthly one Mr. Woodley has supplied to you and solicit the beneficence of your heavenly Master in the one above. The prayers of women, so long as they are truly 'DISCREET, CHASTE, KEEPERS AT HOME, good, obedient to their own husbands' are surely heard." He added, aside, "Second epistle of Paul to Titus, verse five."

"Yes, sir."

"I think I may command your obedience," Mr. Tudge continued, "since I am speaking *as* a husband, although not, of course, as yours. Return to your sphere, woman, and LET MEN DO men's work in men's sphere."

Before Rachel could reply to this, the minister said in a more ordinary tone, "I have already promised you Mr. Woodley will be supplied with counsel and whatever else he has need of, and we will add our prayers to yours, of course."

"I do thank you," Rachel said hesitantly. "But—perhaps if I knew what charges have been laid against my husband..." It was the third attempt she had made to ask the question, and the first she had been able to come near enough finishing to be understood.

Drawing a great breath, Mr. Tudge pulled himself up as though in outrage, ready to sermonize her further; then apparently decided on second thought it was reasonable enough for her to want to know, and deflated. "The charge, I'm sorry to report, is a serious one," he said, looking away. "Murder in the first degree."

"Miss Mary Hale's murder?"

Mr. Tudge looked at Rachel with astonishment. "Mr. Woodley *told* you about her?"

It was evident he had already assumed any connection between Josiah and Mary must have been an improper one.

"Indeed, yes," she said, speaking as strongly as she dared. (Mr. Tudge detested strong speech from a female.) "Miss Hale attended at our church in Seabury. She was not made a member because she had been read out of the Bristol church for...lewd behavior"—Rachel's cheeks flamed at the admission—"but she appeared to be repentant, and Josiah and I were hopeful of her. It appears we were mistaken in our expectations."

Mr. Tudge considered. After a moment he said, "I did not know this of Miss Hale. It puts the matter in another light, to some extent."

Seeing her chance, Rachel said eagerly, "I shouldn't like for Miss Hale to be defamed, of course, but shouldn't the sheriff or someone be informed as to her character, then?"

Mr. Tudge brushed the suggestion aside. "Oh, I'm sure Mr. Woodley's counsel will do what's needed. I have in mind a cousin of mine for the office of your husband's advocate. He's young, but promising—and we must all begin somewhere, of course. Being young, he will make up in energy what he lacks in experience."

Rachel felt her mouth tighten. "Whatever his energy, perhaps for a young lawyer to 'begin' in his career against a charge of murder—"

"Oh, I don't believe my cousin will raise any objection to the charge. He will naturally wish to oblige a man in my position."

"Of course. But—"

"No, no, don't trouble to thank me, Mrs. Woodley," the minister interrupted blithely, extending one hand in a self-deprecating manner while discreetly checking his pocket watch with the other. "Consider the matter settled. My cousin is the very man for the job—faultlessly devout, and very discreet."

Though he rose as if to dismiss her, Rachel, her head lowered, remained as she was. "I *have* heard it said that expertise and long experience in the law are of more use in a courtroom than religious orthodoxy," she murmured.

"A good woman's appeal to heaven, Mrs. Woodley, is of more use than either," Mr. Tudge retorted, putting just enough emphasis on the word "good" to make his point clear.

She would gain nothing further, Rachel saw, from the Reverend Mr. Tudge. Rising herself, she said, "I thank you, sir. Please do what you can for my husband."

Kitty had waited for her in the hall, and for decency's sake, the door to Mr. Tudge's study was left open, of course. It added to Rachel's misery that the girl had undoubtedly heard everything. Kitty made no comment however, until, as they left the church, Rachel turned left, toward home.

Kitty had already started to the right. "Oh," the girl exclaimed, scurrying back to Rachel's side when she saw her mistake. "Are we not going there, then?"

"Going where?" Rachel asked, her head down, trying not to meet the eye of anyone in the street.

"Why—to the—the—the place where Reverend Woodley is. You know."

"To the jail?" Rachel responded in a whisper. "Did you not hear? I am bidden go home and pray, and I will. As never before. I beg you will do the same."

"Oh, surely," Kitty said faintly.

She drew a breath as though to say more. Rachel was grateful she did not.

*

Kitty had lived seventeen—nearly eighteen—winters, which constituted, in her opinion, a wide experience of the world and its creatures. Based on this thoroughgoing conversance with human nature, she had concluded soon after meeting her that Mrs. Woodley was a self-contained type of woman; chilly, devout, submissive, and rather inclined to be particular about unimportant little things, like dust and flies. This assessment served Kitty well—particularly in regard to the dust and flies, with which Kitty had no personal quarrel. But it did not prepare her for the experience of tiptoeing uncertainly up the stairs at midday with the news that a late dinner was ready, and in fact, a bit overdone, and finding Rachel sitting in a heap on the floor beside her bed, sobbing as though her heart had broken. For a moment, Kitty was struck quite dumb by the sight.

"Oh, missus," she cried, running to her mistress and, after only a brief hesitation, dropping down on the floor beside her, putting her arms around Rachel's shoulders and drawing her in. "It's not so bad as that!"

Though "the missus" seemed taken aback by the gesture, she made no noticeable effort to pull away, so Kitty eagerly continued to offer comfort. She said earnestly, "You know what the Reverend Tudge told you, about how all of us will be praying and all. That's bound to help, isn't it?" Snatching the handkerchief from Rachel's hand, she mopped her wet cheeks with it—futilely, for the handkerchief was sopping. "And Mr. Woodley never done what they're saying he done. We all know that." After brief consideration, Kitty added, "I mean, the ones that *know* him know it. Know he didn't. And we won't bother about the ones that *don't*, will we?"

Rachel sobbed harder.

"The sheriff will see he's made a mistake soon," Kitty continued, "and then Mr. Woodley will be set free. Don't you think so? *I* do."

"Oh, I don't know, I don't know," moaned Rachel, distractedly. "Why should anyone believe for a moment Josiah could have done such a thing? He's such a good man. Anyone can see that. He has his faults, of course. He's so... That is, we all have our faults. But to imagine he could have done such a thing as to...hurt...a young girl! I don't understand it. I *can't* understand it!"

"No, because it can't be true," Kitty said, rocking Rachel gently and patting her back. Recalling it was a minister's wife to whom she spoke, she piously added, "It's most likely only one of those trials that's sent us now and then to test our faith, don't you think? I'm sure that's what it is. And what with all of us praying and trusting in the Lord, He'll see we *do* have faith, and then Mr. Woodley will be let go. But it might take a few days yet and more praying."

A long, ragged inhalation was Rachel's only reply.

"Do you want us to pray together?" Kitty asked. "What I mean is, you could *say* the prayers because I know you know how better than I do, but I would keep my heart lifted unto the Lord and all and join in at the 'amen.' I've been praying all morning, as I said I would—but only just while I was making the dinner, and not on my knees. Prayers are better if you make them on your knees." The girl abruptly stopped talking and her eyes went wide. Dinner had been in no very good condition when she left it, and was likely not becoming more eatable while she was upstairs.

On second thought, Kitty resolved not to mention dinner, and resumed her rocking and patting.

After a few moments, Rachel said dully, "It's no good. I can't pray." She sat up straight and turned her head away. Closing her eyes, she added, "I've been trying to pray for hours—for days—and nothing comes. If my faith is being tried, it will indeed be found wanting. All I see is blackness whichever way I turn. Anyway, I've been tried enough already, I think. Let heaven try someone else for a change."

Kitty knew about the Woodley's dead child and understood that this loss was to what Rachel referred.

"Well, I have wondered from time to time why everybody's faith isn't tried all the same," Kitty said. "I mean, I know God has His reasons, but I don't know what they are, so I can't say. Or maybe it *is* someone else's faith being tried, and Mr. Woodley is just a— a— you know; a what-you-may-call-it."

"A bystander, do you mean?"

"Maybe. Does that mean a person who's just got mixed into something by accident? I could go visit Mr. Woodley and see what I could find out, if you like. And maybe take him some dinner. They're awfully mean about what the men in the jail is given for their dinners."

Startled, Rachel turned to look at Kitty. "Are they?" she asked. "What do you know about it?"

Explained Kitty, with perfect cheer, "I took my brothers their dinners every day when they was in jail. They'd near have starved to death if I hadn't. Pa said I oughtn't, and being a little hungry wouldn't hurt them, and they'd learn their lesson better for it, but Ma wanted me to."

"How did they come to be in…"

"Jail?"

"Yes. Was it a serious charge? If I may ask."

"No, not very serious. Only just that they got awful drunk. And broke a window. Well, shot it out, is what they done. But they didn't mean to, and they didn't know anybody was to home when they done it. They might have got off for a fine, only Father wouldn't pay it. He said he didn't need them around the farm that time of year, and it would do them good to be locked up, and save him thrashing them. It was just Election Day," she added. In Kitty's mind, Election Day—

falling, as it did, in cider season—justified high spirits.

Rachel looked at the floor while she mulled over the suggestion.

"It's one of the taverns makes the food for the jail prisoners, and the town pays for it," Kitty explained meanwhile. "The rougher the food, the more the taverner makes, so you can bet he don't give large measures. But you should come and have *your* dinner, at least. You need to keep up your strength." The girl was becoming desperate. The mutton, tough to begin with, would soon be beyond saving.

"I don't think I want anything," Rachel murmured, adding uncertainly, "Wouldn't it be wrong for me to ask you to do something I don't dare to do myself, Kitty? I would like to know that Mr. Woodley had enough to eat, but I can't send you alone. It wouldn't be proper for you to go alone to such a place."

"It wouldn't be wrong if I don't mind doing it," Kitty said quickly, jumping to her feet. "You just come down and have a bite, now," she urged. "I'll see to Reverend Woodley, just like he was one of my own brothers."

Rachel resisted a little more, but Kitty, feeling less timid with "the mistress" now than formerly, was gently insistent.

"I'll see to it all," she repeated several times. "You just eat a bite."

But by the time she ate her "bite," Rachel had reconsidered. Willing or not, Kitty could not be sent on an errand to the town jail as though it were one of the shops. The place itself was an ordinary building, sturdy but ugly, with one room plus a lean-to at the back downstairs and three tiny cells up, and except that it was rather cold in winter, it was not unwholesome. But it was not a place for a lady.

When she said as much to Kitty, the girl complained. Indicating the basket into which she'd loaded the least-burnt parts of the mutton and a great deal of buttered bread, she said, "Now don't go saying I can't go just when I got everything wrapped up nice to take. There's no one at the jail will bother me. If anybody's in the cells but Mr. Woodley, it'll only just be somebody got drunk or in a fight or something like that. You don't need to worry I can't take care of myself, because I can."

"I promised your parents I'd look after you." Rachel's lower lip trembled. "What would they say if they knew I'd let you go to such a place unaccompanied?" Rachel turned aside and began to cry again. "What will they say when they hear what Josiah has been accused of?" she sobbed. "Oh, for shame alone I should send you home at once."

"As if they'd believe it," Kitty scoffed. "Anyway, they don't want me back at home, and that's a fact. My little sister won't learn anything about keeping house if I'm there already knowing how. You just don't worry anymore, Mrs. Woodley, and let me find out what I can about Mr. Woodley, all right? And don't cry. I'm not the least bit afraid."

Kitty soon discovered Mrs. Woodley was (in a ladylike way), as stubborn as she was herself. Since Kitty refused to yield, after further debate—first with Kitty, and then with herself—and further worried consideration of Josiah's state of want, Rachel concluded the only answer was for the two of them to go to the jail together. "I don't know what I will say to Mr. Tudge if he should come to hear of it," she sighed, adjusting her bonnet to rest as far forward on her head as it would go, and putting a veil to it.

"Oh, *him*," sneered Kitty, tying her own bonnet strings. "Well, let's just not fash ourselves over what *he* would think."

As soon as the words were out of her mouth, Kitty recognized that with this remark, she had gone too far. Whatever the circumstances—

and the circumstances were that neither woman liked nor respected Mr. Tudge—one did not *ever* speak slightingly of a minister of The Word. She stopped where she was, braced for a strong rebuke.

But Rachel, distracted with wondering by what words a good wife was expected to cheer her imprisoned spouse, said only, "Let's not dawdle, but get this over with, Kitty. Oh, where are my gloves?"

CHAPTER SIX

The sheriff was clearly appalled at Rachel's boldness in daring to appear before him in defiance of his note saying she should not, and only Kitty's rather saucy challenge ("Look here, we got rights, see?") convinced Rachel to persist in her nerveless demands she be allowed to meet with and bring food to her husband. But when at length she was allowed upstairs after all, she felt suddenly stronger. Her position was that of a wife again. A wife need not make decisions, but only do as she was bid.

She was reassured to see Josiah looked in jail much as he had when she had last seen him in his own home, drawn and low in spirits but perfectly calm, for she was certain at the least sign of fear in him, her own would overwhelm her. His cell had no chair and Josiah was sitting on the edge of the bed, a wooden frame with a thin shuck mattress, not very clean. He was dressed as he had been when he had left her, even to his cloak, for the jail was cold. He was so deep in thought that when his wife appeared he first started, and then stared as if he didn't know her before jumping up to rush eagerly to the barred door.

"I don't know whether I should be here or not," Rachel admitted faintly, reaching for the hands he stretched out to her. After brief thought, she put her cheek to the bars for Josiah to kiss. As she did so, she saw that the sheriff had followed far enough up the stairs to be able to keep watch on them. Kitty noticed the sheriff, too, and stepped boldly in front of the doorway, effectively blocking his view with her skirts. The sheriff audibly snorted, and remained where he was.

Josiah seemed at a loss. "Are you well, Mrs. Woodley?"

His formality irritated Rachel. Her husband could hardly be expecting an affirmative answer, she thought. Not answering, she turned and gestured Kitty forward with the basket. "We brought you food."

The basket itself was, of course, too large to pass through the bars, and Kitty, fumbling with excitement, passed its contents piecemeal to Josiah, who did not conceal his relief and pleasure.

"This will keep me for days," he said, smiling. "I'm sure no one in Milltown makes better bread than you do, Rachel."

At the word "bread," something stirred in the bed of the cell adjoining, and as the three of them looked, a dirty head, eyes wide, poked out from under the blanket. Rachel recoiled, while Kitty and Josiah exchanged glances. At a nod from Josiah, Kitty (with visible disgust) offered a buttered slice to the apparition, who stretched out a dirty palm to receive it, ate it in two or three bites, and afterward withdrew, turtle-fashion, beneath the blanket again.

"Mr. Brown makes an ideal jail mate," Josiah said loudly, putting an arm through the bars and attempting to embrace his wife in a reassuring manner. "He's very quiet himself, but doesn't mind how much I talk." In a lower tone, he added, "As a matter of fact, I think he's rather deaf."

Rachel whispered, shuddering, "His head is absolutely crawling."

"Yes. Lice are one of the least pleasant aspects of this place—aside from missing you, of course. As you can see, I've moved my bed as far from his as it can be made to go. I'm keeping the vermin at bay so far, I think—but only just."

Until then, Rachel had been so overcome with shame and fear that she had noticed neither Josiah's bed nor anything else, but now she forced herself to look around.

"You've no place to wash," she observed.

"No."

"And the light is terrible. Your sight will be ruined."

"No lamps or candles permitted, unfortunately, for fear of the bedclothes taking fire. Longer days will soon be with us, though."

Rachel met his eyes with surprise. "Are you expecting to be here to see them? Will you not be released soon?"

Josiah gave one longing glance at the sky visible through the high window opposite where they stood, then forced himself to look back at her.

"Not very soon," he said. "I need to be given a chance to put together my case, for one thing. And there's some discussion as to whether twelve men in Milltown can be assembled as jurors who haven't already formed an opinion as to my guilt. If not, the trial might have to be held elsewhere. That would delay things."

Rachel went cold, but tried for Josiah's sake (and that of the listening sheriff) to speak out firmly. "What opinion can anyone have but that you have been wrongly detained? No one who knows you can possibly think you have anything to do with Miss Hale's death. This is all absurd."

Josiah seemed heartened by her tone. He even managed a smile. "I'll be given a chance to prove that. Now tell me the news from home. Are you well?"

But when she spoke of home matters, Rachel had a sense her husband could hardly follow her. Doubtless his own situation obsessed his mind. After a few sentences, she dropped the topic and cast about for something to say relating to his case instead.

"You know Mr. Tudge has undertaken to find you counsel?" Josiah made a wry face. "I've had a note from him to that effect. The gesture is—kindly meant, I'm sure."

Until that moment, Rachel had been trying to stifle her own doubts on the matter; but seeing Josiah had some, too, she suggested quickly, "You might decline it."

"I'm not presently in a position to decline any help I'm offered."

Behind Rachel, the sheriff cleared his throat with meaning.

His grip on her hand tightening, Josiah said, "You'll have to go now, I'm afraid."

"So soon? But I've only just come!" Desperation seized her. "I can't just sit at home and wait, Josiah," she said, speaking rapidly and clutching nervously at his arm with her free hand. "What am I to do? Quickly, now: Before I go, tell me what I need to do."

"Why, what you think best," replied Josiah, with evident surprise. "Your judgment is such as may be relied upon."

Rachel saw no compliment to herself in the remark. She only thought angrily that it was like Josiah to shirk his natural responsibility to direct his wife.

The sheriff had come all the way up the stairs by now. Pushing past Kitty, who tried to block him with her body, he stepped up behind Rachel and touched her shoulder.

Rachel shook him off. "Don't abandon me, Josiah," she cried. "I need your guidance! *Tell me what to do.*"

Josiah looked confused. "Well, what do you feel you *can* do?"

"Nothing!" Rachel cried. "And yet—I must do *something*. Tell me what. Tell me what is best, Josiah."

The sheriff seized her elbow. "Come on, now," he said irritably. "Time's up."

"A moment, please, sheriff," Josiah begged. To Rachel, he said, "Bring me something warm to wear, perhaps. Or if you don't like to bring it yourself, send it with Dr. Conrad."

"Dr. Conrad?"

"Yes, he'll do it. He sent word he would come tomorrow. And— write my sister, won't you? Ask after William."

"Of course I've already done *that*," answered Rachel crossly. Letter writing was a woman's natural purview. "But—should I come again? Or should I stay away? I don't know what is right. Should I ask Dr. Conrad to act for me?"

The sheriff tugged at her elbow again; harder this time.

"Just one minute more," she begged, clinging on determinedly to her husband. "Should I come, Josiah? At least tell me whether I should come here again."

"You should not," the sheriff interposed firmly. "Jail's no place for a lady. Especially a lady don't know when it's time to leave."

"Don't you put your hands on her like that," Kitty cried indignantly, squeezing between Rachel and the sheriff. "Here, come take my arm, Mrs. Woodley. Don't worry, Reverend Woodley. I'll look after her."

"Josiah, *please!*" Rachel begged.

"I don't know how to answer that," Josiah said distractedly. "Come if you think you can bear it. Please, Sheriff! A moment, please. My wife is discomposed."

For a short time, all was confusion, with even Josiah's reclusive jail mate registering muffled support—or else complaints at the uproar—from under his blanket. Rachel, frightened and bewildered, refused to leave without instructions from Josiah, while the sheriff was determined to make her go. Kitty and Josiah together competed to reassure Rachel and fend off the sheriff. As both of them had hold of Rachel's person, Josiah holding tightly to her hand and Kitty with an arm twined protectively around her waist, the sheriff was at a disadvantage. As much as he wanted Rachel to go, it was clear he did not care to drag a preacher's wife bodily down a flight of stairs.

It fell to Josiah to break the stalemate finally by abruptly letting go of his wife's hand and folding his own before him, intoning solemnly as he did so, "Let us pray!"

The gesture caught them all up short—the sheriff most of all.

Grumpily agreeing to grant time enough for a damn *short* prayer, he withdrew to the doorway, where he stood glaring down the stairwell with his back to the room. He grunted rudely when, with the flair for drama (though not the physical grace) of a performer upon the stage, Kitty plumped down upon her knees and bowed her head piously over hands tightly folded at her waist. The scene had its ridiculous aspects, but Rachel felt no urge to laugh.

After collecting himself for a moment, Josiah began firmly, "Heavenly Father—"

Rachel started. Unless from the pulpit at church, it was not her husband's custom to pray aloud. As he did not close his eyes, but looked directly into hers, she realized he was talking less to God than to her. "Bless my dear wife," Josiah continued, speaking not loudly, but slowly and audibly enough that the sheriff would not need to approach nearer to hear him. "Lord, I do not ask Thee to strengthen Rachel to bear these trials Thou hast sent, for I know Thou hast created her with strength enough to bear *all* Thy trials."

Despairingly, Rachel wondered whether her husband knew her at all, to imagine such a thing as *that*.

"Instead, I ask that Thou makest Rachel to *feel* the strength that is already in her, so she is not afraid but able to trust in herself as I trust in her." He added, "I thank Thee for giving me such a strong and reasonable creature to be my wife, and pray Thou makest me ever worthy of her." Josiah's subsequent, "Amen," gave the impression of an afterthought.

Rachel was briefly shocked into silence. Then she blurted, "That's *all*? But—what am I to *do*, Josiah?"

Before her husband could answer this—if he even intended to answer it, which Rachel doubted—the sheriff seized her arm again, and she sensed this time he would brook no further delay. She allowed herself to be led away with only one brief glance back. Josiah was standing at the far corner of his cell, straining to keep her in his sight to the last possible instant.

Having gotten his troublesome visitor downstairs at last, the sheriff seemed to imagine the infliction of a little more unpleasantness would ensure he did not have to deal with her ever again. With this intention, he opened his mind to Rachel on the subject of milksop preachers and their pernicious effect on America's young men, in his day tough as hickory, but alarmingly softened since. At the same time Kitty, in a sort of counterpoint, verbally abused the sheriff for his ill manners.

Rachel, lost in her thoughts, did not respond to either of them.

A man's proper role, she believed, was to contend against troubles, while a woman sought refuge from them in prayerful resignation. Instead, topsy-turvy, it was Josiah who was resigned, while she herself longed—internally raged to be allowed, in fact—to strike out in every direction.

When she was finally able to bring her attention back to the present, she found both Kitty and the sheriff had meanwhile become more reasonable. Both having apparently interpreted her silence as a condemnation of their undignified contention, they were even guiltily offering each other concessions.

"I'll see Mr. Woodley gets whatever he needs," the sheriff was saying, his tone less gruff than previously, while Kitty at the same time acknowledged that she knew the sheriff's job was a hard one.

"Long's you don't get the idea you can treat us just any old way," she concluded, gently urging the silent Rachel toward the door.

The two then bid each other cordial "good days," after which Rachel and the sheriff exchanged bows. Rachel's bow was from force of habit, while the sheriff's was reflexive and somewhat unwilling, but each believed the other was acting in good faith and consequently parted (slightly) better friends.

*

Walking homeward, Kitty was excited and inclined to chatter, mostly on the subject of baked treats she might make for the prisoner, but Rachel could not listen. It occurred to her that until she had seen him there with her own eyes, she had not believed Josiah—her own husband, a man whose house she kept and whose clothes she washed and whose voice she could pick out of a roomful of voices, whose bed she shared (or, as she thought of it, who shared her bed) and who had given her a daughter, a man she had imagined she knew better than she knew anyone else in the world—was actually in jail. In jail, and charged with the murder of a slut of a mill girl. The word "slut" came to Rachel's mind easily, though she did not remember ever learning it.

In the same instant she understood her situation, she understood also that nothing she had ever known before had prepared her to deal with it. It had been easier to carry on after Lucy's death than it would be to grapple with the present reality. At least she had known then, without question, exactly what she needed to do. To relinquish the dear, tiny body to be laid in cold earth was agonizing, but inevitable. To accept God's will in the matter was even more difficult, and in fact, she had not yet entirely managed to do so. But at least she had never felt the slightest doubt that prayer (and the passage of time) were the means to that end.

What to do about Josiah was another thing altogether.

She needed advice, but to whom could she turn? Josiah himself was of no help, as usual. Prayers were all very well in their way, but not enough. God was either being maddeningly silent in the matter of Josiah, or else fear had deafened her to His voice. Her mother was inclined, in adversity, to blame adversity's victim, while her father had never cared for Josiah in the first place. As for Josiah's family, his mother was long dead, and his father was—fierce. A good and Godly man, of course—but fierce. Rachel was more than half afraid of him. Josiah's sister had a sick—possibly dying—husband to engross her, and Rachel's sister was too young to confide in. Rachel had no woman friends, and Dr. Conrad and Mr. Tudge, if consulted, would only recommend prayer, patience, and womanly submission.

Or, on second thought, would they? Rachel stopped dead where she was, at the turn of her own street, to consider.

In her mind, she could hear Mr. Tudge's exhortations to obedience and ardent prayer as clearly as though he stood before her making them at that moment. She could see the minister's face, and predict on exactly which words he would cast his eyes heavenward, and on which raise his voice and rock up on his toes—habits which kept the youngest church members attentive during services, keeping count for comparison among themselves afterward.

Dr. Conrad, on the other hand, was less predictable. His sermons were doctrinally so correct as to be unremarkable. Anyone as familiar with church dogma as Rachel was could easily predict from his text what sermon would follow. But in conversation he sometimes surprised her—and not only because he had a sense of humor, which Rachel—largely—did not. Mr. Tudge was a species of preaching automaton, in the pulpit and out, but Dr. Conrad could sometimes be very human. And unlike Mr. Tudge, he was kindhearted enough never to have chided her for appearing to question God's will in the matter of her daughter's loss by grieving for it.

When Rachel could listen to her again, Kitty was saying, "It's gone four o'clock already somehow. I'm wanting my tea, aren't you?"

"Yes I am, now I think of it," Rachel replied. "If we made a meal of it, do you think we might forgo supper, Kitty? I suppose it's ridiculous of me when I really have nothing better to do, but I just don't care to go to the trouble of setting the table again, and washing another plate."

Kitty was never unwilling to adopt a plan to do less work. "I might make it an apple one. We have such a lot of apples still."

"Beg pardon?"

"The pie I'm going to bake for Mr. Woodley."

"A pie?" Josiah liked pie. "You may make it tomorrow morning while I pay a call, then," Rachel agreed. "I'm going to call on Dr.— that is, on *Mrs.* Conrad."

"Oh, she don't hardly see anybody," Kitty warned. "She's never well, and she don't see callers for fear they might expect her to make return of the visit."

Rachel thought, but did not say, that in the stead of Mrs. Conrad, Dr. Conrad would do perfectly well.

CHAPTER SEVEN

*A*t the Conrads' door, Rachel offered her name to Rebecca, the household's pretty maid, who, after warning that her master was not at home, went up to speak to her mistress.

Sophronia Conrad's chamber, which she seldom left, faced the street, and since she was presently sitting as she did most mornings, well wrapped up and near enough an upstairs window to see out without being seen, she knew she was being paid a visit before Rachel pulled the bell. This gave her time enough to change her mind several times as to whether she would receive her before Rebecca arrived to inquire.

Mrs. Conrad was not naturally unsociable—quite the opposite. In her girlhood she had been notably outgoing. But in the years since she had suffered, and her sufferings had made her turn to God. Religious scruples now made callers a trial to her soul. Desperate for heaven, Sophronia felt the company of other women made her too easy a target for the Tempter. The young Mrs. Woodley's abundance of youth and health, for example, engendered sensations of wicked covetousness in her soul, while Mrs. Tudge's obvious ill-breeding enticed her to the sin of pride that her own was better. She had not met any women with whom she could visit, in fact, without putting her soul in danger by sinfully presuming to judge them by their words or by succumbing to lightmindedness or uncharity in the flow of conversation.

Only with men was Mrs. Conrad at ease. Since it was a matter of doctrine that they were all her superiors before God, she did not presume to form any opinions about men at all. But with men, of course, she could not visit anyway.

If anyone had asked her, Sophronia would have denied being lonely. She would have said the company of God was company enough. Perhaps God's company palled a bit on this particular morning. She instructed Rebecca to send Mrs. Woodley up.

Having immediate second thoughts, she said quickly, "No, wait. Or rather—yes. Yes, I think this time I shall. Send her up."

Once seated, Rachel inquired politely after Mrs. Conrad's health.

"I am as well as always," Mrs. Conrad told her, meaning she was unwell. As she spoke, she pulled her shawl more tightly about her shoulders since the draft that had undoubtedly entered at the door with Mrs. Woodley was likely to have followed her up the stairs. Winter, with its twin perils of cold air and fire smoke was an unhealthy season for her—although less so than summer, perhaps, with its heat and flies. The rains of spring and autumn brought their own risks, of course. "But how are you bearing up, dear?" she asked kindly. "It is for you we are all anxious."

It reassured Mrs. Conrad to know there was no danger Rachel might answer the question honestly. Everyone knew that any but cheerful words could overset an invalid like herself.

"I'm well enough, thank you," Rachel said. "A little lonely. It's good of you to see me. I came to get your advice, if you will give it. Dr. Conrad will have told you of my—of our—situation. My husband is—" Unable to bring herself to pronounce the words "in jail," she raced on.

"It's not pleasant for him, as you may imagine, but he's keeping as well as can be expected. We can neither of us quite comprehend how this whole affair should have…come to pass. I came to ask you—" Rachel threw out her hands in appeal. "Can you tell me what to do? You are a great deal wiser than I."

Mrs. Conrad searched her heart, fearing to find some trace of vainglory at having her opinion sought. Though she did not detect any, she risked answering only, "Oh, I have no advice. It is kind of you to ask me, but I know nothing of legal things." Rachel's appearance of desperation made her add, "That is, I know very *little* of legal things." Mrs. Conrad's own father had been a legal man. "I believe Mr. Woodley should have an advocate to speak on his behalf."

"Oh, yes, certainly. I— Mr. Tudge undertakes to supply someone of that description. I meant for myself. What should *I* do under the circumstances?"

"Oh!"

Had she been able, at that moment, to look behind Mrs. Conrad's blue eyes and see even a small part of the hundred ideas that immediately crowded the older woman's brain, Rachel would have been astonished by what she found there. In quick succession, Sophronia pictured herself (in Rachel's position) storming the jailhouse, stalwartly refusing to leave except on her (freed) husband's arm; mounting the pulpit in her husband's place on Sunday and appealing to the congregation for their support; and organizing relays of singers to keep up a steady din of hymns beneath the jail's windows until the sheriff—the whole town—relented and sent the prisoner home.

Instead of suggesting any of these things, she instead—irreproachably—advised Rachel to pray. "I think praying is the best thing any of us women can do. You may be sure Mr. Woodley will have my prayers, too."

"Yes, of course. Thank you," Rachel replied automatically. "Should I visit Josiah, do you think?"

"Visit? Oh! In—jail."

Mrs. Conrad's immediate impulse was to cry, "Indeed you should!" Instead, she only ventured, "It is scriptural to visit prisoners." Lest this not be strong enough to convince her visitor (to whom she must not, however, presume to give advice), she added, "If your husband wants you to come, to visit him would be your duty. We must always do our duty."

"I'm not certain whether my husband wants me to visit him or not," Rachel admitted. "I believe he does, but doesn't like to require me. I thought it would strengthen me to know I would be doing *right* to go."

"*Don't be such a goose, girl! Go to your husband at once,*" Mrs. Conrad said silently. Aloud, she repeated, "Always do your duty."

This, Rachel could see, was as bold a recommendation as Mrs. Conrad was willing to make. She turned the conversation and asked politely after the health of the rest of the Conrad family.

At parting a few minutes later, Sophronia did have one last piece of advice for Rachel—one she could offer without fear or apology. "In these trials, do look after your health," she counseled. "Health is a great blessing."

*

To Rachel's great relief, just as she reached the front door, Dr. Conrad stepped in at it.

"Mrs. Woodley, you are exactly the person I most wished to see," he said at once. "But I observe you are going. Have you a moment more to give me? I'll look in on my wife and be down again at once if you can stay."

"Certainly I can stay!"

"Come in here, then. We don't use this parlor, and I keep it as a sort of office, as you see. I won't be long. It's unconscionable that I should make you wait, but I will be quick."

Dr. Conrad was a few years older than his wife, but the contrast between them was astonishing. His step on the staircase was as quick as Josiah's.

While she waited, Rachel had a look around the room into which she had been shown.

It was not quite a parlor anymore, but not entirely given over as an office, either—to maintain the fiction, Rachel supposed, that Mrs. Conrad might somehow recover her health and require it again one day for entertaining. There was no proper desk. A standish and blotter were set out on an ordinary table in a way that suggested Dr. Conrad sat there to write. Shelves had been put up on one wall, the upper- and lower-most filled with books, and one in the middle displaying seashells and bird's eggs and other curiosities of nature. It was common among clergymen to cultivate—or feign—an interest in such works of God's hand, but Rachel thought Dr. Conrad's interest must be genuine. There were as many books on natural history on his shelves as there were on religious topics. More, even.

When, after not many minutes, she heard Dr. Conrad's step on the stairs again, Rachel hurried to sit in a chair over which hung a miniature of the lovely young girl Mrs. Conrad had once been.

Dr. Conrad closed the door to the room softly behind him.

"Don't let me make you uncomfortable," he said quickly. "You observe that we face the road here and may be seen plainly by anyone passing. It's only that my wife naps at this hour, and any little noise from below is apt to make her restless."

Rachel did not, in fact, feel her reputation was in the least compromised by the closed door. Despite his vigor, Dr. Conrad's clerical band and white hair seemed to her proof against scandal.

"I have been wishing to see you," Dr. Conrad continued, sitting down and speaking low for his wife's sake, but earnestly. "I can hardly imagine what you must be suffering. I wanted to offer you my assurances we in the church will support Mr. Woodley in every way during this difficult time. I am perfectly convinced of his entire innocence of the charge against him."

Rachel began her thanks, and then found she could not go on without sobbing aloud with relief. This was the exact style of reassurance, confident and complete, she had been wanting.

Dr. Conrad waited for her to compose herself.

"I am at such a loss," Rachel said when she felt she could speak quietly. "I have no idea what course of action to follow, or what is needed. Mr. Tudge has kindly offered to arrange advocacy for Josiah, but how is such a thing done, I wonder? And how am I to pay for it? It seems wrong in me to doubt God will provide, but if Josiah is unable to fulfill his duties…" She broke off awkwardly, aware she might be putting a senior minister of the church in an embarrassing position by introducing the issue of Josiah's salary. She had not meant to speak of it. She had not even realized until the moment she spoke the degree to which the matter was weighing upon her.

Dr. Conrad said immediately, "As Mr. Woodley has been convicted of no crime, his salary will continue, of course. And as for his legal representation, it is probably an advantage that the Reverend Mr.

Tudge's cousin is—young. No doubt his fees will be in proportion to his experience. In any case, I had a long talk with your husband this morning, and we agreed that his entire innocence of the charge against him is the best defender he could possibly have."

Rachel nodded agreement with this statement, meanwhile suppressing a secret conviction that without a good legal man directing the case, innocence was of limited value in a courtroom.

"You saw Josiah?" she asked. "He told me you would come. You are so kind to do it."

"Not at all. I think he was probably disappointed it was only me. Yours is undoubtedly the face he most wants before him. But I was able to be of some practical use, and the most important thing is that a prisoner not be left alone enough to imagine he is forgotten."

Again, this was the kind of clear, firm direction Rachel craved. "I will go to him every day," she promised.

Rachel then ventured to ask on what ground Josiah was accused. "His acquaintance with Mary Hale was really very slight, and never of an improper character."

It was her impression Dr. Conrad did not quite like to answer her. He removed his spectacles and toyed with them for a moment before he spoke.

"I have not been invited to examine the evidence against your husband, of course," he said finally. "Woodley— Mr. Woodley feels he first fell under suspicion because of a letter he wrote to the young lady. A brief note that was found among her effects."

Rachel's brow furrowed. She was not aware of any such "note."

"To the effect that he did not like to be the instrument of her ruin," Dr. Conrad finished, as gently as he could. "You will immediately understand his meaning, and he has explained the situation to me, but unfortunately his remarks are capable, under the circumstances, of another construction."

Rachel covered her face with her hands then and moaned aloud—though softly, with a due regard for the invalid upstairs, and the possibility the Conrad's hired girl was the kind to listen at keyholes. "Oh, dear God," she said wearily. "Am I to blame in this, then? It was I who insisted he write, to warn the Methodist elders of Miss Hale's character. Why did he write to *her* instead? I wish he had not written to her. If the letter is the problem, I will testify myself as to what it signified, if necessary."

"Unfortunately, you may not," said Dr. Conrad. "In this state, a wife may not testify in court either on behalf of, or against, her husband."

Rachel digested this unwelcome piece of information in stunned silence.

"Does the—does the court imagine I would *lie?*" she asked finally, her tone indignant.

Apparently, the court imagined she might.

"Then, if *I* cannot," she persisted, "anyone else who knows him might testify to Josiah's true meaning. Of course he meant nothing untoward! Josiah's entire doings are as innocent as a baby's."

"They are, I'm sure," Dr. Conrad soothed. "But there are—well, other things."

Suspiciously, Rachel asked, "What 'other things?'"

Clearing his throat, Dr. Conrad acknowledged that on the night she died, Miss Hale had been seen walking with a tall man in a long coat. This same man had been seen again, quite alone, at a later hour. So far, at least, no one identified this man positively as Mr. Woodley; but—! Dr. Conrad gestured helplessly.

Rachel considered what she had just been told.

Lawyers and clergymen wore long coats. A few pushing medical doctors, eager to ascend from tradesmen to professionals, were beginning to assume that badge. In all of Milltown and the countryside around, there were perhaps only a dozen men who might legitimately wear such a garment.

Josiah was tall, and justly proud of his right to clerical habiliment.

"Anyone might put on a long coat," she said. "And Josiah is not the only tall man about."

"That is so."

"Is there more of this nonsense than just a letter which may be explained away in an instant, and the existence in the world of tall men and long coats? I don't understand why my husband should be kept from me on so-called 'evidence' of this nature."

"There may be more," Dr. Conrad said. "I am not, as I said, privy to it."

Rachel thought for a moment.

"But who was the tall man?" she asked then. "If his identity were discovered, Josiah would be discharged at once, I should think."

"It would certainly…" Dr. Conrad stopped himself. Perhaps, Rachel thought, he did not like to hold out false hopes.

When he did not continue, she added, "Miss Hale must have had friends. She was a young girl, and presumably would have confided in those friends, as young girls do. Will someone speak to them and see what information they could provide?" Blushing to find herself alluding so baldly to the matter, Rachel forced herself to add, "They may know the name of her—her young man."

Dr. Conrad seemed taken aback by the suggestion. "Perhaps they may," he agreed, and seemed to think the matter over. After a moment, catching Rachel's eye, he smiled. "And no doubt his advocate will do exactly as you suggest," he assured her firmly. "I feel certain of it, in fact. I'm sure we may trust to his advocate's legal training in this and all such questions."

Rachel considered whether she could decently ask what Mr. Tudge's young cousin's legal training had actually been, and decided she couldn't.

"Thank you for your help, Doctor," she said instead.

"Don't despair," Dr. Conrad answered kindly. "This unpleasantness will all be soon behind us. Meanwhile, you will be in my prayers, and much better, you will be in my wife's."

Rachel went home feeling more hopeful.

CHAPTER EIGHT

uoyed by the Conrads' advice about prisoners, Rachel continued to visit Josiah, where she found the shock of seeing her husband behind bars wore off quickly. Within two days, a sort of homey routine already seemed established. Leaving Kitty below and brushing coolly by the sheriff, who, as he followed her up, offered no more than token objections to her presence, she took the food basket to Josiah herself. Once upstairs, she shared out the contents between her husband and the alcoholic Mr. Brown, who, like a shy but hungry dog, progressed from hiding beneath his blanket to taking food directly from her hand. She knew Josiah prayed daily with his jail mate to have strength, when he came to be released, to confine himself to beer and resist the temptation to strong drink, but she had an impression her husband's expectations were not high.

"I know his kind. One ale always leads to another," Josiah told her quietly. "And another to a third, and by then he's forgotten all his resolve and takes a dram of something stronger. What can I do for him? He used to be a mechanic. Now he's a hedger—when he's in employment at all. Hedging's thirsty work."

"If one ale leads to another, can he not drink coffee, then? Or tea?"

Behind her, the sheriff snorted.

"Coffee's dear," Josiah pointed out gently. "Tea, too. They're not drinks for a working man."

"God help him, then," Rachel said sadly.

"And his wife and little ones," Josiah agreed.

On the third day, Rachel happened to bring some rather nice meat pies to the jail. While the sheriff was informing her that her husband was alone upstairs, Mr. Brown having been discharged at last (though for how long, no one could say), he seemed to be eyeing the dinner basket, and, on an impulse, Rachel offered Mr. Brown's share of the food to the sheriff.

If all men have their price, the sheriff's price happened to be a meat pie. He was a bachelor who, like his prisoners, was condemned without trial to a diet of tavern food, and when Rachel produced a half-moon of fat, rich pastry, oozing gravy from a carelessly crimped seam, he managed to accept it as though offhand, but not to resist staying downstairs to eat it up at once.

As she went up the stairs, Rachel could hear Kitty jeering that the sheriff was a greedy pig and advising that a change of linen and a scrub with strong soap on his part would improve the view from where she sat, but she doubted he minded. Very few men, she thought, would mind the company of a plump, rosy blonde. And as for the jeering, it did not appear to her the sheriff paid the least attention to anything said by a woman anyway, be she dark or fair.

Alone upstairs, Rachel and Josiah could talk freely at last.

Almost immediately, Rachel brought up the letter Josiah had written to Mary Hale.

"If only you had taken my advice and spoken to her minister, instead! It seems the note is behind all of this."

Josiah did not remind his wife (though she suddenly recollected it herself) that his own impulse to say nothing to anyone of Mary's past would also have served.

"It was found in Miss Hale's hymnbook, along with several other letters I did *not* write, though it is thought I did. I have all this from Mrs. Brown, by the way. She hears all the local gossip in the kitchens where she collects washing and shouts it to her husband on her visits here. I can't help but overhear. It seems the case is much discussed about the town."

Seeing Rachel suddenly look sick, Josiah quickly changed the subject. "What a sad, weary little thing Mrs. Brown is," he said. "And what a foolish law, that confines a husband for drunkenness, meanwhile leaving his family to starve! Do you think we might do anything for her?"

"The little washing we have, Kitty manages to do," Rachel said. Then, seeing that Josiah seemed genuinely concerned, she added, "Agnes Tudge said something about needing more help. I think she was hinting that our Kitty might spare her a few hours in the afternoons, but I certainly don't intend to give her Kitty! Let me speak to Agnes. Oh, I am glad you're not a drinking man, Josiah!"

Her husband laughed grimly. "Oh, never that. I only stand accused of murder."

They stood silent for some time, listening as from far off, the dinner bells rang over the mills to signal to the mill girls to shut down their equipment for the forty minutes they were allowed in which to eat dinner.

On most days, mechanics circulated on the mill floor during those forty minutes, mending looms and spinning machines that had broken during the morning. The mechanics were often too few for the number of machines needing attention, and every day some girls missed the meal in seeing to their frames themselves in order not to lose pay to a broken one. While Rachel and Josiah were talking privately together at the jail, some of the diligent mill girls were observing that on this day, mechanics were fewer than ever.

The night before, after an ale or two beyond his usual custom, one of the younger mechanics at Number Four had been taken with a fit of belligerence, and, after casting about for a focus for his mood, announced to his neighbors that preacher or no, a man who laid rash hands on a woman ought to be thrashed for it. There was general agreement with the statement, in honor of which another round of ale was called for. This led, sometime later, to the formulation of a plan to actually administer the thrashing, which shortly became a horsewhipping, and, before the men staggered home for what was left of the night, a hanging. On a streetcorner, in what they imagined were stern and manly voices, the mechanics agreed among themselves to march on the jail at the dinner break next day and conduct an on-the-spot adjudication of the Woodley case. Most of the men were under twenty-five, and some were only boys. From their point of view, to take part in a lynching seemed an adventure, and a welcome break from routine.

By the light of the next day, it occurred to some of the conspirators there was no real urgency for them to act in the matter. Mary Hale's murderer was safely locked up in jail, and the case was making its way along the usual courses of justice. It might be enough for them to keep a rope handy in the event of an unfavorable verdict in the case. As they went about their work, the men avoided bringing up the topic of the day's planned activities, and nearly all would enthusiastically have seconded a motion to defer action to a later day—any later day, provided it was one on which their heads were not so abominably sore.

But none of the erstwhile conspirators was willing to be the one to suggest a postponement, and when the dinner bells rang, a group of them somewhat sheepishly assembled and set off walking together toward the jail.

Along the way, to their surprise and growing consternation, the mechanics found themselves joined by a score or so of young rowdies who had somehow got wind of the plot (their stern and manly voices of the night before had been shriller and more carrying than any of the mechanics imagined) and were now demanding to be let in on the fun. The newcomers were mostly as drunk now as the mill mechanics had been the night before and were not yet wracked by any sober second thoughts. The hanging that had, in the mechanic's minds, ebbed over the course of the morning to a whipping, then a thrashing, and by the time they left the mills to a stern warning, was suddenly a lynching party in earnest. One of the rowdies carried a coil of rope, and another, drunk as seven lords, brandished a pistol. A few of the mechanics found opportunities to lose themselves down alleys and into shops along the way, but most, however much they might wish themselves elsewhere, felt committed to the plot they had laid.

The sheriff had just stood to shout up the stairs that the Woodleys' time together was up when a change in the usual street noises caught his ear. Kitty, lacking his experience, did not perceive it, and attempting to distract him from his perceived purpose, she quickly introduced a new conversational theme. The sheriff rudely hushed her.

"Be quiet, you ninny," he said roughly, going quickly to the window. Kitty was hurt. She had a great deal to say about how hurt she was. The sheriff was not listening.

After seeing to it both windows were locked, he strode quickly to the door of the lean-to at the back of the jail, closed it, and turned the key. Then he went to his desk and slid open a drawer, pulling from it the pistol he always kept at the ready. This he lay on the desktop before him. He then drew the case with the pistol's mate from another drawer, and proceeded, with steady hands, to load the second pistol as well.

That done, he did not sit down, but continued to stand where he was, with the desk before him, and his arms loose at his sides.

Only then did he spare a thought for Kitty. "Get upstairs," he said, not looking at her.

His tone convinced her to obey him at once.

A moment later, a sort of scuffle could be heard just outside the jailhouse door. Then it opened and a half-dozen men crowded in. Three were mill mechanics, who looked uneasily about themselves, and the three others were town layabouts who had no need to look around since, having been resident in the jail from time to time, they were already perfectly familiar with it.

The sheriff allowed his lip to curl disdainfully. "Ain't seen you of late, Parker," he said to one. "Been from town?"

"You know who we come for," Parker announced.

"And we mean to have him," another jail-familiar added darkly.

"Well, then," said the sheriff calmly, "you'll have a warrant from the governor, I guess. Soon's I see it, I'll make over my prisoner to your charge. Otherwise, you can get on your way."

Their faculties blunted with drink, the toughs analyzed these remarks with difficulty.

Outside, one of the younger mechanics had become somewhat overset with excitement. Pushing his way to the front of the mob he shouted breathlessly, "We need no warrant! Our authority is from God and his angels!"

The sheriff returned promptly, "I'll accept that authority—provided you can produce the angels!"

The crowd laughed, and the young mechanic shrank back, abashed.

Upstairs, after a moment of confusion over what the voices from below signified, Josiah put his arms through the bars and drew the women, both white with terror, to him. Rachel wondered suddenly that the possibility there might be an attempt made at lynching Josiah had not occurred to her before. One heard of such things, in cases like his.

Her voice rising nervously, she begged, "Josiah, what shall we do?" Before Josiah could say anything, Rachel answered her own question. "Hide!" she cried.

The upstairs room was divided with bars into three cells. Josiah's and Mr. Brown's former lodging were equivalently furnished, each containing a narrow bed and small table. The third cell was smaller and held only a chair, for the use of prisoners expected to stay in the jail only a short time before being released to the custody of their families—or the hangman. None offered anything that looked like sanctuary, or even modest cover.

In a matter-of-fact voice, Josiah pointed out, "You can't really hide, I don't think, but you will be safer out of the way. You and Kitty go to the back of Brown's cell, Rachel. The very back, do you see? Push the table aside, and get behind it. Once you've done that—and no matter what happens—don't move from that spot. I don't think anyone will dare to hurt you, but if there is trouble, that will be the safest place for you. And get down low."

He did not specify, "in case shots may be fired," but Rachel understood it as implied.

Rachel looked at him, looked where he indicated, and then slipped her arm under her husband's coat and held tighter.

Josiah tried again. "Kitty, did you hear me? Get Mrs. Woodley and yourself into the corner of that cell." He attempted to push them on their way, but both clung tightly to him.

Downstairs, the commotion grew louder. Someone in the crowd outside was attempting with poor success to lead a chant.

The part of Stern Husband did not come naturally to Josiah, but he tried his best. "Mrs. Woodley," he ordered, "you must do as I say!"

Though Rachel had always wanted Josiah to be more masterful, at this particular moment she was not open to any new persona on his part. An irrational notion had seized her that the three of them were somehow safer together, and she shook her head stubbornly.

Josiah tried another tack. Speaking in his usual voice again, he said, "Rachel, Kitty's frightened. Help her into Brown's cell, won't you?"

Kitty was indeed frightened, too much so even to cry, and clinging as hard to Josiah as Rachel was. Seeing the girl's white face, compassion lessened Rachel's own fear. She pried Kitty's fingers from her own arm and Josiah's coat sleeve, and, murmuring encouragement, gently walked her into Mr. Brown's open cell. Despite her fear and the dreadful shouts from the street, from some strangely calm center of her being Rachel observed and regretted that her skirts brushed against the coarse ticking of a mattress stiff with filth, and undoubtedly buggy.

By this time, the sheriff had assessed the situation with which he was faced, and sensed by the noise and restlessness of the mob an encouraging degree of uncertain purpose among them. Had the greater number of men stood silently by while delegates outlined previously agreed-upon demands, he would have been uneasy, but tavern sweepings and boys prone to attacks of religious fervor did not worry him much. Furthermore, a number of respectable women, market baskets on their arms, had by now collected here and there in the street outside and were observing the scene with the sorts of clucks and headshakes of obvious disapproval to which no man could be immune who has ever had a mother. Already the mill mechanics were exchanging uneasy glances among themselves, and readjusting their neckerchiefs and hats to more respectable angles.

The sheriff stayed as he was, therefore, and again invited the men to leave.

"If you got business with me, I'll see you one at a time," he stated. "Otherwise, be on your way."

Mr. Parker and a few others seemed inclined to take the advice, but a part of the crowd pressed still closer. Someone called out, "Our business is with that base murderer Jo— Joseph—" then stopped in confusion. A neighbor having offered a prompt in a hoarse whisper, he finished, "Joseph Headley. Bring him down."

Other men who attempted to offer the correct name of their intended object were interrupted by a new voice crying impatiently, "Send him out and we'll leave you alone."

"It'll only be the worse for you if we're obliged to take him without your leave," cried someone else.

"See here, Sheriff," a third man began, while the agent of God and his angels, having recovered from his earlier embarrassment, shouted excitedly, "We're coming in after him!"

Murmurs of approval for this plan emanated from the crowd.

Upstairs, Rachel cried, "Josiah, can you not do something? Call to them. Speak to them." His voice, trained for the pulpit, might well reach to the street.

Below, the mob surged forward in a body.

"Yes, all right," Josiah agreed distractedly. "What should I say?"

Blankly, Rachel replied, "Why—that you're not guilty, I suppose. Say something—say something *religious*. Remind them that what they contemplate is *clear sin*."

Josiah drew in his breath, but before he could attempt a sermon, the sheriff called out, with apparent calm, "I got two pistols in front of me say the first two of you sets foot on the stair gets a ball each. Choose lots, why don't you? See who it's to be."

This provoked a rumble of conversation.

"He's only got *two*," Rachel heard one voice say, but there was clearly some disagreement among the men as to which of them should have the honor of being shot.

At that moment, the very drunken man with the pistol suddenly fired it wildly. At the sound, Josiah flinched, and Kitty, with a squeal, threw herself against Rachel, who hugged her tightly and prayed aloud. The men in the street scattered and looked for cover.

The sheriff continued exactly as he was.

A scar high on the back wall of the jail showed where the bullet had harmlessly spent itself, but the incident, though senseless, had the effect of sobering the crowd. There were no other weapons among them, and the drunken man had, by his shot, disarmed himself, since he had not thought to bring more powder and ball along with the pistol. But the general level of interest in carrying out the lynching sharply abated. The man with the coil of rope laid it gently against the garden wall behind where he stood and edged quietly away.

From far off, the end-of-dinner bells rang over the mills.

At the bells' sound, the mill mechanics, most looking sick at what they had started, turned quietly with one accord, and trooped back toward the mills together, thoroughly dispirited. Their forty-minute's adventure was over, and now they would have to go hungry while they made up the work they had left. The sheriff, seeing the mechanics go, bid the men immediately before him a wry "good day," and shamefacedly, they, too, withdrew. The sheriff expressed his contempt for them by courteously seeing them out, turning his back to his pistols as he did so—though when the men were gone, he made certain to lock the door behind them. The boys and tavern rowdies jeered the deserters, but the rowdies had evidently grown thirsty with shouting and shoving, and were soon off as well, returning to their accustomed taverns. The boys stayed by for a time, swaggering about and barracking the sheriff and his prisoner loudly to each other for the benefit of passers-by, and then they, too, went in search of better entertainment. Less than an hour had passed between the first angry shout and the return of perfect peace in the street.

The sheriff sat down behind his desk and enjoyed a pipe, not remembering for some time that there were ladies upstairs.

*

Josiah, listening tensely, ventured finally, "I think they've all gone."

Where Rachel was silent in her relief, Kitty sobbed aloud and begged over and over again for assurance all danger was past.

"The sheriff talked sense into them," Josiah comforted her. "They won't bother us any more." His eye met his wife's with a slight smile, and Rachel guessed he thought as she did, that the sheriff's reputation as a marksman had been his best argument.

By and by someone tried the jailhouse door, and finding it locked, tapped at a window. Looking out, the sheriff saw it was Kitty's father, and opened up for him.

Mr. Stone's greeting was a laconic, "Sheriff."

"Abner," the sheriff returned with equal brevity. "You well?"

"Well enough. Daughter?"

"Upstairs."

"Daughter!"

Kitty jumped at hearing the familiar voice from below, and crying "Oh, Pa!" released Josiah's arm immediately to run down to this even more welcome source of reassurance. Rachel took the opportunity to hang on her husband in a way she would have been ashamed to do before witnesses.

Josiah, delighted in spite of himself, murmured, "Mrs. Woodley, how can I comfort you in such a way that you are, in fact, comforted, and yet don't care to remove your arms from around my neck? The bars must be hurting you, though, pressing against your face as they are."

Rachel blushed. Backing away and straightening her bonnet, she said, "I think it must be safe again, or the sheriff would not have let Mr. Stone in."

Josiah agreed, sounding slightly regretful. "You'd better get home as quickly as you can. And tomorrow, go to your father's."

Rachel blinked. "Why? I don't believe anyone will hurt me. I must send Kitty to *her* home, I suppose. But I prefer to stay here in Milltown."

Since he had given his wife exactly the kind of unambiguous guidance she'd been demanding of him, Josiah frowned to find himself arguing the matter. "There's nothing you can do here. Dr. Conrad will see to my needs until the trial. He has promised he will." Unwisely, he added, "You can't live alone, Rachel. It's unwomanly."

If her husband had said that for her to live alone would be ungodly, Rachel would not have had the courage to defy him further. Josiah's ordained status undoubtedly entitled him to speak with authority on what was and was not pleasing to God.

But—!

"I think I know better than you do what is *womanly*," she blurted. Rachel didn't share with her husband that she'd discovered something strangely heartening in defying a mob. It made her feel less helpless to deal with her troubles.

"Stay, then," Josiah relented, smiling and putting his hand through the bars to rest on Rachel's arm. For the first time since Lucy's death, Rachel had no impulse to throw him off.

*

When Rachel came downstairs, Kitty was still recounting the afternoon's events to her father, hanging on him as she had earlier hung on Josiah. Mr. Stone, a stooped man in a shapeless suit of homespun, seemed uninterested in the tale.

"Yes, all right," he said absently, patting his daughter's hand with his own rough one. "I know already about the trouble here. Now then, your mother said when I started for town this morning that if I saw you I was to say she sends her thanks for them buttons you made, and would like a few more, if you can oblige. Bigger ones this time, she says. Her fingers is stiff, and them small ones get away from her."

He caught sight of Rachel, and encumbered by his daughter, bowed to her awkwardly.

Rachel took a breath and, while her resolve was still high, forced herself to say, "Mr. Stone, I must send Kitty home with you. You know the Reverend Woodley's situation. It's not a fit one for so young a lady to be involved in. I am truly sorry to have endangered her today by bringing her to this place."

Farmer Stone either did not entirely hear, or did not understand what she said.

"Home?" he repeated. "Nobody wants Kitty to home." To Kitty herself, he added aside, "Your sister is taking hold pretty well. She don't have your way with the hens yet, but she's young. Did I say already about the buttons?"

Kitty, whose face had fallen when she heard she was to be sent home, said quickly, "See, Mrs. Woodley? No need for me to go home. Pa don't mind for me to stay."

"*I* mind for you to stay," Rachel insisted. "I can't be certain you'll be safe with me."

Determined not to return so soon to farm life, Kitty repeated that she would stay.

Her father was inclined to be indulgent, but the sheriff took Rachel's part. Kitty should go home at once, he said. That way, Mrs. Woodley could go live with her parents or somewhere.

When Rachel, with lifted chin, asserted she had no intention of leaving Milltown, the sheriff replied as Josiah had: "Ladies don't live alone!"

"Then give me back my husband!" Rachel cried.

"Now, don't you two get to quarreling again," Kitty commanded, hurrying to Rachel and drawing her mistress's arm through her own. "Let's us just get on home now, Mrs. Woodley. And Pa, you tell Ma I'll send them buttons right along. What a day this has been, hasn't it? And couldn't I just do with a cup of tea!"

An hour later, the two women stood in Rachel's kitchen, where of late they had done most of their living. Since getting back from the jail, Kitty had done nothing but tell over the events of the day over and over while Rachel made tea and cut bread.

"I don't know what I'd have done if anybody'd come up the stairs." Kitty shivered. "What would you have done, Mrs. Woodley?"

Rachel was not listening. "Yes," she said vaguely.

Kitty shrugged and went on with her story.

She had just gotten to the part where the shot had been fired—a shot which, in Kitty's telling, had gone but very little wide of the sheriff's heart—when Rachel interrupted, "Kitty, where do the mill girls live? What I mean is, I know they reside in that row of big houses…"

"Boarding houses," Kitty offered.

"Boarding houses, as you say—by the river. But—what is the system? Do the girls from each mill have their own houses? That is to say, if a young lady works in Number Four, does she live in a particular boarding house? How might I find a particular young lady? Or—a young lady's friends. Is it enough to know where she was employed?"

Kitty was perfectly *au courant* in the matter, of course, and explained that the boarding houses were independent of the mills, and let rooms to all comers. "Some's nicer than others, of course, and cost more to live in."

"Would you be afraid to go into that part of town?"

Kitty scoffed at the idea. "I been there lots of times. I got a cousin used to work in the mills. She's married now and has the cutest, fattest little boy! Such a little love! I'll get him here someday so you can see him. It's good luck to bring babies where babies is wanted."

"Will you go there with me tomorrow?"

At this, Kitty stared. "Why should you go down there? Is it something to do with leaving tracts?"

Rachel swallowed hard. "Something of that nature," she said—and then mentally asked God's pardon for the lie.

"Oh. All right, then," Kitty said, and resumed her tale. "And wasn't the sheriff brave! He never turned a hair! I mean, I always knew he was brave. That's why he's sheriff. But I never knew he was as brave as that!"

"Yes, very brave," Rachel agreed. Girls of Kitty's age, she reflected wryly, were apt to fall at least half in love with any plausible male.

"And Reverend Woodley," continued Kitty. "He was brave, too. Did you see how he laughed when those fellows was shouting they'd hang him, only saying 'Joseph Headly,' and 'Parson Woodfield,' and all those other wrong names? It *was* funny, now I think about it, but I didn't think it was funny at the time! I think Mr. Woodley would've laughed in those fellows' faces while they were putting the rope around his neck—just to shame them."

Rachel stopped what she was doing and stared at the young girl.

"You thought Josiah brave?"

"Didn't you?" returned Kitty, looking surprised. "The way he was so calm and all?"

In point of fact, Rachel had been annoyed by her husband's equanimity at the jail. She felt he ought to have shown not serenity, but a manly readiness to fight any would-be attackers who made it up the stairs.

Kitty's words put the matter in a somewhat different light.

Turning back to her work, Rachel said slowly, "I have sometimes failed to resign myself bravely to—trials. Josiah has exactly that kind of courage."

CHAPTER NINE

For an hour, Rachel had been asking where Mary Hale had lived, both at boardinghouse doors and of passers-by in the street, but could not get a clear nor friendly answer from anyone.

Reaching for Rachel's arm after yet another chilly rebuff, Kitty said falteringly, "Oh, missus, I didn't know you meant to ask after Mary when we came down here. I don't think you ought to, really."

"Don't be silly," Rachel returned tightly. "I must, if I want to find Miss Hale's friends. Dr. Conrad said they might have information important to Mr. Woodley's defense." Dr. Conrad had also said Josiah's advocate should be the one to speak to them. Rachel didn't mention this part to Kitty. "Why is that man staring at me? Yes, him. Oh, he's turned away, now, but he looked right at me, quite boldly. And not in a pleasant way. Is it my dress?" She glanced down at herself. "Is something out of order?"

"No," Kitty said. "That is, there's nothing torn or anything."

This was clearly an evasion. Rachel said coldly, "I can see for myself my dress isn't torn."

"No, it's a very nice dress. What I mean is, I think folks around here aren't used to seeing silk dresses except on Sunday, maybe. And being it's clear from your dress you don't want work in a mill, the boardinghouse keepers probably think you're after taking one of their girls away to work for you, and they don't like that. A girl what works for you won't live in a boardinghouse, and that's less money coming to them."

Rachel's face fell. "I didn't think of that."

"And then the places where you said your name... People who know you're Reverend Woodley's wife might think you come down here to call Mary Hale a—call her a bad name. There's people saying all the time working in mills turns girls bad, but the girls want their jobs and the mill owners don't want to be made to hire only men, so they don't like anybody to say bad things against mill girls." Kitty didn't bother to add—because Rachel already knew it—that the mill owners found girls more tractable than men, and much, much cheaper to employ.

When Rachel didn't answer this, Kitty continued, "And then there's Mr. Woodley, too. What he's supposed to have done. There's some hard feelings among these folks that a preacher would do— that. You know. Only of course, you and me know he didn't." The girl finished hastily, "What I'm meaning to say is, it's not that people down here don't like for you to have a silk day-dress, or how you talk, or anything like that. Not really. It's just that Mary was one of them, and you aren't. It might've been better if you had said *my* name at the houses instead of your own, but I didn't think to mention it before. I only thought we were going to invite everybody to Sunday service or something."

"You don't think anyone here would harm us, do you?" Rachel asked uneasily.

Kitty did not. "It's only talk," she said. "You know how folks can be."

Suddenly weary, Rachel sighed. "I'm accomplishing nothing. We might as well go home."

Kitty quickly agreed.

*

Late the next afternoon, when Rachel's visit to Josiah had been paid and the Woodley house "set to rights"—a pointless exercise, in Kitty's opinion, since the house was always perfectly "to rights," and even— again, in Kitty's opinion—over-right, Rachel asked suddenly, "Kitty, when does the shift at the mill let out? At six o'clock, isn't it?"

Interrupted in a long story she was telling, Kitty was slow to understand. "The mill? Why, yes. Six o'clock. Seven in summer. What do you want to know for?"

"I'm going down to Number Four, Kitty. I don't want you to come."

"Number Four?"

"Yes. It suddenly came to me that I went about things all wrong yesterday. If I expect to speak to the mill girls I'll have to go to see them when they're not at work, won't I?"

Kitty's eyes went dark with shock. "You're never going off to the mills *now*," she protested. "Why, it's almost nighttime! What about all those men came to the jail the other day wanting to…hurt…Mr. Woodley? They were millhands, some of them. They live right down there where you'd be going."

"Surely no one would hurt a woman."

"Somebody hurt Mary!"

Rachel swallowed, but said, "This is different. I'm sure I'll be perfectly safe. Anyway, I've no choice. If something isn't done to help Mr. Woodley, he'll be convicted at trial and then those men who came to the jail will get their wish and see him hanged. I don't know who's to help Josiah if I don't." After thinking for a minute, Rachel added, "I won't say anything against the sheriff. He's a good enough man, in his way. But he doesn't care whether it's Josiah or someone else who hangs for killing Mary Hale. That's not his concern."

"How's talking to mill girls going to help Mr. Woodley, though?"

"It's my idea that the man who killed Miss Hale was—may have been—" Rachel, stopped—then recollected suddenly that Kitty was not quite such an innocent as she had once imagined she was, and was already perfectly aware of what Mary's situation had been. "That he was the father of her baby, in point of fact," she finished bluntly. "And I mean to find out his name."

"Do you think he's in the mill?"

"I think Mary's friends at the mill will know the name."

Kitty considered. "It's a good plan," she said finally. "But like I said before, I don't know who'll talk to you. You being—well, who you are, and all."

"Yes, I've thought about that," Rachel replied. "Will you let me have your clothes, Kitty? That gown, anyway. And—your cape, I think. And bonnet. I'm sorry to ask it."

Kitty glanced down at herself, as though to see for certain that her dress was still only her second-best gray one—a little faded—and had not transmuted itself into something fit for a preacher's wife to wear.

"What do want this old thing for?" she faltered. "My Sunday one's in my box. I'll just get it, shall I? It's much nicer."

"No, it's that one I want. You don't mind?"

"Oh, you may have anything you like of mine, but it'll be a bit short on you. And big in the—" Kitty gestured vaguely to indicate the problem.

Rachel forced a laugh. "I shall look like a scarecrow, in fact," she admitted. "But maybe that's all to the good. If the mill girls are reluctant to speak to a minister's wife, perhaps they wouldn't mind speaking to a farmer's daughter."

Kitty was dubious. "Oh, they won't think you're only *that*," she said sincerely. "Anyone can tell you're a lady."

"If I'm going at all," Rachel said, glancing at the clock, "I'll have to hurry, so give me the dress, if you would. I should have left ten minutes ago, in fact. Do you have something else to put on?"

It seemed that Kitty's other gown was presently on the line. "Sunday best, then," the girl said, sighing. "Though it seems like I can never put it on I don't right away find myself in dust or lamp-black or something."

"Well, sit like a lady, then," Rachel recommended through the door behind which her maid had modestly withdrawn. "Stay away from the lamp, leave the dishes until I get back, knot those buttons for your mother, and think improving thoughts. If I'm to pretend I'm you, you might as well pretend to be the wife of a minister of the church."

Kitty, patting her tumbled hair back into place before her tiny looking glass, muttered something that sounded to Rachel very much like, "I'd think I'd rather be a corpse in the graveyard than that," before calling out, "Be careful then, Mrs. Woodley."

"Oh, certainly. And as for you," Rachel returned, "keep the stove going here, and if anyone comes to threaten you, fire the broom, and wave it right in his face. Set the house alight if you have to. That ought to bring help in a hurry."

CHAPTER TEN

I t was a habit with certain of the young men of the town to have
an evening stroll along Water Street when a shift at the mills was
letting out, for the purpose of enjoying at close range the prospect
of the young ladies as they passed. The boys walked slowly or idled
about in groups, sometimes calling out admiringly or rudely to the
ones they thought prettiest, and the girls made a show of scorning the
attention, or answered back smartly, as they were inclined.

Rachel arrived rather late in the area of Number Four, and the
night's performance was nearly over. Though she had not taken time
over the fit of Kitty's clothes and, having slipped out at the back of the
house, walked as quickly as she could on the way, the late February
night was raw and the mill girls, for the most part, did not linger on the
streets to garner compliments, but got inside their respective houses
as quickly as they could. The few laggards were not inclined to stop in
response to Rachel's timid requests for a moment of their time. One
or two slowed enough on their way to hear her out—she was, because
breathless, brief—but none admitted to knowing the name of Mary
Hale. A certain anxiety crept over Rachel. In another five minutes, the
street would be entirely empty of young ladies. She had accomplished
nothing with her inquiries so far, and she had no further plan for how

to proceed should this one fail. To compound her anguish, the young men, being generally hardier, were still in the streets, and having no other target, made Rachel the object of their banter.

Nothing in her life before had prepared Rachel for such attentions. Tears stung her lids, and she pressed her lips together tightly so no involuntary shake of the lower one could give her away.

"You want work?" a voice from some distance behind her demanded.

Rachel turned.

"Go in there if you want work." One of the young men was walking up upon her, and indicating by a jerk of his thumb the door of the mill just opposite. "No sense asking the girls about it. They don't own the mills." If he touched his cap to Rachel at all, it was only to push it back, the better to look her frankly up and down. "Or is it you need a place for the night?" he continued. "Because if that's what it is, I can fix you up. Maybe. If you treat me nice, that is."

The impulse to tears left Rachel in a hurry. "Are you addressing me, sir?" she inquired distantly. She straightened and stiffened her body in a way intended to convey her indignation, not reflecting that, as Kitty's dress was already too short on her to entirely cover the flannel petticoat beneath, the gesture might have another effect.

The young man who had accosted her now compounded the outrage by frankly laughing.

"No need to come all the lady on me," he said. "I won't hurt you. If you need a place for the night I'll fix you up, treat me nice or not. You ought to treat me nice, for I'd be doing you a favor, but I'm not going to leave you on the street either way. And in the morning, just walk in the front door of any mill if you want work and ask for it. There's nobody will bite you."

Something in his look, suggesting amusement tinged with pity, made Rachel suddenly remember the considerable difference between her own well-fit good clothes and shorter, stouter Kitty's second-best.

She said quickly, while attempting to compact her spine into a better fit for her gown, "You are under a misapprehension, sir. I am not in need of either work or lodging."

"You look like you're in need of something," the boy answered her back impertinently. "The wit to get yourself to a fire when the night's a cold one, maybe. Is that it?"

Burning with fury, Rachel started away. Before many steps, however, she had cooled enough to reflect perhaps that she oughtn't to neglect any possible source of information.

Meanwhile, the young man had apparently decided it was unkind of him to tease even a girl wearing a gown that looked like she'd stolen it off a clothes-line, for as Rachel turned back, he caught up with her, anticipating the apology she was about to make him with one of his own.

"Don't mind me," he said quickly. "I don't mean anything. If you need help, miss, just say so. My name's Dan, and I've got sisters of my own at home, see?"

Not entirely appeased, Rachel asked under her breath "Would you have sisters of your own at home if your name *wasn't* Dan?" Then she added aloud, "Thank you, sir." She bowed slightly, which had the effect she intended of reminding Dan that custom obliged him to answer it by uncovering his head. "It's information I require. I wonder whether you can help? Oh, and please do put your hat on," she urged. Now that he'd amended his manner, she had no desire to punish the boy further. "No, do, please. It's dreadfully cold."

The young man hesitantly replaced his cap. "What information would that be?" he asked, warily. "If it's anywhere in town you need to go, I can take you there, if you want."

"I want—I think the most useful thing would be to know in which house Miss Mary Hale lived," Rachel said, growing eager at such a promising response. "Do you know it? Were you acquainted with Miss Hale? Do you—are you employed in a mill, sir?"

Dan studied her briefly before answering. "What do you want to know all that for?"

"Did you know Miss Mary Hale?"

"No. She's been talked of. What was she to you?"

Rachel evaded the question. "I know she worked at Number Four mill. But I don't know which house was hers. I am looking for her friends."

"What for?"

It was apparent that Dan was suspicious of her motives. Rachel cast about for a diversion. Putting out her hand, she asked suddenly, "What is your name, please? Your surname. I am—I am Mrs. Stone," although she had not actually requested of Kitty the loan of her name along with the gown. "Thank you for your trouble. Do you know where Miss Hale lived?"

The hat came off again, from force of habit, while the young man gingerly touched her proffered hand. "Gage, miss—missus, I mean. Missus"—Rachel prompted him gently—"Mrs. Stone, that is. Daniel Gage is my name."

"Do you know—?"

"No, miss—that is, Mrs. Stone. I know where another girl lives who works at Four. I'll take you there, if you want. She might know."

Rachel managed to maintain a gracious, rather than elated, expression.

Though the parlors of the boardinghouses she and Dan visited were packed and overheated with young ladies, none of the girls in any of them admitted to having known Mary Hale personally. To Rachel's mortification, many of them looked her coolly up and down, and replied to her queries with perceptible disdain. While she wore Kitty's homely gown and bonnet, the mill girls saw Rachel as someone no richer (nor older) than they, who for some reason was affecting the manners and speech patterns of her betters, and they didn't scruple to hide their scorn.

At each establishment, Dan Gage waited while Rachel asked her questions, and nothing she said could induce him to leave her.

"It might not be safe," he said; adding innocently, "Folks are all stirred up. Didn't you hear? The other day, there was almost a lynching."

Mary Hale's house, when Rachel found it, turned out to be one of the smallest and poorest. Mary had been in Milltown for a relatively short time, and Rachel surmised that places in the newer, finer establishments were harder to come by. Like the mill girls, the dour-faced landlady seemed mistrustful of the way Rachel's genteel manners did not match her dress and bonnet. Even as she regretted it, Rachel admired her discernment.

On the other hand, there were certain undeniable advantages to a genteel manner. When, stammering a little, Rachel offered to pay any little debt Miss Hale might have owed, the landlady immediately stepped aside and waved her in. Once in the vestibule, she assessed Kitty's worn gown and plain bonnet again, and named a modest sum. Though from Dan's muffled guffaw behind her, Rachel understood that he judged it unlikely any such debt truly existed, Rachel accepted it willingly as the price of admission, and paid.

Thrusting the coins into a pocket under her dirty apron, the old woman waddled to the door of the parlor—which, Rachel observed, contained neither a piano, as many others had, nor even a good lamp—and shouted for someone.

Rachel, meanwhile, was formulating a desperate plan. Young Kitty, she reflected, was the very pattern of sociability. She was wearing Kitty's clothes. Could she not wear—just for an hour—Kitty's smile and easy manner, too? Though Rachel's whole being shrank from the mental picture of putting herself boldly forward as Kitty did, face decked with smiles and friendly nothings bubbling on her lips, she also feared going home again with nothing accomplished, and decided to make the effort. When a tall, toothy young lady, older than most of the other girls (in fact, older than Rachel herself), detached herself from the chattering group in the parlor and started toward her, Rachel assumed what she hoped was a bright smile, and tried to recall the exact cadence of Kitty's "good evening!"

Growled the landlady to Rachel, "This here's Polly. She'n Mary used to share the last room back. Polly, this here girl wants to know about Mary Hale."

"Thank you," murmured Rachel, in her usual voice—and then quickly reassumed her bright smile. Recalling that Kitty and her friends were all very interested in dress, she added, "What a pretty dress you have on, Polly!"

This would have been a more effective icebreaker had Polly felt able to return the compliment.

"I can't say I knew Mary real well," Polly admitted, shyly taking the hand Rachel had unconsciously offered. "None of us did. She only came here last summer. I'll tell you what I know, though. Come into the kitchen, why don't you? It's quieter in there."

The young woman's friendliness convinced Rachel she had found the way to her ends at last.

Once they were in the kitchen, however, Polly seemed to feel a few formalities needed to be observed before they could speak freely of the dead, and Rachel immediately found herself back in difficulties.

Began Polly, "Poor Mary! But she's gone to a better place now;" and when Rachel, unfamiliar with the ritual, merely nodded, the smile frozen on her lips, Polly gave her a sharp look.

After an uncomfortable moment, Rachel finally comprehended that a *grave* aspect was now required, and let the corners of her mouth fall.

Reassured by this, Polly began again, "She's gone to her last, best home." Then she waited expectantly.

"Yes," said Rachel nervously. "Her last, and as you say, best home."

This response elicited a further suggestion from Polly that the present world was one of sin and sorrow, followed by another awkward pause it took Rachel a moment to understand was again hers to fill. She hoped the ritual would not continue long. Her supply of comforting nothings was not extensive.

"Heaven's mercy upon us all," Rachel ventured, and since this seemed a little bloodless, added, "Our sister is safe from all trial now."

The reference to Mary Hale as a "sister" evidently pleased Polly. She repeated "our sister" several times, gravely, and afterward seemed ready to converse.

She invited Rachel to sit down, and set a chair for herself beside Rachel's.

"You shared a room with Miss Hale?" Rachel began.

"Shared a bed," said Polly, nodding. "Us girls all share with somebody. It's warmer." Further questioning on Rachel's part elicited the information that the boarding house was (as Rachel had already guessed) one of the least expensive in town, and mostly tenanted by girls who, like Mary, came to Milltown without savings or parental subsidy.

"Not me, though," Polly proudly announced. "I could live anywhere. I been in the mills three years, and I've saved."

"For your marriage?"

Polly permitted herself an unladylike snort. "For old age. I don't mean to marry, but be independent. There's never a moment's rest from husband, house, and children, but when my shift's done at the mill, my time's my own."

The Reverend Tudges of the world were convinced that working in mills turned girls "bad." This, Rachel suddenly saw, was because "bad" and "independent," when applied to women, were equivalent terms to Mr. Tudge. Rachel imagined herself spending a lifetime facing down the Tudges of the world and murmured faintly, "Miss Polly, you are very brave."

Miss Polly basked in the compliment.

"You were friends with Miss Hale," Rachel probed then. "As a friend, did she confide in you?"

Polly did not know the word "confide."

"Speak to you frankly," Rachel clarified. "Tell you—private things?"

"Like as to the baby she had coming? Lordy, she didn't have to tell me *that*. We tie our aprons back in the mill to keep 'em out of the way. It was clear enough she was swelling. Why do you want to know? Are you kin to Mary?"

"No," Rachel confessed. "I was just a—friend. Like you."

Polly eyed her. "I don't recall Mary mentioning the name of Stone. Are you from Bristol?"

At any moment, Rachel sensed, the present conversation would end just as the others had, with a word of dismissal, coldly spoken. A lie might save the situation. If she were to agree that she, like Mary Hale herself, was a Bristol girl, it might allay Polly's evident suspicion.

It was not in Rachel to lie. "No. I knew Miss Hale in New Seabury."

"You ain't a friend, then," Polly said flatly, and started to rise. "Mary told me there wasn't a single person in Seabury was her friend when she needed one."

Rachel caught her arm. "That's not true," she said quickly. "Mary did have a friend. My husband was her friend. He was her friend, and her pastor, and he was sincerely interested in Miss Hale's well-being. And now he's accused of killing her." Before Polly could speak, she added, "I'm his wife. I'm Josiah Woodley's wife."

"You?"

"Yes. My husband didn't kill Miss Hale. And he didn't… That is, he didn't father her child." (Frank words were always difficult for Rachel to pronounce.) "But I believe the man who *was* her child's father may have killed Mary, and I thought her friends might know who that man—the guilty man—was."

Polly sat back down, and a long silence ensued.

"You've got some nerve coming *here*," Polly finally said. Her tone was unexpectedly friendly. Polly apparently admired "nerve." "I can't tell you any name, though. I would if I could, but Mary never said a name." After a minute, she added, "Wait here. Maybe she talked more to Hitty."

Before Rachel could react to this, Polly darted back into the parlor, returning a moment later with a second girl.

"This is Hitty," she announced, pushing forward another chair to accommodate the newcomer. "Hitty, what was the name of Mary's beau? Did she tell you?"

To Rachel's disappointment, Mary had never mentioned any name to Hitty, either.

"Did she describe him to you at all?" Rachel pressed. "Did she say what he looked like?"

"No. I think he was a tall fellow. At least, I saw her with a tall fellow once."

Rachel did not quite like to hear this. Josiah was tall.

"What else besides his height did you notice about him?"

"Oh, I didn't see anything else about him at all. It was dark. Mary got letters from him sometimes. His name might've been on the letters."

"Letters?"

Polly and Hitty explained together that the sheriff had found letters in Mary's hymnbook at her inquest.

Rachel recalled that Josiah had mentioned letters—letters besides his own. She hadn't paid attention at the time. "They were signed, you say? By whom?" Josiah would not have sent his warning without subscribing his name to it.

The mill girls looked blankly at each other. "The yellow one was signed anyway," Hitty said. "I don't know what name it said. I don't know if the other letters were signed or not."

"Yellow?"

"Writ on yellow paper. There were letters on blue paper, too. That's what I heard."

Rachel decided she would not trust anyone else to make Josiah's advocate aware of these letters. She would do it herself. "Does the sheriff still have them?"

Hitty didn't know whether he did or not. Neither girl, in fact, appeared to have any more information to give.

Before they would accept Rachel's thanks and goodbye, the two mill girls—and, unavoidably, Rachel—repeated the earlier ritual of solemnly committing the murdered girl to a better place where trouble could not reach.

The three women then returned to the parlor, where Rachel found Dan still waiting for her. As he insisted again upon being her escort, Rachel was relieved to discover that the streets, by this hour, were all but deserted, since a storm of gossip would certainly have resulted had she been seen walking late in the company of a young man.

An even louder and more virulent storm of gossip would ensue were she to be seen walking alone, of course.

Lost in thought, Rachel was poor company for Dan. They were almost at the Woodley house before she even remembered the thanks she owed him. "I'm afraid you'll have a long, cold walk back," she added.

Dan grinned. "Oh, I guess you'll make it worth my while," he said. "Or I'll be rewarded in the Hereafter, anyway. Whereabouts is your house?"

"Just here, lucky for you," Rachel said, turning in at the alley. "Come into the kitchen and warm yourself at the fire. You'll be satisfied with a modest remuneration, I hope? I'm not a rich woman." From Dan's face as he glimpsed her house, Rachel guessed he thought otherwise.

When she heard them at the door, Kitty hurried in from the parlor. She must have taken Rachel's recommendations for her evening's activities to heart, for she looked clean and rosy, as though she had been sitting warm and at her ease.

"Oh, Mrs. Woodley," she exclaimed. "Let me just build up the fire! You're froze through."

"Make tea, will you?" Rachel said immediately, regretting that she had not thought to ask Kitty in advance to have a pot waiting. She explained, as an afterthought, "Oh, and—this is Mr. Gage."

Kitty made no move toward the wood box, but stood smiling shyly, face turned half away, studying their visitor from the corners of her eyes. "You will have guessed," Rachel continued to Dan, eyeing her maid, "that my name is *not* Stone. I hope you will forgive me the deception. I am, as you heard, Mrs. Woodley. This is *Miss* Stone."

No prompting was necessary now to remind Dan to remove his hat, although he seemed not to remember how to talk. Kitty's Sunday gown suited her, and she seemed to have done something nice with her hair, as well. Even her sudden bashfulness at Dan's frank perusal was pretty.

When Kitty moved at last toward the stove, Dan suddenly found his wits again and leaped to the task of filling it for her, fumbling at the firebox door, rattling the shaker until he was enveloped in ash, and stammering apologies throughout the operation. Rachel, suddenly feeling hundreds of years old, left the room. Her presence was clearly not required in the kitchen, and there was a fire already in the parlor. She could leave the two young people unsupervised for at least long enough to warm her hands there.

Returning some time later, wearing her own gown and with a lace cap over her newly becomingly arranged hair, she found Dan seated comfortably at her kitchen table drinking tea, a plate strewn with crumbs before him. Kitty might dispense with refinements like china dishes and table linen when she was alone, but for strangers, it appeared, only her mistress' daintiest wedding plates would do.

Kitty saw Rachel looking and became rather flustered, but Dan inadvertently mollified Rachel by rising at once at her entrance and begging politely to take his leave. His good manners had the effect of weakening Rachel's resolve to chide Kitty later for her overzealous hospitality.

Nor would Dan take any money for his earlier assistance. "I've eaten up all you might have owed me for it," he said—rather winningly, Rachel thought. "I'll just be going now, and if I might help you again, Miss Katherine knows where to find me."

Dan was so reluctant to tear his eyes from "Miss Katherine," that in leaving, he nearly fell off the back steps.

Kitty giggled.

"That's a nice young man, to be so helpful to you and all," she said, beginning to clear away and handling the china with a show of great care. "His father has a farm west of here that Mr. Gage thinks to take over one day, but he stays in town winters, and works the docks for pocket money. He don't spend all he gets there, neither, but is laying-by properly."

"The two of you got well acquainted, then," Rachel commented dryly, looking into the teapot.

"Oh, yes," Kitty said. "He's got a brother and two sisters at home, and a sister who's married and lives in Providence, and his brother don't seem to take to farming, but wants to live in town and work at a shop or something."

"Making the farm all young Mr. Gage's to claim, I suppose."

"Well, if his brother don't want it... Oh, is the tea stewed? You made such a face!" Kitty giggled. "I'll make more. It'll just take a minute."

But when fresh tea had been brewed, it developed that the milk jug was empty. Kitty was certain there was more in the can, but there was not—nor, it seemed, was there any sugar in the house beyond a few crumbs stuck to the paper.

Rachel said wearily, "Is there any bread, then? I've had no supper."

Mr. Gage had eaten all the bread.

"Well, as he was so kind to you, I thought you would want me to be nice to him," Kitty said, becoming defensive. "Oh, there's a piece of cheese! The fire's low, but there's enough still to toast it. I could do with a piece of toasted cheese myself, now I think of it."

"Toast it then, and bring me mine in the back parlor," Rachel said. "And don't let it fall off the fork, for heaven's sake! I'm ravenous. I'll be writing a letter."

Or rather—two letters, Rachel resolved. She had not written to ask after her brother-in-law William for days.

CHAPTER ELEVEN

The jail was unfortunately situated in the shadow of taller buildings, and by five o'clock on a winter's evening it was quite dark within. So long as the sheriff was at his desk below, a little light made its way up the stairwell, and there was sometimes a moon, of course. But because no lamp or candle was permitted upstairs, by seven—earlier, sometimes—Josiah sat in absolute darkness.

While Mr. Brown was resident, the sheriff had often, as he left for the night, heard his prisoners passing the evening hours away with conversation. The preacher, he noticed, true to his calling, was the principal speaker. Mr. Brown was hard of hearing, and even under the stimulus of strong drink, not a great talker, but he apparently had no objection to the sound of Josiah's voice, and when he could make out the words, sometimes answered them. Josiah talked whether he was answered or not. He had nothing else to do.

But with Mr. Brown gone, Josiah was silent, too self-conscious to talk to himself.

Yet he did not sleep.

It was the sheriff's experience that with nothing else to occupy them, most men reverted in confinement to something like an infant state, napping in the day and sleeping soundly as soon as the sun was down. It unnerved him slightly that, however quiet his step on the stairs, when he came up with his candle for a last check of the cells before resorting to a nearby tavern for his supper, Josiah was always wide awake and, moreover, usually bade him a cheerful goodnight. The sheriff was not certain he was doing his job properly if he was not briskly disliked by his prisoners.

One evening soon after Mr. Brown's departure, having, in his usual way, wished the sheriff a pleasant evening, Josiah also asked the hour. His watch had been taken from him, along with his other property, when he had been put into the cell, and now, as the sheriff clearly saw, Josiah had embarked upon a campaign to have it returned to him. His direct request for it having been denied, the prisoner made a point of asking the time often—especially when it was least handy for the sheriff to ascertain it.

The sheriff, who had no intention of returning the watch or any other subsequent item for which the preacher might afterwards hanker, was on a campaign of his own. However often and however politely Josiah asked the hour, the sheriff as politely told it to him. Eventually, the sheriff supposed, Josiah would become bored with his game and give it up.

This time, before the sheriff could be much inconvenienced by having to shift candle and keys to pull out his watch, a muffled tone from the sheriff's pocket answered for him. Josiah, despite having been thwarted in his intent, laughed.

"You're cheerful tonight, Woodley," the sheriff said irritably. He would have thought his practice of regularly omitting to give the minister his proper title would have had an effect by now. "This life suits you, does it?"

"Will you be offended if I say I've had quite enough of your hospitality?" asked Josiah. "No, it doesn't suit me. I've always wanted more time to read, and now when I've got all I could ask for, I've no light to read by."

"If that bed tick takes fire after I've gone for the night, there'd be nobody handy to bring up the keys to let you out."

"I'd be willing to take the chance."

"You might. I wouldn't. You'll have to wait for your fire until you get to the next world. There'll be plenty there, so I been told."

Josiah understood the insinuation and did not answer, and the sheriff felt obscurely ashamed. "Why don't you sleep?" he said. "Morning'll come quicker then."

"Or seem to," agreed Josiah.

"Write—Think up a sermon. There's nothing like a sermon for putting a man to sleep. What sermon was you to give your next Sunday in the pulpit? Think about that."

"I was to speak on the nature of heaven," Josiah answered. "Not my choice. It was suggested by Dr. Conrad, as I remember, in balance of one delivered by the Reverend Tudge earlier on the nature of hell."

The sheriff's candle was bad, and smoked. "Pick a different thing, then," he said, grimacing and waving the smoke away with one hand. "I've never heard anything about heaven myself made me want much to go there. Not that I'm in danger of it, I suppose you'll say."

"I don't know," replied Josiah. "Why shouldn't you? Or perhaps in your case, the greater your sin, the *likelier* you are of heaven, since it would be a punishment for you to be sent somewhere you didn't want to go. But, since you bring it up, what *have* you heard of the place? Everyone seems to agree as to hell's torments—the smoke and the smells and the fire and whatnot—but all anyone says of heaven is that it is a pleasant land, and we shall be very happy there."

The sheriff, who had been turning to leave, stopped to consider this.

"Angels," he ventured.

"Yes," Josiah agreed, nodding thoughtfully. "There are angels there. And apparently a lot of music, for the Bible speaks of trumpets sounding out of heaven. But are the angels the souls of our own dear departed, as some maintain, or are they separate beings, created by God to serve Him? The point seems unclear."

"It's said we'll meet up again with our folks and such there," said the sheriff slowly. "I don't know as they'll be angels. Don't the Bible make it plain, one way or the other?"

"It seems to me the Bible states that we shall *like* heaven, and that's all," Josiah answered. "Even such as you will like it, I believe. In fact, perhaps that's why Holy Writ is rather vague upon the details of it. Perhaps every man's heaven is different, according to what he likes."

The sheriff did not think much of this remark. A heaven of tobacco chewers free to spit, curse, and ogle the ladies as they pleased did not fit his picture of the divine however much he might have enjoyed it. He turned again to go.

Josiah said quickly, "On another subject—I am concerned about Mr. Brown's family."

The sheriff turned back again. "I don't know as I follow you," he said. "You were talking about angels, I think. I missed where the name of Brown came up."

"It's Mrs. Brown I was thinking of principally," Josiah said. "There are half-a-dozen children in the household, I believe, and very little to keep them on. Mrs. Brown takes in washing, and the bedding in these cells is very dirty. Might you not bring the two together, the impecunious Mrs. Brown and the filthy linen, to both of their advantages? My wife has found her some work, but she says Mrs. Brown would welcome more. You might be able to persuade the city councilors to put something into the budget for the purpose, and then it would cost you nothing for your charity. Or I'll pledge my watch against the expense. It's of no earthly good to me anyway, where it is." This last was said with detectable bitterness.

The sheriff considered for a moment.

"You're an odd one, Parson," he said finally. "I'd have thought you had troubles enough of your own to occupy you without making a charity out of the town drunkard's wife and brats."

Josiah returned promptly, "It's sitting alone in the dark that leads me to think too much. I've nothing to do here, no light, and no means of keeping track of the hours. Besides," he added, smiling, "why *not* make a charity of someone? It's not as though by forgetting my duty to others I can make my own situation any better."

The sheriff's candle was getting short, and he wanted his supper.

"I'll consider the matter," he said, and went down.

*

Next day Mrs. Brown, a shabby, sad-looking creature, came up to ask timidly that Josiah strip off the covers from his bed and push them through the bars to her.

"I'll take your shirt, too, if you will, Reverend," she told him. "Sheriff said I might."

Amazed, Josiah complied. He had begun to be troubled with lice, and disliked to tell Rachel for fear she might not like to come, or to come close. Hiding himself as best he could in the corner of his cell—Mrs. Brown considerately turned away—he stripped off his linen and handed it out. A louse scurried from one fold to hide itself in another.

"Washing won't do nothing about them," Mrs. Brown explained in a mournful tone when she saw it. "They must be squorshed with a heavy iron." And then, without meeting his eyes, she added bashfully, "I do thank you for all you've done for my family, Reverend Woodley."

That evening, the sheriff returned Josiah's watch.

CHAPTER TWELVE

Rachel was in the kitchen, as usual. The rest of the house, save for sleeping, and—to Kitty's regret—sweeping and dusting, now seldom saw either of the women from one week to the next. She and Kitty were sorting through the last of the winter's root vegetables brought up from the cellar to separate out those that were beginning to rot and boil up the rest for immediate use. Kitty thought this an unnecessary economy, as there were plenty of sound potatoes and turnips to see them through to the summer. The girl's apparent inability to understand Rachel's patient explanations as to how the practice of unnecessary thrift was an exercise of virtue somehow had the effect of introducing doubt on the matter into Rachel's own mind and, troubled, she finally sent the younger woman off to the shops with the market basket on her arm to be rid of her.

"You're back quickly today," Rachel commented when Kitty returned. She had expected, in fact, that her maid would make a whole morning of the job, as she usually managed to do. "And where's the thread I asked for? I don't see it here. Did you forget?"

Kitty seemed slow to answer, and kept her face averted. "No. That is—I didn't forget, exactly. I didn't buy any, is all."

"Didn't buy any?" Rachel repeated. The purchase of thread had been the primary objective of the whole expedition.

"I couldn't," Kitty said, adding quickly, "I will, though. I just need to go to another shop. That mercer's was out."

"Out?" As the thread was a common kind, and made in the local mills, this seemed an improbable story. Then, with sudden comprehension, Rachel demanded, "Kitty, did you go to the mercer's on Water Street?"

Though trying to wear a brave face, the girl was not entirely able to keep the shake from her voice as she admitted, "Yes. I know you said I ought not to, that I ought to shop on this side of town, but it's a penny cheaper on Water Street for the same thread, and I don't mind the extra walking." (Not to mention, Rachel thought, there was always a chance of meeting with Mr. Gage on Water Street.) "But when I got there, the shop boy said at first that they hadn't any of the kind I asked for, and then when I told him I could see it myself on the shelf right behind him, he said they did, but it was already promised to someone else. So I left. And then I thought I might as well bring home what I had bought already, so as not to have to carry it. I'll go out again in a minute."

"You certainly won't," Rachel told her. Timidly, in a manner contrary to her nature, Rachel put an arm around her maid and squeezed gently.

Abruptly overcome, Kitty clung on hard, and cried.

"It's nothing to do with you, Kitty," Rachel soothed. "No one has anything against you, dear. It's because of the accusations against Mr. Woodley. I should have told you plainly why I thought you should avoid the Water Street shops, but I never imagined anyone could be so cruel as to refuse you service."

"Have they been hateful to you, too?" Kitty asked from the shelter of Rachel's shoulder. "If they have, you just say so, and I'll speak to my brothers. *They'll* make those fellows understand they can't treat you that way."

"No, no," said Rachel quickly. "No one's been rude to me, really. I just had an impression— Well, you know. That my patronage wasn't wanted."

The shop boys found it easier, Rachel guessed indignantly, to be overtly insolent to a girl of their own class than to a silk-gowned "lady."

Kitty, though she had stopped weeping, remained draped like damp laundry over Rachel's shoulder. "There, there, now," Rachel murmured, attempting to ease the younger girl into a more upright position. "Everything will be all right. Here: Take this."

The sight of Rachel's pocket handkerchief made Kitty raise her head at last.

Having dried her eyes on it, Kitty then examined the article minutely. "That's a nice bit of work," she said, studying the stitches which joined the handkerchief's broad, black border to its white center. "I wouldn't like to have to pick *those* out." (Rachel did not reveal that when she had applied the mourning border it was not with any intention of later removing it. Ever.) Kitty sniffed, "I don't know why I should go down to Water Street anyway. The shops are much nicer this end of town."

"Remember that it's nothing to do with *you*, Kitty," Rachel repeated. "It's—it's the nature of the charge against Mr. Woodley, as I said."

Kitty attempted to return the moist handkerchief. "Well, those folks just ought to withhold judgment, that's all *I* want to say! Why, they don't even *know* Reverend Woodley."

"They do not," agreed Rachel. "Put that in the wash, will you, dear?"

*

After the incident in the shop, Rachel felt she should no longer require Kitty to accompany her to the jail on her daily visits. The sheriff's start of surprise when she arrived for the first time all alone made Rachel think she had better apprise Josiah of the change. It would not do to have her husband imagine she was losing all sense of decency without him at home to guide her.

Josiah heard the tale of the Water Street mercer in grave silence.

"I'm surprised," he said, when Rachel finished. "And I'm sorry."

Rachel waited for more, but her husband seemed to have nothing to add to this. After a moment, she asked him quietly, "If the mill workers have already judged you, do you think they'll ever let you stand trial?"

"Here, do you mean?" Josiah asked.

"Anywhere."

He understood her. "Of course, of course," he said quickly. "The sheriff still has those two pistols, doesn't he?" Josiah's smile begged for an answering one from Rachel, but she could not oblige. "I think a lot of wild talk is circulating, but in the end, I've no doubt cooler heads and the evidence will prevail." He added, with a short laugh, "I just wish, when the time comes to make my case, that I had more and better evidence to present! Something to counteract the letter I wrote to Miss Hale, at least. I made a bad business of that letter. I'm sorry. I meant well, but in as far as I can remember what I wrote, I can understand how, under the circumstances, it might seem to point a finger of blame in my direction."

"Did you write only the one?"

Josiah seemed surprised by the question. "One letter? Oh, certainly," he said. "I had nothing to say to her that might have made her welcome further correspondence between us. I wrote once, telling her I felt myself obliged to acquaint her present pastor with the information that she had not relinquished her membership at Bristol church voluntarily, and that was that. What else had I to say to her?"

"And she did not write you in reply?"

"Oh, no. Why should she?"

"What—what color was the paper on which you wrote?"

Josiah laughed out loud. "Well, white, I suppose," he said. "I don't know. Why do you ask?"

"Might it have been blue?"

With smiling astonishment, Josiah briefly considered. "I don't think so," he said then. "Why? Was it blue? Let me remember for a moment…We have white paper at home, don't we? But I didn't write Miss Hale from home. I have a great stack of yellow paper in my office at the church that I write my sermons on. I probably used that."

"Have you blue paper as well?"

"You're very persistent about this, Mrs. Woodley," Josiah said, still smiling. "What is your point? No, I don't think it was blue. I have no blue paper that I remember. Now that I reflect, I'm certain I used the yellow paper in my office. I wrote Miss Hale from my office; I brought no paper from home; so presumably I used the paper I had at hand there."

"You did not borrow any blue paper? I don't mean only for the letter to Mary Hale. At any time, have you ever written to anyone on blue paper?"

"No blue paper," Josiah assured her. "I have no blue paper, and I know of no one else who has blue paper. Nor pink paper, nor green. Are you satisfied?"

Rachel did not reply until he had asked twice.

"Yes, certainly," she said absently. Following Josiah's gaze, she turned and saw that the sheriff had come up the stairs—his custom when the Woodleys' time together was up.

"You'll come again?" Josiah asked sadly. "I don't like to require you, but it is lonely here."

"Of course I'll come."

On an impulse, Rachel put her face to the bars and kissed Josiah's cheek. Let the sheriff look if he liked it, she thought irritably. She was lonely, too. "I'll come tomorrow," she promised.

Josiah did not, as he usually did, watch her out of sight, but instead addressed the sheriff.

"You're looking unusually spruce today," he commented. "Like a man who's going courting."

The sheriff flushed and, rather than answering, stopped where he was and let Rachel go down without him. Only when the two men heard the street door slam below did the sheriff admit, "Seems that Brown woman won't take a 'no' even when it's said plain to be heard. She—washed my shirt. Both my shirts."

"Would I have committed a solecism by taking a sheet of blue paper?" Josiah asked the sheriff then. "Women see these things better than we do." On Rachel's visits, Josiah stood facing the stairs. He knew exactly, therefore, at what point in their conversation the sheriff had come up.

The sheriff's reply seemed to Josiah not much to the point.

"A lot of women is rattle-brained, and I got no use for rattle-brained women," said the sheriff. "But some ain't."

"I beg your pardon?"

"You might ask Mrs. Woodley more about that paper."

Astonished, Josiah replied, "Thank you. I will do so."

The sheriff went down.

Unlike Josiah, Rachel did not own a watch, and therefore did not realize until after she stepped into the street that their daily visit had been quite a long one. The sheriff had either been inattentive to the time or unusually kindly disposed today, she thought.

As she turned from the jailhouse door in the direction of her home, a woman was walking toward her. Rachel, in her usual manner, shyly averted her glance.

As she approached, the woman—one whom Rachel would have characterized as a "lady" under most circumstances—ostentatiously drew her skirts aside, as though she thought they might be contaminated by contact with Rachel's.

Tears stung Rachel's eyes, but she lifted her chin defiantly.

"Good day to you, madam," said she clearly, as the woman passed. "And isn't it a fine one?"

CHAPTER THIRTEEN

"Kitty, I'm going out today," Rachel said a few days later. "As no one visits, it can present no difficulties for me to be away for the afternoon."

"I don't know how you can say that," Kitty said, looking up in surprise from the knife she was cleaning. "I think you have ever so many visitors here in town. At home we don't see anybody for weeks, sometimes. Mrs. Tudge came only yesterday, and Sister Birdwell the day before. And that other lady who I never remember the name of, with the horrible bonnet. *She* came. Oh, why don't she at least put some new ribbon to that awful thing? Something in me just wants to snatch it off her head and rip it to pieces every time I see her."

"Oh, yes, *those* ladies," Rachel muttered, turning away. From the pattern of the visits, she suspected that calls to the Woodley house were being taken in turn by the wives of the senior church members exactly as they visited among the aged and indigent of the congregation. Calls she herself had once helped to arrange, for charity's sake.

"If any of those ladies should happen to come today, you may tell them I am not at home," Rachel said firmly. "But say it in such a way as will make it seem I am only not receiving, please."

Kitty did not understand.

"That is to say, I *will* be out," Rachel clarified, "but I would rather it were not *known* that I am out. I would rather it be thought that I am *in*, but not to callers. Is that clear? Can you do that, do you think?"

"Oh, I know the sort of thing you mean," Kitty said, becoming comfortable again. "I can do that. But tell me who's to go with you. I'll need to let her come in first, before I turn anybody else away."

This obliged Rachel to admit she intended on going out quite alone. Kitty immediately objected to this.

"You just go and see to those floors," replied Rachel severely. She had clearly permitted Kitty to become too familiar that she now imagined she could dictate to her mistress.

But before Rachel could add, as she intended to, that she was *quite* old enough to look after herself, she remembered she meant to beg the loan of Kitty's cloak and bonnet again by way of disguise. It would be extremely awkward to scold the young woman only to ask a favor of her immediately after. "I'll be fine," she finished weakly.

Kitty gave her a sharp look. "I'm coming with you," she informed Rachel, putting aside the knife. "There's no floor in this house has as much dirt on it as will be put to your name if you go frisking about town all by yourself. Anyhow, I'd rather come than stay by the door to tell lies. Or rather, something *like* lies—only not exactly, since you really *would* be gone."

"No."

"Why? Why can't I?"

"Because—because I might be going where it wouldn't be proper for a young lady to go."

Kitty scoffed at this. "You never would. I don't even know but three such places hereabouts—well, four, really—and you wouldn't go *there*."

Unless it was to deliver tracts or something, which I might help you to do, if you like. That's not unproper."

As sometimes happened, Rachel found herself unconscionably amused by Kitty's remarks. "No, I'm not going *there*, as you put it," she said, trying hard to think where the fourth "such place" of which Kitty spoke could possibly be. "I'm going down to the ferry landing."

"That's not unproper either," Kitty said. "And anyway, I've been to the landing before."

"Yes, but surely with your father or brothers to protect you. After I go to the ferry, I believe I shall also need to visit a—tavern. As I do not know for certain at which tavern I should inquire, I may need to step in at several. You mayn't go with me to a tavern for the simple reason that I don't know how, if I let you, I should face your mother—or God—afterwards."

Rachel then hurried from the room to forestall any possibility of Kitty making some announcement to the effect that she was quite accustomed to taking her recreation in taverns. Her intimacy with Kitty was making Rachel increasingly aware of the great many differences between what her own, and people of Kitty's class, considered acceptable behavior in a woman.

"Well, my ma needn't know, and God will understand," Kitty said, determinedly following Rachel to the stairs. After a glance at her mistress' face, she added hastily, "What I mean is, I'm sure you don't have any reason for going anyplace that isn't so good as to make it right for you to go there. What do we care how it might look to the likes of those who are always wanting to mind other people's business for them? Most folks in taverns is only there to wash the dust from their throats and have something to eat and maybe talk a bit. I don't see what's the wickedness in that. What do you want to go to a tavern for, then?"

"You remember when I told you I didn't know who would inquire into the evidence to support Mr. Woodley's case? Well, it seems no one will, in fact. Therefore, I must do it myself."

Kitty started up the stairs behind Rachel saying cheerfully, "Oh, yes, that's a good idea. Like when you went asking after Mary Hale. I'll come, then."

"No, you won't either. And what do you know about my inquiries concerning Miss Hale?"

Rachel guessed from Kitty's blush what her answer would be.

"Mr. Gage told me. He said he took you to five places asking after Mary before you found the house where she lived, and then you were gone an hour talking to girls there. Oh, don't mind that he said so, for he didn't understand what you were about before I explained it to him, and after I told him, he promised not to tell another soul. His word is one you can take, too, like Mr. Woodley's is."

She folded her arms and assessed Rachel's appearance. "If you don't want folks to see who you are—which I'm guessing you don't— you should wear something in a color. No one in Milltown's ever seen you wear anything but black. There's a nice blue gown I laid away in the press the first day I worked here. You'd be like a different woman, almost, in blue."

Rachel stopped where she stood, remembering how she and Josiah had laughed together when, upon her putting on the gown one day long ago, she had discovered it would no longer button at the waist, nor across the bosom. "Why, he's a great strapping little fellow already, isn't he?" her husband had cried, fondly kissing her. She had never worn the dress since. Rachel turned away from Kitty, her hand to her mouth.

Behind her, the young girl said gently, "You mustn't think I'm not sorry about your little girl." Stepping closer, she patted Rachel's shoulder. "I am, really. And I know your heart is broke. But it's only a dress, if you think about it. And there'll be other babies."

"Not like Lucy," Rachel whispered.

"No. That's what my ma says, too," Kitty agreed. "'One don't replace another,' she always says. 'They're all different.' Even when we lost little Tom, and she named the new baby 'Thomas,' too, she said we mustn't get the idea he'd be just like the first one because he had the same name. It was only that she wanted one called for her father is all." Kitty waited for some comment, and when none was forthcoming, added, "I'll get the dress, shall I? Or if you don't like that, I'll give you mine—though I think it isn't fit for you to be seen by light of day in, owing to how it don't cover up all your petticoat."

Rachel was taken aback by Kitty's straightforward manner. It was true that other women had endured what she had, though the loss of no other child, of course, could be as much a loss as Lucy's. How they then went on afterwards—as they did, and she must—she could not understand.

Drying her eyes, she said slowly, "I don't think it's fit, either. You're right, of course. It's but a dress. I'll wear my blue."

As Kitty started happily toward the clothespress, Rachel added, "And—another bonnet, perhaps. Is it too early for straw? And then *you* go down and see to those floors, girl. Under no circumstances are you coming with me today!"

Better blue now, in spite of Lucy, she told herself, *than black for Josiah later.*

*

Rachel saw at once why the ferry landing, where she had never previously been, had a reputation in some circles as an unholy venue. It had nothing to do with the actual business of ferrying men and goods across the river. But lying, as it did, outside of the regular jurisdiction of Milltown, convenient to another state and passage as far as the sea beyond while still within an easy walk of town loafers, it was a magnet to rootless wanderers, men wishing to evade their natural duties, and those wanting to conduct business of a surreptitious sort.

Nevertheless, as the nearest bridge was at some distance, the ferry was also the quickest way to towns on the opposite shore, and always busy. Rachel approached the dock warily, scanning the faces of those boarding for any she knew. At her side was Kitty, who had obtained permission to come by the straightforward expedient of outwearing her mistress.

The ferry master stood on the dock overseeing the ferry's loading, and as they drew near him, Rachel and Kitty kept close to one another and clutched nervously at each other's arms. Judging by the torrent of oaths issuing from him, the ferry master's humor was evidently bad. Rachel's courage had been wavering since she first set foot off her own front steps, and now it almost failed her altogether. If she did not turn back, it was only because she could not quite think how to explain the decision to Kitty.

After observing the scene for some time from the steps above the landing, Rachel decided it might—possibly—be safe to approach the ferryman after all. His temper was—perhaps—not as bad as his language implied. Even as he was occupied in pointing the resemblance between one man's efforts to maneuver an unwieldy barrel with that of a broke-back, three-legged jackass donkey attempting the act of coition, the expression on his weathered face remained serene. His earnest tone even suggested he imagined he was offering not abuse, but advice from which the clumsy dockhand might profit.

"Come on, then," she said nervously, with a glance at the stunned and staring Kitty. "But mind where you step. If you fall down here, we shall have to burn your clothes." It was evident the men who worked the dock were much given to tobacco "chaw."

After a glance at the faded signboard to ascertain the name, Rachel called out, "Mr. Cockburn, may I have a moment of your time, please?" Her voice was only a little tremulous, and she came forward boldly.

As the ferryboat, at that moment, was just drawing creaking away from the dock, Mr. Cockburn did not immediately hear her, but when at last he turned and saw two women, he instantly transformed. After visibly starting, he squared his shoulders and attempted to straighten his collar before remembering he wore none. These things done, he bowed, then came briskly forward, removing his cap with one bare hand and wiping the sweat from his brow with the other—with which he then promptly and vigorously wrung the gloved hand Rachel mechanically half-offered.

"You didn't want to cross, did you?" he bellowed. "Next crossing in two hours, if she's back on time, damn her. Pardon my language, ma'am, miss." He replaced his cap—apparently for the purpose of removing it again with a flourish immediately after. "A fine day, ma'am. I believe I may guarantee you a smooth crossing. That is, the Lord willing, damn Him! Beg pardon, ma'am, miss. Not going across? What may I do for you, then?"

Rachel faintly repeated that she wanted a moment of his time to talk.

Mr. Cockburn's lifted eyebrows suggested he was puzzled, but perfectly well-disposed. "Time? Talk?" he roared. A roar seemed habitual to him. "Well, come in, then. Come in, come in. Ma'am. Miss. Don't stand in the wind, damn it. Pardon my language, ladies, please." Having ushered them in to the lower room of the tiny cottage that served him as business office and residence, Mr. Cockburn attempted to explain himself to his visitors.

"You'll have to pardon my language, ladies," he said, thrusting forward a dusty chair—there was only one in the room—for their accommodation. "A bachelor all my days. No woman's gentling influence and all that, damn me."

Rachel pressed Kitty down into the chair. Kitty's gray gown, she thought, would not show the dirt from the chair so readily as her blue one would do.

"Mr. Cockburn," she began, and then hesitated, thinking how to proceed.

Before she could continue, Mr. Cockburn's attention was suddenly diverted to the window and events outside.

"*Damn* me!" he breathed, his eyes widening. Throwing open the door, he engaged in a brief, profane exchange with a loafer attempting to light up his pipe in the lee of a few dockside bales of cotton.

Turning back and wiping his brow again, the ferryman apologized for the interruption.

"You were saying, ma'am?" he enquired politely, at a volume that would have been better suited to the open air.

Rachel had had enough. "Mr. Cockburn," she expostulated, with a gesture toward the fascinated Kitty. "If you have the least care for your soul's preservation, you will not expose an innocent young girl to further such indecencies!"

Beneath his tan, Mr. Cockburn flushed perceptibly. "I do beg pardon, ma'am," he said quickly. "A lifelong bachelor. I've lived rough and I talk rough, but I mean no offense. Pardon my language, please. You was saying, ma'am? Miss?"

"You are transgressing against God and His commandments every time you take His name in vain, Mr. Cockburn! You are offending your Heavenly Father, to whom you are indebted for every blessing of your existence—and for existence itself!"

"Yes, ma'am, I sure am. And I do beg pardon for it." Mr. Cockburn's face glistened with sweat.

"It is not *my* pardon you should solicit!"

"No, ma'am."

"Surely you could conduct your business without recourse to—such language. For your own soul's sake, and for that of your men. As their employer, it is your responsibility to bring them closer to God, not to lead them by the shortest road to—to Perdition!"

Mr. Cockburn, who had been appropriately subdued and humbled to this point, scratched his chin thoughtfully at this last remark.

"Well, ma'am," he ventured cautiously, "I'm not so sure I agree with you there. I believe you may have the right on your side when you say I ought to be more careful in my language before the young lady—such a nice, pretty young lady she is, too. Damn pretty! Where'd you get them blue eyes, girlie? Damn pretty blue eyes—pardon my language, ma'am. But as to whether I could hope to get such a drag-tailed, dog-lazy, good-for-nothing crew of low-living, high-drinking—beg pardon, ma'am, miss. Lacking a woman's gentling touch is what I am. But as to whether I could get such a bunch to God when I can't get them to earn half their pay without scalding their ears, I doubt it could be done by anybody, unless maybe with a sharp whip and a hot poker stuck—beg pardon, ma'am. Which I've got no taste for the use of. But I've heard it said that God don't give a man a job to do that

He don't give the man tools to do it with, and it appears the only tool He give me was my tongue. Which I use the best way I can. But I do apologize to you ladies. I'm a rough man, and I've lived rough, is all. I mean no offense."

Kitty giggled, and hid her face behind her hands—to Mr. Cockburn's evident enjoyment.

Squeezing the girl's shoulder until both of them winced, Rachel said sternly, "I will not lecture you further, sir. I'm sure you know what it is you ought to do."

The spiritual health of Mr. Cockburn was a subject Rachel knew she had a moral duty to explore further, but time pressed, and furthermore, she needed the ferryman's good-will. Therefore, she continued, "Mr. Cockburn, I have information that you have given evidence in the case against Mr. Woodley to the effect that you saw him here accompanied by a young lady on a certain Thursday evening of January last. Is that correct?"

This information Rachel had gotten—along with the letter from Mr. Tudge's cousin—from Mrs. Tudge, who, though she hated gossip, thought it her duty when she visited to inform *dear* Mrs. Woodley what stories were circulating about her husband.

"Say again?" asked Mr. Cockburn blankly.

At first, the ferry master remembered nothing of the matter, and even insisted he had never heard the name of Woodley before in his life. But when Rachel reminded him of the facts of the case, he said, "Oh, him. The murdering parson." Rachel flushed, but when Kitty made as if to fly to Josiah's defense, pressed the girl's shoulder again to warn her not to speak.

"That has yet to be determined," Rachel said, with dignity. "I only enquire as to whether that is the statement you made. I only heard it secondhand," she admitted, thinking guiltily, *or third or fourth, perhaps,* "and I wish to be certain of my facts."

Mr. Cockburn had to ponder the matter.

"No," he said finally.

Rachel's heart leaped with hope.

"I don't believe I said I knew the fellow's name. A tall parson and a little woman in a calash bonnet. They come by here just after dark. I never asked the fellow's name, damn him."

Rachel despaired.

"Are you certain the man was a minister?" she asked. "Or did you only think so because he wore a long coat?"

"Oh, no, he was a parson, all right. He said he was. It was a pretty young lady with him. Dark, though. I favor the fair ones, myself."

Kitty preened.

"And you are certain of the date you saw them? It was not another day?"

"Oh, no," said Mr. Cockburn positively. "I know the day. 'Twas the day before that same young lady was found hung at the woodyard, is what the day was. One of them broke-down, God-damned, do-naught cripples calls hisself a sailor brung me the news. He was up at the woodyard himself and saw the whole thing, damn him."

He had a few more details to add, and did so, flirting outrageously with Kitty the while, and making a genuine effort that a fair percentage of his words were ones that could cause no offense. Rachel could not think of anything more to ask. The situation was not as she had hoped.

Finally, it occurred to her to inquire, "Did they wish to cross the river?" It might do Josiah some good, she thought, were the ferry master to answer in the affirmative. To cross and to return—even without allowing any time for such activities as they might have engaged in on the opposite shore—would have taken Josiah and Mary several hours. Were she to investigate carefully, she might find witnesses to say Josiah was not away from office and house for long enough to have made such a trip and then to have hanged poor Mary after.

But Mr. Cockburn said, "Oh, no. Just passed by, damn them. Had her arm through his, and talking like lovers. Never came down this far at all."

A silence followed, until Kitty asked doubtfully, "Well, how did he tell you he was a parson if they didn't come down? You have got me all mixed up, Mr. Cockburn."

Mr. Cockburn thought things over.

"No, 'twas the next day he said it," he explained. "Passed by Thursday night without stopping, then the parson come back alone next day—come bold as you please, too, like he'd never laid a hand on a woman in his life, damn him—and crossed. When I asked him what manner of work gave him such pretty, white hands, damn them, he told me he was a preacher. Tall man with a dog-skin valise, as I told the sheriff. I saw him again when the sheriff brought him back the next week, and it was the same man, and the same valise. Tall man, brown eyes, damn them."

Rachel asked, heart pounding, "The man who passed by with the girl had brown eyes?"

It was Mr. Cockburn's turn to be confused. "I never said so, damn it. I couldn't see what color his eyes was in the dark, could I?"

"Mr. Cockburn, think carefully," Rachel ordered, white to the lips. "Are you certain these two men of whom you speak are the *same* man? The one who passed on Thursday with the young lady, and the one who made the crossing next day? Might it not have been two *different* men you saw?"

"Oh, no. Tall man, long coat."

"But you could not see him clearly in the dark. You said so."

"No," Mr. Cockburn said slowly. "It was the same man crossed on Friday that the sheriff brung back. I know *that* for sure, damn me. Dog-skin valise."

"He was going to visit his sister."

"Yes, that's what he said! I remember now he told me so."

Speaking as distinctly as her growing excitement allowed, Rachel asked, "Mr. Cockburn, do you feel you could give evidence in a court of law—under oath, on peril of your soul, remember—that the tall man in a long coat who passed by with Mary Hale on Thursday night was the same man who crossed the river on Friday evening? Under oath, Mr. Cockburn. Would that be the testimony you would give?"

"Now who's this Mary What-say-you?" Mr. Cockburn inquired, rubbing his bald head confusedly. "I don't recall when *she* was brung up, damn her."

It fell to Kitty to explain, since Rachel could not get her breath.

When Kitty was finished, Mr. Cockburn pronounced an especially violent oath, and paused to consider the matter.

"Tall man, long coat," he said finally. "That would be what I would say. Wore a fur hat, now I think of it."

"But not necessarily the same…"

"Oh," said the ferry master impatiently. "Might have been another tall man dressed like a parson, if you say it was. Might have been Lucifer, but I didn't see he had no tail. I couldn't say more than that, damn me, if you was to—"

It would be better not to specify what Mr. Cockburn suggested would be necessary to elicit further testimony from him.

Despite this lapse in his speech, Rachel thanked the ferry master with a warmth that probably surprised him, for she was too truly grateful for reserve. She offered her hand again and allowed Mr. Cockburn to hold it for longer than was necessary (strictly speaking), repeatedly expressing her appreciation. As they left, the ferryman invited both women back at any time to make the river crossing or another attempt at his conversion, either one.

"Damn fine females," Rachel heard him saying loudly after them. "Damn them!"

*

Kitty had not quite followed events.

"You look almost happy, Mrs. Woodley," she commented. Kitty was breathing hard, for Rachel had taken the stairs up from the landing so quickly the maid had to scramble to keep with her. "He's not such a bad fellow, is he? Mr. Cockburn, I mean. Not so bad as you—I mean *we*—thought at first, anyway."

"I *am* happy," Rachel said, hurrying on. "No, not happy. I'll wait to rejoice until I've made further inquiries. After all, Mr. Cockburn could not say it *was* Josiah, but neither could he say for certain that it was *not* Josiah."

"Is that it, then?" Kitty panted. "Does that prove Reverend Woodley never killed Mary?"

"No, it doesn't prove it," Rachel conceded. "But Mr. Cockburn's testimony cannot do Mr. Woodley any harm, at least."

Taking her maid's arm suddenly she said, "Thank you for your—support, Kitty. I'm sorry to have exposed you to such dreadful language. Really, one wonders why such a man is not stricken dumb!

But I was glad to have you with me, nonetheless."

"Oh, I quite enjoyed myself," Kitty admitted happily. "Mr. Cockburn is so funny!"

"Is that how you found him? 'Funny?' Well, maybe he was, a little. Are you ready to step in at a tavern, then?"

"Oh, yes," said Kitty confidently. "In fact, I own I could do with a little glass of something just now."

Rachel wailed aloud. "Kitty, we are going for information only! Not to—tipple."

"I wasn't thinking of a tipple, really I wasn't, Mrs. Woodley," Kitty replied quickly. "Only beer, and small beer at that. There's no harm in that, is there? My mother's beer is the best, but I could do with any just now, I'm so dry."

There was probably no point, Rachel thought, in trying to make clear to Kitty the great difference between taking a glass of beer at home and having the same beverage in a tavern. "We'll see, then," she sighed. "If we come upon a respectable establishment."

"Oh, lovely," Kitty said happily. "What a nice day this is turning out to be!"

Rachel was surprised to note the number of drinking establishments along the road on which Mary Hale had been seen taking the last walk of her life, and down which a man alleged to have been Josiah had returned alone. She had never thought before to count, or even notice them, but had always kept her face decently forward. For her own sake and Kitty's, she made the assumption that anyone enough like a minister in appearance to be taken for one would not have called in at a mere grog shop, and asked for information only at places she and Kitty could agree seemed "respectable." Kitty, owing to her thirst, was more flexible than

Rachel as to what features constituted respectability.

On their third attempt, the two women struck upon the tavern at which Josiah had allegedly been seen on the night of Mary's death. The information Rachel received there was much like what Mr. Cockburn had provided. A tall man in a long coat had come in, the proprietress informed Rachel, and asked for a bite of supper. She remembered he was wearing a fur hat.

"Beaver?" Rachel asked. Josiah's hat was felted beaver.

"No," the woman said. "A *fur* hat." She mimed stroking an animal. "Rabbit, probably. Might have been squirrel. Didn't take notice at the time."

Josiah had no such hat. "Did you speak with this man?"

"Only to tell him he'd come too late, so there was nothing left in the kitchen. When I said that, he went away."

"Was this man the Reverend Josiah Woodley? Could you swear that it was?"

But the tavern keeper, a Methodist, had never seen Mr. Woodley.

"He was a very tall man," she said. "I remember that. In and out in five minutes, he was. Wanted nothing to drink, only food, he said. I didn't ask his name, and I know I never saw him before—nor since, come to think of it."

Kitty, who had caught on to things by now, smiled broadly.

Rachel repeated what she had said to Mr. Cockburn relating to oaths and legal testimony.

"The sheriff asked me, and I told him: A tall man in a long coat," the woman said firmly. As a regular churchgoer it clearly offended her to be reminded of what oath-taking entailed. "I never said he was a preacher, even, only that he was dressed like one. And I never said I knew the man's name. And that's what I would say in court—or before the throne of God. A tall man, in a long coat, with a fur hat. That's all I can tell you. It's twelvepence for the drinks, missus."

Rachel was not ready to agree with Kitty that the day was fine, but for the first time in weeks she acknowledged a slight break in the clouds, at least.

CHAPTER FOURTEEN

The custom of the church was that all clerical duties, whether sermons, christenings, weddings, sick-visits, or funerals, should be taken by her ministers in strict rotation. The system was good in theory, ensuring a fair distribution of work and an equal opportunity for experience among the clergymen, but in practice, the strident Mr. Tudge was not popular. When choosing a wedding date, courting couples became intent upon the cycles of birth, sickness, and death in the town, angling for a day when Mr. Tudge was likeliest to be fulfilling some other church duty.

The families of the dead, of course, had no flexibility as to scheduling at all. Therefore, it must have seemed to them that God showed a tender mercy in the way in which funerals fell disproportionately upon Dr. Conrad.

But in fact, if the hand of God was in operation, it worked through the ministers themselves. Mr. Tudge did not much care to preach funerals, whereas Dr. Conrad preferred them above weddings, and the two had in fact been in the habit for some years of making an unobtrusive "swap" of clerical duties where they thought it would not be noticed. A funeral many years before had led John Conrad to the ministry in the first place.

The circumstances surrounding Dr. Conrad's "call" was one of the few details of his life of which Rachel was sure. The minister never talked about himself, or his background—abjuring the sin of pride, she assumed. This left Rachel free to imagine whatever she would about it, and what she imagined was that his background was like her own, one of—if not wealth—solid comfort, at least. From their first meeting, Rachel sensed the existence of a special bond between her and the doctor. Not carnal. The bond was not in any way carnal. It was one of shared good breeding and natural distinction. Rachel's people, while not wealthy, were among the first citizens of Boston, and "class will out," as Rachel told herself.

But in point of fact, Dr. Conrad had started life as the third son of an immigrant farmer and his weary, bent little wife, who were poor in everything but offspring. The entire Konrad family (as the name was originally spelled) ate, slept, and worked in one room when the boys were not laboring with their father in the fields or trudging long miles to a country school that was in session for only a few weeks of the year.

Little Hans, as Dr. Conrad was then, *knew* nothing higher or better than relentless farm work and food eaten from a knife's blade out of a common pot, but an innate sense told him there *was* something more, and he longed to have it.

The first hint he got of the direction in which the road to this other sort of life lay came from the schoolmaster. The schoolmaster, Hans observed, wore a coat of "boughten" cloth, and the farmers removed their hats to him. Little Hans, therefore, resolved to become a schoolmaster himself. The schoolmaster (who was by other measure a poor man), saw a kindred spirit in the book-loving boy, and recommended he study the law instead.

Hans had no clear idea of what "the law" comprehended, but when he broached the idea to his father, the old man did not dislike the notion. Old Mr. Konrad had found himself from time to time at a disadvantage from his own want of legal knowledge, and when the old man thoughtfully knuckled a brother for jeering, Hans understood he had struck upon an acceptable means of escape from the farm.

At fifteen, wearing a suit of homespun his mother and sisters struggled to make presentable, Hans Konrad began an apprenticeship with a country lawyer.

In his two years in the lawyer's household, John (as he now called himself) made poor progress at the law, but acquired a thorough familiarity with his mentor's style of life, which he thought the more important subject. The lawyer's home, he observed, had several rooms, including a parlor, in which there was a bed, it was true, but also a harp, upon which the family daughters played. The son of the house, like his father, wore a broadcloth coat and yellow gloves. The gentlemen's manners were subtly graded according to the quality of the person with whom they interacted, and the ladies' apparent fragility generally overlaid cold steel.

John was most attracted to the life by the fact that, compared to his own family, members of the household seemed to have to labor very little to earn the daily bread that the daughters baked and served out on plates of painted china, one to each person, thrice daily.

The only drawback to his situation, as John saw it, was that he was required to put in regular Sunday appearances at church, where the minister was a plodding and poor speaker. The young man had no interest in the divine. He occupied his mind during services by mentally rewording the sermons to better effect and plotting ways to better his earthly lot.

The lawyer and his neighbors gathered one morning in the

churchyard to lay a friend to his last rest, where throughout the service the man's widow, sadly unreconciled to her loss, wept without intermission. When the moment came for the corpse to be lowered into the earth, the woman threw herself upon the coffin and clung on. This was not an uncommon gesture in the region, but in this case the local minister's attempts at comfort were clumsy, and she resisted his efforts to lead her away.

The woman's sons were having no better luck when, on a sudden impulse, John stepped forward. Embracing the woman, he quoted, "'Why seek ye the living among the dead? He is not here; he is risen.'" Growing up in a backwoods community, the one book John had reliably been able to get his hands on was a Bible.

The gesture was theatrical, and it was presumptuous. It was also bad doctrine, as the local sect was one which preached the Last Trump, and resurrection at a later date. Nevertheless, it had its effect. The sobbing woman allowed herself to be led aside, and the burial of her husband proceeded without further incident.

Any, that is, aside from the admiring glow which began to radiate in John's direction from the lawyer's eldest daughter. John modestly affected not to notice it.

The lawyer had no intention of marrying his daughter to a penniless boy, particularly one who—if he ever managed to be admitted to the bar—would one day be a professional rival. When his daughter gushed to him that she thought Mr. Konrad specially touched by God, her father took advantage of the remark to ask the former Hans whether he would consider continuing his education at the local seminary. When the boy hesitated (and his daughter's adoration continued, and even grew), the lawyer bettered the offer by promising to endorse an application to a proper College of Theology.

John accepted the deal.

Since he was not yet of full age and knew, furthermore, that his father would never accede to such a plan, John enrolled at the college in New Haven under the name of "John Conrad," and registered his status as "orphaned."

There were consolations for this sudden "loss" of his family.

A seminary master and his wife, for pious reasons or for pity at his lonely condition, took him into their home and acquainted him with genteel fashions. John's fees and expenses were paid by a generous endowment funded by lay citizens whose charitable impulses were strongly acted upon by a belief that God took particular notice of Good Works performed in reference to His personal servants. Best of all, to his own surprise (and satisfaction), from being thin and gangling, the young man matured tall and good-looking. At his ordination, it was generally agreed that young Reverend Conrad looked every inch a minister and that a handsome face was useful in securing postings to the better churches.

Equally useful would be the presence of a suitable wife at his side.

This presented no difficulties. John found he attracted without effort the attentions of many pretty and well-off young ladies, whose parents found it awkward to insist upon their usual worldly standards in a potential suitor who was, though poor, demonstrably a Man of God. Among these pretty and well-off young daughters of compliant parents (the lawyer's daughter was long forgotten), Sophronia Hancock was the prettiest and richest.

Rachel knew Dr. Conrad had received his call at a funeral. She also knew—because the doctor often said so—that the day on which Sophronia accepted his offer of marriage was the happiest of his life. The only other thing she knew for sure about him was that, as one of her ministers, he could be applied to for advice in matters of conscience. A week after her experience of "frisking about the town," as Kitty had expressed it, Rachel gloomily concluded that time alone was not going to heal the pricking of her conscience in the matter, and decided to seek out Dr. Conrad again.

The minister was in his study reading when Rachel arrived. He was clearly not expecting visitors, for when Rebecca appeared noiselessly at the parlor door, Rachel behind her, he started. Then, rising quickly, he gestured Rachel in, and Rebecca shut the door on them softly, as she had been taught.

"I am so sorry," the doctor said. "I did not hear you knock."

Flushing, Rachel told him, "I came in at the back, through the kitchen. I didn't like to disturb Mrs. Conrad, but I need your counsel."

"Of course, of course." Courteously waving Rachel to a chair, Dr. Conrad said, "I hope it is not that you are distressed by the fact that Mr. Tyrode cannot come sooner to consult about Mr. Woodley's defense. It seems one or two other little matters need his attention right now. I assure you it's not at all unusual for legal business to be conducted this way."

Mr. Tyrode was the Reverend Mr. Tudge's cousin, and (so far, only nominally) Josiah's advocate.

Rachel replied dryly, "Are you going to tell me preparing for court on short notice often has the effect of wonderfully sharpening a legal man's faculties?"

Dr. Conrad was not quite able to dissemble his amazement at this remark.

"Why should I?" he asked, looking aside. "Is that so?"

"Josiah told me this morning that it was," Rachel answered. "I thought you might have been the one who said it first."

Dr. Conrad was forced to smile sheepishly. "I did, in fact. I thought it would reassure him. I'm not acquainted with Mr. Tyrode personally, but I'm certain he knows his business. He trained with a very good man." The doctor quickly changed the subject. "But what may I do for you? Has something happened at home?"

Rachel hesitated. Now that she had her chance, she was not quite certain how to explain what brought her to the minister's study.

After a moment, Dr. Conrad asked delicately, "Is it that you are experiencing some—uncomfortable degree of physical longing for your husband, perhaps? If that is the difficulty—"

"Oh, no, no!" exclaimed Rachel, blushing. In fact, she *was* longing—a bit—for Josiah, but she would never, under any circumstances *whatsoever* have mentioned such a thing to anyone. "It's something else. Something quite different."

"Desire is perfectly natural," persisted Dr. Conrad. "You need not be ashamed."

Rachel did not agree with this, and could not meet Dr. Conrad's eye. "It's another matter entirely," she repeated, her head down. "In fact, you may already have been told about it by...others." By "others," Rachel specifically meant Agnes Tudge. Bravely looking up again, she admitted, "I have canvassed the town looking for evidence to clear Josiah's name, and in doing so, I've visited various...dubious places. Of course, it was all on Josiah's behalf."

"I see," Dr. Conrad said, without much interest. As he spoke, his left hand moved involuntarily toward his watch pocket. Though he caught himself and stopped it, Rachel detected the gesture.

"I will be brief," she said immediately. "Sir, I confess I am less troubled in my conscience for what I have done, than because I have lied to Josiah about it. I thought a man in his position—confined as he is, I mean—ought not to be given reason to worry. My intentions were good. I beg you to believe they were. But the result is exactly as I should have foreseen from the first. I have told lies, and now I have become entangled in them. Should I confess, Dr. Conrad? Or was I right all along to protect him?"

Dr. Conrad, when Rachel looked up, was smiling. "What were your lies?" he asked.

"You can imagine them," she answered, suddenly weary. "I have lied about where I have been, how I have spent my days. I have led Josiah—Mr. Woodley, I mean—to imagine I am keeping quiet at home and trusting in God and his own innocence to vindicate him, when I am not."

Rachel waited to be chastised for her lack of faith. Instead, Dr. Conrad asked, "What did you learn in your 'canvass,' as you called it? Have you gathered useful evidence?"

"Oh yes! That is, I believe I have. I haven't found any single *great* thing that would clear Mr. Woodley immediately, but I have learned a few small things of which I believe Mr. Tyrode, and possibly the sheriff, should be made aware. But there is my difficulty—or another difficulty beyond my troubled conscience. Since Mr. Tyrode cannot come to Josiah, and since"—Rachel's tone became bitter—"it seems Mr. Tyrode will not accept information from *me*, Josiah must pass on my information himself, in a letter. But for Josiah to be able to do so, I would have to confess to him where the information came from, and, therefore, that I have…lied to him."

Her hands folded in her lap, Rachel sat back with relief and waited to be told whether—and what—to confess to Josiah.

Instead, Dr. Conrad continued for a few moments to question her, wanting to know every detail, it seemed, of whom she had interviewed, and what she had learned at each visit. His questions were pointed and exact. He seemed disappointed she could not remember Polly's last name, though he added, "The testimony of a mere mill girl would not have much weight with the court in any case, perhaps. Or that of a tavern keep."

"Perhaps not," Rachel conceded. "But—Mr. Cockburn's?" Mr. Cockburn, though dirty and profane, was a man. "Do you think nothing of what they told me is worth risking Josiah's peace of mind to communicate to Mr. Tyrode?" She added glumly, "I see I haven't properly appreciated Josiah's faith in my judgment until now, when I risk destroying it."

"Oh, we cannot have him lose faith in your judgment!" Dr. Conrad said immediately. "Never that!"

He leaned back in his chair and steepled his fingers to consider the matter further.

Finally, he said, "You asked for my advice, Mrs. Woodley, and I will give it. First of all, don't let your conscience trouble you unduly. You have been a little adventurous of late, but only because of your anxiety for Mr. Woodley. God will surely understand and forgive you for that. Secondly, let your husband enjoy his peace of mind as well, and do not feel you have to confess any of this to him. Thirdly, when Mr. Tyrode arrives in Milltown, I will tell him myself what you have discovered. That way, he may judge what information may be useful to him in making Mr. Woodley's defense, and your name need not come up at all."

This was just the kind of solution to her difficulties for which Rachel had been hoping. It left her with nothing to do and no (further) lies to tell, and yet advanced the cause of Josiah's defense.

Modestly deflecting Rachel's thanks and picking up the book at his elbow, Dr. Conrad said, smiling, "I'm sorry to have to hurry away from you, Mrs. Woodley, but as it happens, I have a funeral to preach in an hour, and I like to be in good time to have a word with the family beforehand. You will send a note around to me, won't you, if you should think of anything further you learned through your interviews? Anything at all."

Rachel took the hint, and rose immediately.

"Yes, of course. My compliments to Mrs. Conrad, if you think it right to mention my visit at all."

"Thank you, yes, I will tell her. I am just going up to say goodbye to her now, in fact. She should be awake, and I like her to know at all times where I will be, in case she should need me."

They had stepped into the hall by this time, but on the verge of putting out her hand, Rachel stopped and stared.

Dr. Conrad's eye followed hers. "Yes," he agreed, "it's in rather bad condition, isn't it? This prayerbook was given to me at my ordination, and so has seen many years of service. I can't bring myself to buy another, somehow. We have grown old together, as it were." Indicating the slips of paper inserted here and there, he added in a confidential tone, "Bookmarks. It doesn't do to be groping for a verse when souls are at stake."

"No, of course not," said Rachel automatically. "Good day, sir."

As she turned to go out, Dr. Conrad was already darting up the stairs.

CHAPTER FIFTEEN

"Good day to you, Mrs. Woodley. Are you here quite *alone*?"

Ten years' practice in the pulpit had so strengthened the Reverend Mr. Tudge's voice that his accustomed Sunday message of the inescapable damnation of sinners was easily heard by the deafest churchgoer in the farthest pew at the back of the upper balcony—that is to say, Mr. Brown. Unfortunately, it had also seemingly left him unable to pitch his voice at a level suited to a single auditor in a small, enclosed space. When she heard him behind her, Rachel first started and then shivered, confirming more certainly than words could have done that she was, indeed, alone.

"I—that is, *Mr. Woodley* requires something from his office, Mr. Tudge," she said, quickly shutting the drawer through which she had been searching—and heaping sin upon sin, in fact, for she was lying. Josiah knew nothing of her visit. Rachel had not only come alone, but to satisfy only her own curiosity. She wished to know the color of Josiah's writing paper. "I did not know anyone would be here."

Mr. Tudge looked as though he might be about to sermonize her, but to Rachel's relief, he only said good day again, and passed on.

At such a near miss, Rachel's knees gave way, and she sank into Josiah's chair, rested her arms on his desktop, and dropped her head onto them. From a peaceful and ordered one, her life had become an unending sequence of trials, alarms, and humiliations, and Rachel was worn out. Gloomily, she wondered why, since God had seen fit to make her a woman, he had not also seen fit to give her the submissive nature appropriate to her sex. Even as a child she had been prone to contend against authority with balled fists and outthrust chin.

After a few moment's dismal reflection on this, Rachel began again to search her husband's desk.

Keeping in mind that many people in Milltown might have blue writing paper available to them, Rachel initially allowed herself to understand only that she was coming to search Josiah's office to ascertain, once and for all, that he was not one of them. It was a sensible thing for her to do, she felt, before Mr. Tyrode made it a point in his defense strategy. Once in her husband's office, however, she could no longer pretend to herself that she would do nothing further there than to open his desk, note the color of the paper, and leave quietly. Guiltily, in haste, but thoroughly, she sifted through his sermon notes, his daybook, his bookshelves, and even his waste papers—neatly twisted into spills. Josiah had been raised to practice thrift—supernaturally alert for any reference, by name or inference, to anyone who might have been Mary Hale.

Rachel had always rather disliked the girl, though she could hardly say why. The stories that had followed Mary from Bristol were a factor in her prejudice, certainly. Josiah might say they amounted to no clear evidence of a deformed character, but "no smoke without fire" was Rachel's motto. And then, the time had not been right for any new acquaintance. First pregnant, and then newly bereft of her child, Rachel had wanted all of her husband's attentions even as they irritated and disappointed her. She resented the time Josiah gave to answering the pretty, carefree-seeming girl's so-called religious questions. Not that Rachel doubted the questions were religious in their nature. She only wondered whether it was really for the sake of her soul's comfort that Mary asked them, or because she found the minister himself good company. Josiah kept a record in his daybook of every visitor to his office, and "MH" appeared there several times during his Seabury tenure.

Once, also, Rachel had observed the two conversing on the church porch. They did not see her. As Rachel watched, Josiah, at one point, turned away from Mary, looking suddenly lost and rather embarrassed—rather like a scorned lover, it seemed to Rachel. She told herself, then and after, that she trusted Josiah; trusted him absolutely. But there was no denying the sharp prick of jealousy she experienced at seeing her husband with a woman who was, in her liveliness and cheery self-confidence, everything Rachel herself was not.

Seeing nothing among his other papers that so much as hinted at Mary, Rachel studied the daybook carefully.

Josiah's notes since coming to Milltown were briefer than those he had kept in Seabury—he was busier—but still quite complete. Though it was true that there was no record anywhere comprehending Miss Hale's last hours, in the daybook's cataloguing of the name of everyone with whom he had met or to whom he had written ("letter-MH" appeared in its proper place) there was no indication of any communication at all with Mary Hale beyond that one brief, unfortunate, note.

In court, Rachel reflected, it might logically be argued that Josiah's relationship with Mary was something conducted entirely outside the chronology represented by his daybook, but Rachel was satisfied with what she discovered. Though her domestic appointments did not include any means for Josiah to note down his evening activities, she herself knew without any doubt that, aside from an occasional hike about the fields, her husband spent the hours he was not at the church at home, with her. Relief made her almost weak—though she did not know why she should ever have doubted him.

Thinking that Mr. Tyrode might make use of the daybook in preparing Josiah's case, Rachel put it into the bottom of her market basket, carefully spreading her handkerchief atop, since it was nobody's business but her own what she carried out the office door. Then, seeing Josiah's Greek testament lying by, she reached for that, too.

Josiah's father had given the volume to him when he left home for the seminary, and, as Rachel was aware, it represented much more than a book to her husband. Though old Mr. Woodley was a religious enough man, he had not been pleased to have his son choose the church over the family farm. Josiah was his only boy, and the land was something wrested by his father and grandfather before him from the grip of Raw Nature and turned into a fit and bounteous home for Godly people. It was Josiah's duty, the old man felt, to stay and work it. Josiah had an obliging nature, but in this one thing he had stood firm. His sister Anne and her husband William, he maintained, should have the farm. William was a farmer born, and Anne had never imagined any life for herself than that of a farmer's wife. The parting gift of the testament represented a long-delayed and otherwise unspoken acquiescence on the part of the old man to his son's decision.

Aside from considerations of sentiment, it was Josiah's favorite book, and would undoubtedly be useful for passing the long jail hours.

As she laid the volume in her basket, an edge of paper slipped out at the top, catching Rachel's eye. It was a common thing, just an edge of paper, but it aroused her curiosity nevertheless. Without thinking what she was doing, Rachel withdrew it. On a folded sheet of white notepaper were written the initials "MH," and within was a long lock of dark curling hair.

CHAPTER SIXTEEN

Rachel sat at Josiah's desk for a long time, too hurt even to cry. Then she walked home, climbed the stairs, and lay down fully clothed on her bed, staring at the wall opposite with burning, unblinking eyes until Kitty, who had been calling to her for some time, came up and found her there. Rachel said she was ill, and Kitty summoned a doctor who, noting Rachel's pale lips and rapid pulse, recommended rest and a light diet.

On a light diet, therefore, Rachel rested, spending her days like a certain other lady, sitting well wrapped up before a low fire in her bedroom, near enough a window to see out without being seen and listlessly refusing, through Kitty, all callers.

Kitty was solicitous, but clearly did not approve Rachel's self-imposed isolation. "You been up here for a week," she hinted. "I think you might just see some of these ladies that come visiting you. Mrs. Birdwell, maybe. She's nice. She don't ask a lot of questions about what's none of her business."

"Another time I will."

"All right. And of course I can hardly keep Mrs. Tudge out. She'd like to have come right up the stairs without my leave! I won't let her, though."

"Thank you."

"And Mr. Woodley keeps asking about you, every time I go to see him. I told him this morning I thought you were better."

"Yes."

Kitty's fists went to her hips. "You could write him," she urged. "I wouldn't mind taking a letter from you to the jail. He writes to *you*, after all."

Rachel's expression hardened at the mention of Josiah's correspondence.

In the first hours of her "illness," Kitty had, on her own authority, carried word of Rachel's condition to Josiah in his cell, along with the basket containing what she had collected from his office. In return, the girl brought back a note that ended, "Love and thanks for the Bible, and the hair. I loved her so much, as you know, that any little token of her is the greatest comfort to me."

Mentally, Rachel raged that Josiah should write such a thing to *her*, of all people! Was he simply shameless, or could he actually be insane? Her head aching with unshed tears, she searched in her memory for any hitherto undetected pattern of madness in Josiah's behavior and was almost sorry to find none. If he were sane, then what other conclusion could she reach but that what he had written to her was the work of someone both brazen and wantonly cruel?

Rachel closed her eyes. "Kitty, I'm very tired. I think I'll rest now, if you don't mind."

With Kitty gone and nothing to do, Rachel passed the time replaying in her mind her earlier life with Josiah.

He had been a shy but ardent wooer. His perseverance in courting her in the teeth of her parents' obvious disapproval had eventually won even her father's grudging respect. A girl as headstrong as she was, Rachel's parents had long told her, had no business choosing any but a *masterful* husband. But though Rachel knew her parents were right about her need of firm discipline, what attracted her most about Josiah was his gentleness.

People often did want what was worst for them, she now thought, bitterly—just as babies wanted sugar-sticks instead of healthful pap.

Still, if Josiah had never been a properly masterful husband, he had at least not been a cruel one. Since Lucy's death, something in him must have changed for him to love another, and openly announce the fact to her. She acknowledged to herself, reluctantly, that while she was grieving their child, it was possible she had neglected Josiah just a little. Mary must have taken advantage of that to flatter his vanity, and soothe his injured pride.

Or had their estrangement, Rachel wondered, sprung from another source entirely? Had she alienated her husband by her self-will and unwomanly drive? If that were the case, maybe he'd be satisfied now that, like Sophronia Conrad, she kept meekly to her room, saw no one, and prayed.

She did not recollect that Josiah had no way of knowing *what* she was doing, since she neither visited nor wrote to him.

Josiah, meanwhile, wrote regularly to his wife, covering pages and pages with all the news he heard from anyone, the story of his days, and as warmly phrased expressions of his affection as he thought would not disgust Rachel and yet still give his heart relief. Each letter ended with a delicately expressed confidence that his wife would soon feel well enough to write him back. As she was said to be ill, he did not like to press—but he was lonely.

Rachel read none of the letters, putting each as it arrived into her writing box unopened.

*

Time was passing, and, exactly as Rachel had once feared would be the case, it was passing with nothing whatever being done to prepare Josiah's defense. Strangely, just as Rachel became indifferent about it (Josiah continued serene), the sheriff began to feel concerned.

It occurred to the sheriff one day that when the Reverend Woodley was condemned, as it appeared he would be, it would be his own duty to sit with the minister in his last hours, lead him to the gallows, put the rope around his neck and, finally, when the last prayers had been read, to spring the trap beneath him. This was a part of his job, and the sheriff had always accepted it as such.

But the sheriff had come to like Josiah, and to feel that any woman who had pushed a man as mild as the young minister to the point of murder had probably been fit to be hanged herself. And was Mr. Woodley even guilty? The sheriff, who would at one time have been ready to swear he was, had begun to have doubts.

In the locked drawer of his desk, beneath the pistols, the sheriff held the letters found in Mary Hale's hymnal against the day of his trial. Better men than he (specifically, the members of the tribunal who issued the indictment against Josiah) maintained that the two unsigned letters on blue notepaper had been written by the same person who wrote the letter written on yellow paper, though "in a disguised hand." There was no doubt as to who had sent the letter on yellow paper. The signature was clear, and in any case, Josiah had owned it immediately when it was shown to him. The letters on blue paper Josiah had denied, a denial the sheriff thought at the time was merely the self-serving lie of a man who had murdered in a panic when he found himself in the snares of a harlot. The three letters together, since they suggested the motive for the murder, were held to be strong evidence of Josiah Woodley's guilt.

Since the day he had heard Mrs. Woodley interrogating her husband about the color of his paper, the sheriff had examined the letters many times. At first when he did so, the tribunal's decision appeared to him an inescapably correct one. The sheriff was a man of wide experience, but little education, and instinctively deferred to the judgment of those more learned than he.

But over time he had become less certain, and by now he was absolutely convinced that such was not, in fact, the case. He believed now that the letters on blue paper had not been written by Josiah "in a disguised hand," because they had not been written in a disguised hand at all. The sheriff was no detective. He was unfamiliar with even the word "detective." But he had been sheriff for some years, and he had seen "disguised hands" and every other sort of bad writing before. He had examined the work of forgers. He had deciphered the scrawls of the nearly illiterate. He had been witness to last wills penned in the shadow of the gallows by men whose hands shook from fear. To his practiced eye, the letters to Mary Hale appeared to have been written by two *different* men, each in nothing more or less than his usual handwriting. Neither writer had disguised his writing because neither writer saw any reason to do so.

The man whose paper was blue asked Mary for patience, and discretion, and further meetings (though he admitted having failed to keep meetings past), in order for the two of them to settle together on a plan for dealing with Mary's "predicament." He offered his assistance, contingent upon her continued circumspection, including the destruction of the letters themselves. He wrote familiarly, even intimately. If he made no secret of his feelings, why should he disguise his hand?

The man whose paper was yellow—which Josiah Woodley had

unhesitatingly confirmed was none but himself—expressed regret he should have "ruined" Mary, but alluded to no meeting, past or future. He offered his regards, but not help.

The implication of the word "ruin," in Mary Hale's case, was problematic. Josiah's explanation, given before the Tribunal, was that he had meant only to say that by informing the Methodist clergy of Mary's checkered past, he would spoil her chance of making an entirely new start in Milltown with an unclouded reputation. The sheriff was of a suspicious nature and doubted the explanation when it was made. Now that he was better acquainted with Josiah, it seemed perfectly plausible.

The consequence of all this slow, methodical pondering was that the sheriff now wondered who—if it were not Josiah Woodley—actually *had* been dallying with (and writing on blue paper to) Mary Hale, and whether it was not *that* man who ought to be occupying his time in the cell upstairs by reading his testament and looking to his soul's preservation.

Rachel, practicing passivity and virtue in her bedroom at home, would have been surprised to know how often the sheriff thought of her—and with what impatient oaths. The sheriff, meanwhile, was equally surprised to find himself wishing her back; but—damn her!—aloof and irritating though she was, Mrs. Woodley had demonstrated she was not one to be easily balked from doing what she set her mind to do. When she had been out to prove her husband had never killed Mary Hale, there seemed some hope that the evidence necessary to clear him would be amassed. With her away, Josiah's best chance was gone, too.

But that was like a woman, the sheriff thought: Never *where* they were wanted, *when* they were wanted. It was for that very reason he himself was a bachelor.

CHAPTER SEVENTEEN

"**B**ear in mind the first time I find that lit and you sleeping will be the last night you'll have it," the sheriff announced sternly, reaching through the bars to slam down upon the table in Josiah's cell a candlestick in a glass with a few inches of candle in it, and a bit of flint to light it with. "You've got paper enough, I guess."

Josiah, who had gotten into a habit of lounging on his bunk to read, since there was no chair in the cell, sat up in surprise.

"Yes, thank you," he said, beginning to smile delightedly. "Oh, my! Yes, that'll do nicely. It's amazing to me how, though the days have undoubtedly gotten longer since I've been here, the nights somehow don't appear to have grown correspondingly shorter. To what do I owe this welcome change in your policy, sir?" Automatically, he moved the candle and writing implements around on the table into a proper semblance of a writing desk.

The sheriff eyed his prisoner with evident dissatisfaction. "Well, now, it's not so's you can write sermons," he growled. "Court day is coming up. It's time you were making up your case."

Josiah's face fell and he was still for a moment. "Excuse my ignorance," he said. "I had imagined that would be my advocate's responsibility."

The sheriff declared flatly, "Well, he don't seem overeager for the job! You better get on by yourself the best you can. Then when he shows up, you might have something to show your lawyer that he can make your defense *of*."

"I see," Josiah said. "I admit I had been trusting in God until now that my entire innocence of the crime of which I'm accused would be defense enough. But then, I've stood on that all along, and here I am in jail still, aren't I? What more do you suggest I do, then?"

The sheriff stirred impatiently, thinking that though the Reverend Mr. Woodley was a good man by most measures, he didn't seem to take hold, somehow. It was good and Godly and all to go on loving your fellow man even when he was trying to put your neck in a noose, but any man with a proper degree of enterprise would make a better effort to *avoid the noose*.

Irritably, he said, "Now look here, Woodley. This is a regular trial in a regular court you're called up to; not the Last Trump. It might be that God will know if you're guilty or not without you saying nothing, but there's going to be twelve men in that jury box who don't. Now, nights when it's quiet, what you need to do is to light up that candle and write down on that paper what you remember about things that will convince them twelve men. Ask God to tell you what to write, since you set such a store by Him. But don't wear out your knees praying instead of doing what you can to help yourself first."

For a moment, Josiah said nothing.

Then, not looking up, he answered, "Perhaps I deserve the reproof. It must appear to you I've done very little to help myself. But as a matter of fact, I've considered my situation pretty thoroughly since I've been here, and my problem, as I see it, is that I have absolutely no idea what I could possibly say to convince a jury of my innocence. If the light is intended solely to allow me to write my defense against a charge of murder, you had better take it away."

"You saying you done it, then?"

"I'm saying I can offer no *proofs* I did not. It will not take me the light of a quarter inch of candle to write the words, '*I did not murder Miss Mary Hale*,' and I have nothing but that to offer. I did not kill her. I spent the night of her death like any other, at home with my wife. I have no witness but my wife to that fact, but so it is."

"Well, your wife can't testify," the sheriff said flatly. "You need something better than that." The state's legislature had long before ruled that a wife must not be put into the position of having to decide whether it would be better for her to betray the interests of her earthly master, her husband (should he be guilty of a crime), or God, her heavenly one, and Witness to the oath she had sworn to speak the truth. A *man*, perhaps, could not serve two masters, but women were understood to do so, and accommodation made for the fact.

"Yes. But what?" Josiah asked.

The sheriff understood it would be an unwise policy to allow Josiah, or any defendant, to know in advance of his trial exactly what evidence would be brought against him there, since such foreknowledge might permit him to "adjust" his alibi (which ought to be nothing but plain truth) to refute it. The account of his activities during the time Mary Hale had been murdered that the Reverend Woodley had given at his arraignment would be read out in court, and it was assumed if it were a true, complete, and honest deposition, "evidence" presented to the contrary would show itself false against it.

Such was the principle.

However, as even Josiah might have admitted, in Josiah's particular instance neither this principle nor his own religiously correct policy of trusting in Providence and his own innocence to refute the charges against him seemed tending to secure his acquittal. As matters stood, the thing most apt of any to prove unconvincing in the courtroom was Josiah's alibi.

"I have done everything I know to prepare myself for what's ahead," Josiah continued. "I think I've prayed myself into a condition to accept either martyrdom or a miracle, as heaven sees fit to bestow."

The sheriff was not as entirely satisfied as Josiah that this constituted the most thoroughgoing defense strategy. After mentally casting about for some way to stimulate his likeable but unsatisfactory prisoner to a more vigorous course of action, the sheriff abruptly inquired, "You ever get around to asking your missus about that paper, Woodley?" He had decided that to speak of the letters, at least, could not be considered a violation of any rule pertaining to the dissemination of evidence, since Josiah had been shown them already.

"Paper?"

Impatiently, the sheriff said, "That paper she was all after asking you about one day. Whether you had blue paper or white paper, or pink or yellow or what. I said to you at the time you might want to find out what she wanted to know for."

"Yes, you did," Josiah said, brightening. "I forgot all about it when I heard she was ill. Why *did* she want to know all that?"

"There, now!" exclaimed the sheriff. "That's the kind of thing I'm talking about! Don't just sit with your nose in a book all day. Mrs. Woodley had a reason for wanting to know that, and you should be asking her what that reason might be. That's a gumptious woman! She asked because she's looking to find things out that might help you, see? *You* should be looking to find things out that might help you, too."

"All right," Josiah conceded pleasantly. "I shall inquire of her when I write. Anything else?"

The sheriff's countenance rather fell at this.

"You might want to write it some way gets her to write you back," he ventured. "Seems to me I been seeing plenty of letters going out of this jail, and not too many coming back the other direction."

It seemed that way to Josiah, too.

His manner subdued, he said, "I think she must be much more unwell than Dr. Conrad indicates, to so neglect—" He was about to say "me," but did not like to seem self-absorbed, so he finished with, "her duty," instead.

The sheriff suppressed his instinctive snort. His self-control was heroic, at times.

"If your missus is poorly, then maybe you might want to talk to somebody else about that paper," he said. "What about that cheeky bit of girl your wife has got maiding for her? No, never you mind I said *that*. What you want is somebody got a brain bigger than her— Somebody with a brain."

After musing for a moment—the situation was a trickier one than he had first thought—the sheriff hazarded, "Well, now—what do you remember about them letters yourself, then?"

"What letters?" Josiah asked vaguely.

"*What* letters?" the sheriff exploded. "Damn me, what letters do you *think*? *Them* letters! Them letters likely to get you hung, of course! What letters am I *going* to be meaning?" He drew a breath and let it out slowly, to calm himself. "I'm talking about the letters to the Hale girl that was in her hymnbook. There was some on—" Briefly, he reflected, but concluded it was necessary to go on. "Some on one color paper, and some on another. What do you think of that?"

To his relief, Josiah's look became keener.

"I see," he said immediately. "I cannot recall what the differences were—color, you say?—but I do recall that the letters I did *not* write were on a different kind of paper from the paper of the one I did write. Sheriff, in all my life I have committed not a single criminal act. I beg you to believe that."

"I told you before it don't matter what I believe," the sheriff said firmly. "I can't be on the jury hears your case."

"Of course," Josiah said. It was his turn to draw a long breath. "Of what were we speaking?" He frowned. "Oh, the paper... You mean to imply, I believe, that by proving I had no ready access to paper like that of the spurious letters, I would prove I had not murdered Miss Hale. Or at least, that I had not written her. Forgive me for saying I can't see a great deal of value in that. I was not invited to read the letters, only to identify the hand as my own—which it certainly was *not*—but if my information from Mrs. Brown is correct, they only suggested an illicit connection between the writer and Miss Hale, which is not the charge against me. And in any case, how would the paper prove I did *not* write them? Anyone might buy any sort of paper at the stationer's."

"Be going too far to say it would prove your case," the sheriff agreed. "If you showed you didn't have a drawer full of blue paper down at the church, nor at home, nor right to hand, it might help you in the juror's minds, though."

"I see. Blue paper? Ah, it was blue. I remember Mrs. Woodley saying 'blue,' now. I noticed because she is particularly lovely herself when she wears blue. No, I don't believe I have any blue paper." He turned narrowed eyes on the sheriff. "What is in those letters? The ones I did *not* write? Are they dreadfully incriminating?"

The sheriff felt this question approached very near the sort of information he was not authorized to impart.

In a compromise with his conscience, he said finally, looking at the floor, "Say you met her." It was the smallest fact he could offer that he thought might still be of use to Josiah.

"Met Miss Hale? I certainly did not," Josiah said indignantly. "I did not know her to be in Milltown at all until a few days before—before she died. And when I saw her, I resolved immediately that she should not see me, nor I her."

"Not the kind of gal a parson wants it known he has the acquaintance of, I guess," the sheriff said, smirking.

Josiah flushed.

"I did not mean to be speaking ill of her," he said uncomfortably. "I thought her—a decent girl. And sincerely desirous of spiritual rebirth."

"Not so 'decent' but that she was looking towards another kind of birth," the sheriff said. "And half the town has you the pa of it."

"There's no question of that," Josiah said impatiently. "I had some occasions to speak with her at my former church, yes. Miss Hale came several times to see me there. But I assure you her concerns were entirely to do with religious matters."

"Well, what *I* know about the girl is that Old Adam and Mistress Eve was the kind of Bible story she liked best to play at. What you want is some way to make them jurymen know she wasn't playing at it with *you*."

Josiah exclaimed suddenly, "Oh, I see! I thank you for that remark, Sheriff. I was wondering why my wife sent this to me." From beneath the bed, he produced the daybook Rachel had taken from his office. She had intended it for the use of Mr. Tyrode, but not knowing this, Kitty had assumed that, like the testament, it was meant for Josiah himself, and brought it to the jail.

Josiah continued, laughing a little, "I really could not imagine why Mrs. Woodley thought I would want this, but I see now she must have deduced it would be a way to demonstrate what you have suggested— that I was not in the habit of meeting with Mary Hale."

He showed the book to the sheriff, who studied a few pages with apparent suspicion.

"You write a pretty hand," he acknowledged, after some moments spent spelling over the volume. "This looks to be the kind of thing I'm talking about, now. It's good for you that it owns up to the letter got you in trouble. Makes plain you didn't think you had nothing to hide about Miss Mary there. Your missus give you anything more?"

"Nothing I can see a use for in regard to my legal case."

After seeing that Josiah had nothing more to add, the sheriff cautiously urged, "What you want to do now is decide how to put what she found out for you to work."

"How?"

"What about that bloodsucking leech supposed to be lawyering this case? Don't you think maybe he ought to know about that book and that blue paper?"

"Oh! Yes, that would be useful, I suppose. Should I write him?"

"Unless you think you can shout to be heard all the way to Boston!"

Josiah grinned suddenly. "I'll bet Herbert Tudge could do it," he said, wickedly.

The sheriff was obliged to smile at this.

"See what you can do for yourself besides reading a book, then," he said. "What book is that, anyway? I never see you read nothing else, now you've got it."

Josiah showed the testament to him. It was a handsome volume, with smooth limp red covers stamped in gold.

"It's a Bible," he said. "A New Testament." He handed it through the bars.

The sheriff, after examining it briefly in a manner suggesting he expected it to bite, or lightning to issue from it, handed the book back, saying, "My eyes is old. I can't read such small letters no more."

"They're Greek letters," Josiah explained. "Lovely, aren't they?"

The sheriff peered through the bars at the print Josiah showed him. "What's it Greek for?" he asked.

"That's the language the Bible was written in," Josiah explained. "This part of it, anyway. The testament one usually sees is a translation of this."

The sheriff's habitually mistrustful expression returned. "I thought 'twas written in English," he said. "It wasn't written in English?"

"No, Greek. It's very beautiful in the original, but Greek takes rather a long time to learn, and not many people care to undertake it."

Asked the sheriff testily, "Well, if it wasn't written in English, how did You-Know-Who expect we should read it? That don't make sense." He grunted, "Near eight-o'clock. I want my supper. You get on with your letter, then, Parson."

"Thank you. I will. And thank you for the light, sir. I am more pleased than you could know to have it."

The sheriff went downstairs, thinking again it was rather more a pity than a relief that Mrs. Woodley no longer came to the jail. While she might lack her husband's good heart, she would instantly have comprehended and quite possibly already acted upon the information it had taken the preacher half the evening to ponder.

In his cell, meanwhile, Josiah, his candle lit and paper laid before him, dipped his pen and began another letter to Rachel. "My dearest, 'gumptious' wife," he wrote, smiling to himself. "This will be but a short note to let you know I have decided to write to Attorney Tyrode…"

CHAPTER EIGHTEEN

The sheriff's concession in the matter of the light was well-timed. Josiah had spent enough dark nights searching his soul, and was now ready to concede that being properly spiritually *prepared* to die did not absolutely require he resign himself to do so at once, nor did exerting himself to secure an acquittal at his trial constitute a failure of trust in the Almighty. To busy himself making a defense was more absorbing even than his testament—which, after all, he had read many times before.

The fact that he would be continuing work begun by his wife was also a recommendation of it. It did not occur to Josiah that his appraisal of Rachel's initiative and intelligence was more admiring than her own.

Mr. Tyrode, therefore, soon found himself in receipt of a letter from his client pointing him to weaknesses in the prosecution's case.

The small effort of writing this letter invigorated Josiah. Intellectual strength, the only kind he had ever displayed, was not much valued on his father's farm, and from his boyhood, Josiah had been aware he was regarded as ineffective. He was loved for his good nature, but considered of limited practical use. When the sheriff (who read it before sending it on) acknowledged that the letter to Attorney Tyrode was well done and likely to help his case, Josiah felt himself seized with new energy.

One evening, when the sheriff came up as usual to take his leave at the end of the day, Josiah said, "When you have time for me, I should like very much to talk to you."

"What about?" asked the sheriff, eyeing his prisoner warily. From time to time, denizens of the jail had been known to introduce, by means of friendly conversation, the topic of the sheriff's salary, and the amount by which they, the inmates, were prepared to augment it in return for certain "concessions."

Josiah said instead, "I want to know what the scene was at the woodyard on the morning Miss Hale's body was discovered. You may find this hard to believe, but I really know almost nothing of the details of the crime of which I'm accused."

The request took the sheriff by surprise. He stopped to consider it.

Seeing his hesitation, Josiah added, "I won't press you to tell me anything I'm not entitled to know. I only want to gain the advantage those who believe me guilty assume I already have—of knowing what the site of Miss Hale's murder was like."

This seemed to the sheriff a reasonable (though slightly dangerous) request for Josiah to make. The reluctance he felt over the danger, however, was overcome by his sudden inspiration that to describe the scene would allow him to lay traps for Josiah which might prove his guilt or innocence once and for all—at least, to the sheriff's own satisfaction.

Therefore, he said with heavy humor, "We can talk now, if you don't have somewheres else you need to be. What do you want to know, exactly?"

Josiah seemed pleased. "I'm keeping you from your supper, though," he said quickly. "Will you share mine? Kitty brought me a basket full of good things today. She's not the cook Mrs. Woodley is, but it all looks very nice." When the sheriff hesitated, Josiah added, "You'd be doing me a favor to take it. It's more than I can eat. Anyway, I'm tired of eating alone."

The sheriff, who was also tired of eating alone, obligingly fetched the chair from the empty small cell, placed it on the opposite side of the table from Josiah, and sat down, the cell bars between them. Watching as the minister laid out the food Kitty had brought, he exerted himself not to let his irritation show that his prisoner usually ate better than he did.

"What d'you want to know, then?" he asked.

"I suppose I want to know," began Josiah thoughtfully, "exactly *how* Miss Hale died. I've heard she was hanged. But how? What were the circumstances?"

"Well," the sheriff lied calmly, his mouth already full, "she was strung up in the shed at the woodyard."

Josiah considered this. "That makes sense," he said, missing the sheriff's pitfall by a wide margin. "I've never visited the woodyard myself, but I've been by it, and I don't see where else one could be hanged."

The sheriff's answer to this was a non-committal grunt.

"All right," Josiah continued, "and how did you arrive at your estimation of the *time* Miss Hale was hanged? I hope you don't mind my asking. I'm not questioning your judgment in the matter, you understand. It's just that this point seems to me of some importance to my case. I was informed the hour she died corresponded to one for which I have no witness to my whereabouts but Mrs. Woodley.

But how does one know when a death occurs? Are you allowed to tell me?"

The sheriff wiped his mouth with the back of his hand and studied his prisoner.

"Was a man in this town once, years ago," he said slowly, "got so tore up in a fight he died of it, laying all alone in an alley. Had a watch in his pocket had been broke by a blow with its hands at eight of the clock."

Josiah smiled. "Are you going to tell me Mary Hale's watch was stopped at ten o'clock?"

"No. Didn't have no watch I'm aware of. What I'm telling you is, I been sheriff twenty years and that's the only time it's been exactly clear, when there weren't no witness, what time a murder was done. Commonly, there's some guessing to it. Ten o'clock is a guess. At nine o'clock you and her—her and a man looked like you—was seen walking. At six next morning she was froze stiff. Sometime between nine at night and six next day, Mary Hale was hung, and it was likely earlier than later, or she wouldn't have been froze hard." He added, "Don't do you no good whichever way, though. You can't prove where you were anytime after seven or so."

"That's true, sad to say," agreed Josiah. "What about this man with Miss Hale, though? Why is everyone so certain it was me?"

"Well, he was a tall man..."

"I am tall."

"Had on a long coat."

"I do wear a long coat," Josiah conceded. "Anything better, or more precise? It seems to me I'm not the only tall man about."

The sheriff grinned suddenly. "You're the only one's a *young* man," he said. "And you two was acquainted. You said so yourself."

At this, Josiah leaned back on his bunk, where his face was obscured in shadow.

The sheriff, though with feigned unconcern, pushed the candle across the table to where it shown full on his prisoner. "Pretty dark now," he said, slyly. He was determined to keep a close eye on the minister's every expression as they spoke.

"It's those letters make it look bad for you," he continued, watching Josiah carefully. "The man seen walking with her and the man wrote to *ask* her to walk with him is the man that most likely hung her. Stands to reason." He did not add the information that he was no longer at all certain Josiah was the one who had written the letters.

After a moment's silence, Josiah said, "Here's another question for you: What makes you sure Mary Hale was murdered at all? What I heard first was that she was a suicide."

The sheriff nodded vigorously, and, for the first time since he had sat down, stopped eating. The question struck a nerve with him. "I said it was from the first," he declared. "'Twere the millworkers got another idea. Couldn't rest unless somebody else was made to blame for it, as if no girl in trouble ever done away with herself before. I've seen it a dozen times—no, more—while I been sheriff. It's usually by drowning themselves, but I suppose it being January made it look to her like the river was too cold. A man fixed on dying don't care: He'll blow his brains all over the barn. But ladies like to go easy if they can."

"This sounds promising," Josiah mused. "What elements of the scene at the woodyard suggested to you it was a suicide?"

To answer the question seemed to the sheriff dangerously close to imparting evidence to which Josiah had no right, and therefore he did not immediately answer.

"I'm not asking you to share your secrets," Josiah said quickly, apparently noting the sheriff's confusion. "Since it didn't occur to me that morning to go to the woodyard myself, all I want to know is, what would I have seen if I had? Describe it to me, and let me see what, if anything, suggests suicide to *me*. I've been told there were dozens of witnesses to the sight. Or if you don't like to tell me, whom do you recommend I ask instead? Clearly, I need to widen my circle of acquaintances to include a gossip or two, don't I? Then I wouldn't have to bother you."

The sheriff realized it was he, and not Josiah, who had caught his foot in a trap. An accurate description of the murder scene—whether from him or a gossip—must begin with the news that Mary Hale's body had *not* hung in the shed.

The sheriff didn't care to be exposed as a liar. Beginning to eat again, he said cautiously, "No need to ask nobody. I don't mind saying some things. Make of them what you can, I guess."

Josiah nodded. "Thank you, sir."

"She was hung, like I said," the sheriff said, "and the rope was tied above her. She was a little woman, but it wasn't tied higher than where she might've reached to string it herself by just stepping up a bit. And there was a place next to her she might've stepped up easy to do it from, too."

"That seems straightforward," said Josiah. "What about a scene like that *doesn't* suggest suicide?"

The sheriff, his mind still on the interfering mill workers, waved his hand with annoyance. "Only that her feet touched," he admitted. "And there might be ten other reasons for that than murder."

The sheriff had not meant to reveal the detail about the feet. He was so distressed by his blunder he swallowed a mouthful whole, without chewing. To his relief, Josiah, his brow contracted in thought, gave no indication he had heard the remark. The sheriff breathed again.

"Go on," Josiah said after a minute.

"No place more to go. She was dressed in her walking clothes, with no pocketbook,"—which was, of course, another lie—"and didn't leave no note. Which is too bad for you she didn't, of course."

Every witness to the scene, including the murderer, would have observed Mary's pocketbook lying near her body, the sheriff thought, and noted with interest that Josiah's face did not register any wonder at the statement concerning the absence of one.

"Is that all?"

The sheriff shrugged. "That's all me or anybody saw or knows about it," he said, adding wryly, "though I see them gossips you mentioned a minute ago have colored the picture up so's those of us was there don't recognize it no more."

"They always do," murmured Josiah.

Before the sheriff could reply to this, the young minister evidently caught the implication of the sheriff's earlier revelation that Mary's feet had touched the ground. "Miss Hale strangled, then," he said sadly. "It must have been a terrible death. Terrible."

The sheriff abandoned his efforts to trip Josiah up with lies. "No," he admitted. "Her neck was broke."

Josiah started slightly. "Broken? But how?"

The sheriff thought for a moment about how he wanted to answer this.

"Be a good question for a lawyer to ask somebody in court," he said finally. "If he asked it the right way. Not me, though. All I can do is say what I saw. I can't state no opinions." He threw discretion to the wind.

"Like, I can't say I don't see how no murderer could've talked Miss Mary into climbing up on a wood stack and putting a rope round her neck so's he could push her off and break it."

Josiah answered this absently, but a moment later, to the sheriff's relief, caught on. "Surely an attacker would have found it easier to simply strangle her on the ground!" he exclaimed.

Then he stopped himself and looked away. "Forgive me for forgetting for a moment I was speaking of a human life."

Though the sheriff sensed the remark had not really been meant for him, he said, "No harm done. Time for me to go. Why don't you write that all down in a letter before you forget it?"

Josiah was staring at his candle. "Yes," he said dully. "I will write."

Not until the sheriff was half-way down the dark staircase did Josiah remember to call out his thanks, and in his usual gentlemanly way, to wish the sheriff a pleasant evening. It occurred to the sheriff then that the evening had indeed been a pleasant one—though more, he suspected, for himself than for his prisoner. In gratitude for it, he paused and called back over his shoulder, "Person's neck gets clean broke like that, parson, they generally don't feel a thing."

He was not actually certain this reassurance was true, but he sensed it was the one the young minister wanted most in the world.

*

After a week of practicing hard at resignation and womanly submission, Rachel was forced to admit to herself the experiment was only making her, if anything, more rebellious in soul than ever, and Kitty found it easier to persuade her mistress to leave her silent bedroom for the much cozier kitchen. Rachel even agreed to see select callers, though she would not go farther and visit her husband.

"Why can't I be like Sophronia Conrad?" Rachel complained. "Why can't I be good, and trust in God, and stop wanting to manipulate events I ought to leave in His capable hands?" It was through trying to "manipulate events," of course, that she had discovered Josiah's treachery.

"Well, I have heard that Mrs. Conrad's good and all," Kitty answered, in a tone suggesting she did not entirely believe it. "It's easy to be good when you don't *do* anything, I guess."

"She does as much as she's able," Rachel said quickly. "It's certainly not by her choice she's confined to bed. No doubt she'd love to leave her room and be active in the world again."

"But then maybe she wouldn't be able to be as good," said Kitty. "Anyway, what do you call good? Maybe you don't like to stay at home and trust to God to do everything, but it says right in the Bible that the Lord helps them that helps themselves, don't it? That means we're supposed to do things ourselves, instead of only praying."

"The Bible says no such thing," Rachel informed her maid. "Mr. Aesop said that, and Mr. Aesop was a pagan."

"Oh." Kitty seemed downcast by this observation—but only for a moment.

"Well, my mother says it all the time," she told Rachel, becoming cheerful again. "And my mother's a *very* religious woman!"

The last apples of the previous autumn were withering in the barrel, Kitty then informed her mistress.

"I've made pies and pies with them all winter, until I don't think I ever want to look at an apple pie again. But there's still a lot of them in the cellar."

"We'll turn the rest into apple butter and jelly," Rachel decided. "I'm tired of apples, too, but maybe we can give the jelly to the poor or something. The Brown children would like a nice apple jelly, I think. We'll make apple butter first and save the peels for making jellies after."

To make the dull work of peeling more interesting, Rachel and Kitty amused themselves in traditional ways, with competitions to see which of them could skin an apple quickest, or produce the longest unbroken strip of peel.

"My sister and I used to have contests like this at home," said Rachel. "It seems a long time ago now."

"Did you ever try to find out who you would marry by saying your alphabet while you peeled, and seeing what letter the peel broke at?" asked Kitty, blushing as she said it. "I've done that, though I don't like to say what the letter was I got!"

Rachel favored an alternative means of prognostication. "Where I come from, we pare until the strip breaks of itself, and then throw the strip backward over our left shoulder and look to see what letter it forms when it lands."

"Oh, I know that way," Kitty exclaimed. "That's a good one." She quickly added, "Not as good as the other way, maybe."

Rachel suspected Kitty preferred her own way because by her method, the smallest movement of the knife ensured that a strip of peel broke at whatever letter was wanted—in Kitty's case, a "D" or a "G." Rachel was reconciled to Dan Gage's surreptitious kitchen visits because they were discreet, and because, for Kitty's sake, the young man kept the household's wood box filled. How she would have managed without Dan's help, Rachel wasn't sure.

"Try it, and see," she suggested, smiling to herself.

The peel was cut and thrown, whereupon Kitty discovered what Rachel already knew—that a long curl of apple peel could represent almost any letter one was determined to see in it. With relief, Kitty announced, "I think it's a 'D'. Don't you?"

"Oh, certainly," Rachel said without bothering to look. "The pot's just about to boil. I'll stir and you pare the rest, will you? There's only a few."

Far from objecting, Kitty had already begun on another apple, saying excitedly as she did so, "I wonder who my cousin is going to marry? I know she has a fellow, but she won't tell me who it is. I'll do her next."

While Rachel watched to see that her apples didn't burn, Kitty explored the love-lives of her sisters and female cousins.

"I don't know who this could be," she said finally. "A stranger, maybe. I don't know anybody whose name begins with 'A.'"

Rachel glanced over. "Andy?"

Kitty did not know any "Andy."

Rachel hazarded, "Albert? Alphonse? Adam?" Headshakes from Kitty. "Well, then, maybe it's a 'V' and not an 'A' at all. Yes, that's it. It's a 'V'. See? You're looking at it upside-down."

"It might be a 'V,'" Kitty decided, cocking her head. "Though I don't know who *that* could be neither, come to think about it."

Then, looking up, the girl exclaimed with concern, "Why, whatever's the matter, Mrs. Woodley? Are you sick again? Should I run for the doctor?"

Rachel was frozen, her face set and her spoon suspended several inches above her apple butter. As Kitty started for the door, she came suddenly to life again. "No. I'm well. I'm perfectly well. Come take the spoon and keep stirring. I just thought of something I must do."

Rachel managed to walk out of the kitchen with a proper dignity, but as soon as the door closed behind her, she snatched her skirts up indecently high and ran up the stairs. Her writing desk had been placed at her bedside—a broad hint from Kitty to answer Josiah's letters. Throwing it open, she uncorked the inkwell with a hand that shook, snatched up a pen, and dipped it. On the back of Josiah's last letter to her—still unopened—Rachel scrawled the initials "MH," and then rotated the paper to see how what she'd written looked upside down.

Josiah's mother's name had been Harriet, and it was from her that her son had inherited his dark, curling hair.

Her legs weak beneath her, Rachel sat down on the edge of the bed. "Dear God, I've been a fool," she murmured. "Forgive me, Josiah." It was the first sincere and unforced prayer she'd uttered since Lucy's death.

Whatever her husband's faults—not that, at the moment, she could recall he had any at all—Josiah had never betrayed her with Mary Hale. His heart and mind were both clear as water, and the deceptions necessary to practice betrayal were simply beyond him. She was ashamed ever to have doubted him.

Kitty, when she heard her mistress's pounding feet on the stairs, had left the kitchen and come up.

From the doorway she asked doubtfully, "Mrs. Woodley?"

Rachel raised her head, showing wet cheeks. "Go back down and keep stirring, Kitty. I'm getting dressed, and I'm going out."

"You're not well enough for that," Kitty instantly objected—though she began nonetheless to lay out Rachel's clothes.

"Nonsense. I've had a long rest, and now I'm perfectly fine. No, not the black. I'm wearing the blue one today."

Looking up, Kitty inquired blankly, "But—where are you going then, Mrs. Woodley?" The blue dress had hitherto only been called for when Rachel required a disguise.

"To the jail. What are you still doing here? I'm perfectly capable of dressing myself. Do as I said and see to it the apple-butter doesn't burn! Mr. Woodley is *particularly fond* of apple butter!"

CHAPTER NINETEEN

At the jail, the sheriff did not meet her as he usually did. Instead, his voice came down to her from the floor above, along with Josiah's, both of them at nearly the volume of a shout. Rachel paced the floor restlessly until amid the commotion from upstairs she thought she discerned a *woman's* voice. Then, curious, she started up.

A few steps from the top her way was blocked by a washbasin, towel, and pile of muddy clothes, but by standing tiptoe she could observe the scene from the sheriff's customary vantage. The sight that met her eye was a strange one.

Mr. Brown was back, it seemed, and in a very bad condition.

To Rachel's amazement, Josiah was out of his cell. The door to it stood wide open, as did the door to the second cell, in which Mrs. Brown, wearing her customary mournful expression, was apparently preparing the bed to receive her husband. Josiah and the sheriff meanwhile were supporting the inebriated Mr. Brown between them, maneuvering him into a clean shirt. The chair that had previously stood in the tiny holding cell was now, for some reason, positioned outside of Josiah's, and a can of coal oil rested on it. A strong smell emanating from Mr. Brown's head suggested the lamp-oil had been employed as a remedy against lice.

Mr. Brown was at the lachrymose stage of drunkenness and whimpered—to the sheriff's evident disgust.

"Don't give me none of that," he scolded, loudly enough to have some hope Mr. Brown would hear. "This here's no more'n what you deserve. You got yourself too drunk to get home and was found laying in the road like a hog this morn, down amongst some other hogs. And I'm surprised the hogs would have you. In my young days, pigs was more respectful of theirselves, and what the company was they kept."

Mr. Brown's reply to this was incoherent, but did not seem to constitute any attempt to justify himself.

Josiah (as usual) exerted himself to cheer the downcast man. "Oh, come now," he shouted smilingly. "You've stumbled, but not fatally. From this moment, you must just begin again, that's all. Yesterday— or the last two or three days, or whatever it was—a week, you say, Sheriff? Well, then, the last week—was folly, but today you repent and renew your vow to be wiser and more temperate hereafter." He added, "Remember that the Bible tells us 'joy shall be in heaven over one sinner that repenteth, more than over ninety and nine just persons, which need no repentance.'"

"Would ninety-nine be the count of the just for the whole world then, Parson?" the sheriff inquired acidly aside. "I don't recall there's more'n two or three in this particular town."

"Yes, and it's what makes Milltown a great favorite of heaven," Josiah returned, still smiling. "Our citizens provide so many opportunities for rejoicing there."

Sad-faced Mrs. Brown finished her work in the cell and came forward to say into her husband's ear, "Come here, Philly, and lie down. You'll feel better when you've had a good rest." Between them, Josiah and the sheriff got Mr. Brown into the bed, where the drunken man closed his eyes with a sigh and slept at once. Mrs. Brown, shaking her head sadly, declared that her husband would likely have a terrible head when he woke. "I don't know why he should drink so," she said mournfully. "It only makes him suffer."

She started for the stairs, then, saying, "I'll take that washing down, sir."

As she stooped to gather the clothes, Mrs. Brown caught sight of Rachel.

She gasped, and the sheriff, locking Mr. Brown's cell door with his back to the stairs, whirled about, instantly alert.

Josiah turned too, though more slowly. Catching sight of his wife, he cried joyfully, "Oh, my dar—!" stopping himself just in time from pronouncing before witnesses an endearment he knew Rachel considered appropriate for her ear alone. Though he likewise restrained himself from reaching for her, his shining eyes begged her to come.

The sheriff glanced between the two, then looked away.

"Mrs. Woodley," he greeted the wall behind her politely.

After another slight hesitation, he added gruffly to Mrs. Brown, who was still standing dumbstruck, "I'll help you with them things."

As he spoke, he started forward, reaching for the keys on his belt (Josiah had already stepped meekly back into his cell), and then, unexpectedly, seemed to change his mind. His hand dropping back to his side, he said, "You come on and have your visit, Mrs. Woodley. I'll be up again in a while."

To Josiah he added a warning—rather perfunctorily issued—"Just so's you know it, I'm reckoned a dead shot." Still avoiding Rachel's eyes, the sheriff went quickly downstairs, pushing Mrs. Brown before him.

For a moment, neither Rachel nor Josiah knew quite what to do. Josiah, still standing in his cell, reached suddenly for his wife, but then, as she started toward him, drew back.

"I'd better not," he said awkwardly. "I'm afraid I'm not very clean myself, after assisting to wash Mr. Brown. He's unfortunately relapsed a bit, as you can see."

Rachel said quickly, "I don't mind you." She entered her husband's cell and shyly put out her own arms. Josiah walked straight into them.

After a first, eager kiss (which thrilled Rachel strangely), the Woodleys were as self-conscious with each other as in the days of their courting, on the rare occasions when they briefly found themselves alone in the family parlor. Gradually, when the sheriff did not return, they became more comfortable.

Josiah initially insisted Rachel should not sit on his bed.

"The armies of lice and bedbugs have been reduced to skirmishers," he told her, "but they are not yet entirely beaten. You'll be safer on that chair."

Rachel objected to this, Josiah did not insist, and the brief argument ended with them sitting side by side, hands linked.

Rachel looked about her. "It's cleaner," she noted with surprise.

"Mrs. Brown's work," Josiah said. "The sheriff allowed her to do it. Fortunately for me, his interest in conditions up here has recently become personal. We have gotten into the habit of whiling away part of every evening together, talking."

Only one possible topic for such conversation suggested itself to Rachel. "Do you think you'll convert him?"

"As a matter of fact, the subject of religion has hardly arisen," her husband admitted sheepishly. "Unless you count the discussion we had about King Solomon's seven hundred wives and three hundred concubines. The sheriff's curiosity was purely professional, you understand. He wanted to know how the king kept the peace among so many. I was forced to say I didn't know, though I thought Solomon's wisdom was proved by the fact that he could do it. For the most part, our conversation is on secular matters. Our sheriff, it seems, is the son of a sheriff, and the grandson of a constable of colony days. He has a wealth of stories, as you might imagine."

As Josiah was speaking, he cautiously slipped his arm around his wife's waist, and when she did not object, gently drew her nearer— though he held her in such a way that the two of them could quickly move apart at the first sound of a step on the stair or a break in Mr. Brown's steady snores.

Rachel mentioned the lock of hair in Josiah's testament, referring to it as his mother's—an identification with which Josiah agreed without realizing his wife had ever imagined anything else.

"My father gave it to me," he said. "I believe I have not heard him speak five times of my mother since she died, but he has a tender side." (Rachel doubted this.) "I wrote to him, as you know, and explained my present circumstances."

Rachel did *not* know this, in fact, but rather than reveal she had never read her husband's letters to her, she nodded.

"I delayed too long to do it," Josiah continued, "but I was afraid of what he'd say. I thought he might blame me for my situation. Somehow, I've never measured up to his expectations. I don't know why."

"Because you didn't take the farm," said Rachel, slowly lowering her head to rest on her husband's shoulder. "He hoped you would, and you didn't. You'd have been a good farmer. You were just called to something else, that's all."

Josiah said tightly, "No, he was right. I *should* have stayed. Not as my father thinks, so that the farm kept the Woodley name. What does the name on the deed matter? Anne is as much a Woodley as I am. I should have stayed because William's not strong enough for farming, and I knew it from the first. He's ill every winter, Rachel. If the farm hasn't killed him this time, another year it may."

Rachel pulled away to look her husband in the face. "Do you blame yourself for William's weak chest?"

"No."

"Yes, you do. I can see you do. But you shouldn't. William must work at *something*; we all must. And farming was what he wanted. I never saw a man happier in his work than William." She added, in a practical tone, "And anyway, if something should happen to William, the farm will be your sister's mainstay after."

"As Anne herself is my father's," Josiah agreed, sounding relieved.

Something suddenly occurred to Rachel. Abruptly, she demanded, "When you were leaving to go to Anne, you said something was on your conscience. Is this what you meant? Did you mean you felt responsible for William?"

Josiah admitted he had. "I went intending to offer my help to Anne in setting William up with a shop or something—assuming he recovered."

Rachel didn't want to speak further about this. Though William still lived, his condition, Anne's recent letters indicated, seemed to be settling into one of chronic invalidism.

Forcing himself to sound more cheerful, Josiah told her, "I wrote to Mr. Tyrode about the blue letter paper you mentioned. It was clever of you to see the importance of that."

"It's not a woman's place to be 'clever,'" answered Rachel automatically. It was how her mother had taught her to respond to comments that, unchallenged, might have tempted her to pride.

"It's a woman's '*place*' to be as God made her," Josiah responded.

This was an argument Rachel would never have dared to advance on her own behalf but loved hearing her husband make for her—so much so that she snuggled closer.

"Tell me what more I can do to help my case along," Josiah begged, kissing her hair.

The two talked until downstairs, the sheriff grew unusually heavy-footed, and his chair seemed to need a great deal of noisy adjustment in its position. Rightly interpreting this as a warning to them, the Woodleys drew apart, though Josiah could not seem to relinquish his wife's hand.

"You see I have a candle now," he said, pointing it out to her proudly.

Rachel had already noticed and marveled at it. She had stayed so long, she suddenly realized, that it would soon be time to light it.

Josiah cocked his head for a moment, listening to the sounds from below, then said quickly, "I hate to ask it of you, but the sheriff suggested something that might help my case. I wouldn't ask you to involve yourself in it, but time is short, and I think it's too delicate a matter for a letter."

Rachel paled. "How short?"

"The fifteenth of next month is the opening of the court session. Mr. Tyrode writes that I should expect my case to be heard within a day or two of it."

Only a few weeks, then.

"Yes, of course you may ask me anything. What can I do?"

Another scrape of the chair downstairs.

"Call upon the doctor who examined Mary's body." Josiah withdrew a paper on which a numbered list of questions was written and offered it. "Will you do that? Can you? If the doctor will speak to you at all, which he may not, I'm afraid you may have to listen to some…unsettling things."

Rachel hesitated. Josiah was referring, she guessed, to Mary Hale's pregnancy—and remembering Rachel's. "Of course I can do it," she said firmly.

The sheriff, half-way up the stairs and advancing slowly, was clearing his throat loudly now.

Rachel hastily smoothed the marks of their bodies from Josiah's bed then stepped out of his cell, but she did not—she could not bear to—close the cell door upon him.

That remained for the sheriff to do. Rachel noticed he did not look at either of the Woodleys as he turned the key in the lock.

"Time to go, Mrs. Woodley," he said.

"I'll come tomorrow, Josiah," promised Rachel, reaching between the bars to take the paper from his hand. "And I'll get the information you ask for. If it can be gotten at all, I will get it!"

CHAPTER TWENTY

The front parlor of Dr. Brown's house—Brown was a common name in the area—had been turned into a consulting room, done up in the modern style. It had a worn carpet, a desk and a case of medical books, a glass-fronted cabinet of drugs and instruments, a pair of wooden chairs, and a sofa gracefully curved at one end and covered in faded damask and stains. Operations where much blood was likely to be let were performed on the table in the dining room opposite—if they could not be performed in the sufferer's own home. Medicaments were formulated by the doctor's wife in the kitchen, alongside the doctor's dinner. A woman who married a doctor could expect, like it or not, to function as needed in the capacity of nurse and pharmacist. In short, the house was a thorough-going medical establishment.

Restless, Rachel rose and approached the bookcase. Cullin's *Treatise,* and Cowper's *Anatomy* were placed prominently at the front of the shelves, along with something in Latin, a language Rachel did not know. Smaller volumes with ragged paper covers peeked out half-hidden from behind.

Rachel was just, furtively, reaching to move a Galen slightly aside when movement outside the window caught her eye.

Dr. Conrad was passing, a woman of about Rachel's own age with him. The minister was carrying his hat and his countenance registered grave and kindly concern. It seemed the same grave and kindly concern he always showed to *her*, in fact, and Rachel blushed for the twinge of jealousy she experienced at the sight. A step in the passage behind her made Rachel jump, and she quickly returned to her chair.

The doctor, when he entered, proved a still youngish man, and in his manner to Rachel, impatient and irritable.

"I've no intention of giving testimony at Mr. Woodley's trial," he said firmly as he entered, waving Rachel's earlier note to him in the air. "I gave my opinion at the girl's inquest, and I have nothing further to add to it now."

"But—will you at least speak to *me*, if you won't speak to the court?" begged Rachel.

"What point would there be in your having such information?" retorted Dr. Brown. "I assure you, I have nothing for you to share in the parlor with your friends. I doubt you would even understand what I said."

Though her cheeks burned, Rachel managed to keep her voice level. "Whatever you tell me, the only person I will share it with is my husband's advocate," she said. "He may understand it. I hope he will. Or can I persuade you to write to him yourself?"

Dr. Brown sat down at his desk and drummed his fingers. "What do you want to know?" he asked finally.

Now that she had gained her point, Rachel's shyness reasserted itself. Instead of speaking, she brought out a list of questions Josiah had formulated and silently handed it across the desk.

The doctor, when he had looked it over, seemed taken aback. "I hope you haven't read this."

His tone warned Rachel not to admit she had. "Will you answer the questions?"

"Not before a lady," said the doctor firmly. "Your husband had no business putting such a document into your hands!"

"He only asked me to give it to you."

"Well, if you looked at it, you did wrong."

To spare herself from telling an outright lie, Rachel lowered her head in a way she hoped suggested she had not only not read the document, but might, in fact, be too illiterate to do so. "You need not speak to me," she said. "If you like, you may write instead to Mr. Woodley."

The doctor hesitated, reread the paper, then ran a thoughtful finger down one cheek.

"I'm an obliging man, I think," he said finally, "and I would like to help. But a patient's medical history is, and ought to be, a private matter."

"Yes, of course," said Rachel immediately. "Though—"

"A private matter," Dr. Brown repeated.

Rachel discovered she was not too proud to beg. "Your patient, Miss Hale, is dead," she pleaded. "Whereas my husband is alive and quite innocent of the charge against him." Thinking quickly (since the doctor still frowned), she added, "You are in the business—that is, the *profession*—of saving lives, Dr. Brown. Will you not save Mr. Woodley's, if it is in your power?"

The doctor cleared his throat, clearly touched in a tender spot. "I hardly see that it *is* in my power," he replied uncomfortably.

"The situation is this, sir," said Rachel. "Five months before Miss Hale died, my husband and I were living at Seabury, and Miss Hale in Milltown. If, as you said at the inquest, Miss Hale was five months…"

Here, Rachel was obliged to stop. She had never before in her life pronounced aloud the bald word "pregnant." "If when she died, Miss Hale was five months—*along*, Mr. Woodley could have had no possible motive for killing her, for he could not have been the father of her child. Forgive my forthright speech, but my husband will soon be on trial for his life, and I have no friend or brother to act for me in this matter."

At this appeal, Dr. Brown sighed, and seemed to soften a little.

"I'm an obliging man, as I said," he repeated, more kindly. "But I've been to court before, madam, and I can tell you it's not an uncommon thing for two lawyers to pull a witness between them like dogs with a soup bone. I can't afford to be made a fool of. I have my practice to think of, and my family."

"But you need not go to court!" Rachel repeated. "Only write a few words!"

Despite her pleas—and, in the end, tears—the doctor would not be persuaded.

"It is all in the notes of the inquest," was the most he would say.

A rap at the consulting-room door finally put an end to the argument, and Rachel left with her handkerchief to her eyes.

*

Sophronia Conrad was trying to pray. She prayed every day, on behalf of her husband, children, and every other family connection; and also for all of the ill, bereaved, and troubled citizens of Milltown generally, whether known to her personally or not. Suffering in Milltown went on at about the rate usual everywhere, and consequently it often required several hours for Mrs. Conrad to point out to the Almighty each particular case requiring His attention.

On this day, however, she was finding it hard to elevate her thoughts. Mr. Tudge was in the back parlor discussing church business with Dr. Conrad, and though the younger minister began every sentence in a low murmur, by midway through it his voice had typically begun mounting toward its accustomed pulpit roar. Dr. Conrad was then obliged, with weary regularity, to remind his fellow clergyman to lower it again, for which consideration of her invalid condition Mrs. Conrad as regularly thanked God, the provider of so good a husband.

But in fact, her real regret (though she would never have admitted it even to herself) was that she could not hear Mr. Tudge more clearly. Her room was furnished with everything possible to ease her infirmity, and was, of course, a blessed refuge from worldly temptations—but Mrs. Conrad was bored.

Following an inarticulate comment from her husband, Mr. Tudge's reply built until Mrs. Conrad heard him plainly proclaim, "...and furthermore, I believe it is only by the practices of INDUSTRY, ECONOMY, AND VIRTUE that anyone merits plenty and the right to wear handsome clothes. Christian charity is all very well, Dr. Conrad, and I hope I am as charitable as the next man. BUT WHEN I SEE a woman like Mrs. Olney, who, in *clear defiance* of my sermons on the topic, does *not* practice industry, economy, and VIRTUE, I DO NOT BELIEVE she has any right to appear other than appropriately MEANLY DRESSED!"

Putting this remark together with other intelligence Mrs. Conrad had recently gathered regarding the Olney family allowed her to deduce that financial reverses had resulted in Mrs. Olney asking for a remission of her church tithes. Mrs. Conrad made a mental note to pray for Mrs. Olney.

Dr. Conrad replied to this in a low voice, following which—to her relief—Mrs. Conrad distinguished in Mr. Tudge's answer the word "leniency" pronounced in a grudging manner.

The topic of church funds generally then came under what Mrs. Conrad surmised was close discussion. Money, she had noticed before, was a matter in which Mr. Tudge took a consuming interest.

From a low rumbling start, Mr. Tudge's voice built quickly to a full-throated "…not so much as we *would* have were THOSE METHODISTS not…" before Dr. Conrad managed to shush him. Thereafter Mrs. Conrad could make out nothing further for some time.

Then the name of "Josiah Woodley" was spoken.

At this, Mrs. Conrad—setting her efforts at prayer entirely aside—inclined her ear toward the door. She wanted very much to know how Josiah Woodley did.

In a voice that became more audible with every word, Mr. Tudge said, "I have refrained, for charity's sake, from making this suggestion before, Dr. Conrad, but far from obliging the *church* to undertake to pay for his defense, I think it is time instead that we consider casting the unprofitable servant INTO OUTER DARKNESS, as the LORD recommends."

There followed a murmur from Dr. Conrad, to which Mr. Tudge replied firmly, "I do. By his transgressions he shames the church."

From a certain change in the sound of his voice, Mrs. Conrad knew her husband had risen and was now walking the parlor floor—a habit of his when distressed. His steps evidently carried him near to the door, for she caught without difficulty his next comment, spoken deliberately: "The crime of which Mr. Woodley stands accused is a serious one, of course, but we should keep in mind he hasn't been convicted of it yet."

Mr. Tudge apparently did not think this an important distinction. "It only makes us look worse, the longer we delay," he said impatiently. And then, after some further brief remark from his superior, "Yes, yes. Well, we need not strike him from membership in the church until after the trial, if you think it's wiser not to, but certainly the man ought to be struck from the *clergy*. We know he's guilty. Just look at the evidence: A tall clergyman, in a BEAVER HAT—"

"Was it a beaver?" asked Dr. Conrad. Sophronia rejoiced at his mild tone.

Mr. Tudge asserted in reply, "It's the CHURCH I'm thinking of here, Doctor. Not myself. All that money being spent out on the defense of a man entirely likely to be GUILTY AS CHARGED would be better spent, I think…"

Mr. Tudge was prevented from saying what he thought the money would be better spent upon by Dr. Conrad's quiet reminder that all funds disbursed upon Mr. Woodley's defense were, in fact, going to Mr. Tudge's own young cousin.

Mr. Tudge cried, "But out of *church funds*, Dr. Conrad! That was NOT my expectation when I suggested him for the job!"

Mr. Tudge, it was apparent to Sophronia, would have had no complaint if the lawyer's fee had been twice as much, had it only been coming from Josiah Woodley's pocket.

Though Mrs. Conrad could not make out any more of the conversation, it was apparent moments later, when Mr. Tudge at last took his leave, that he had not been entirely mollified, for her husband said at their parting, in a pacific tone, "I will consider your recommendation, Herbert."

At that moment there lay at Mrs. Conrad's right hand a note from Rachel Woodley, newly risen from her sickbed. The note was to thank

Mrs. Conrad for a piece of advice Mrs. Conrad did not remember giving—that Rachel should do what she felt bidden to do without regarding the practical difficulties of her actions or other people's opinion of them.

Mrs. Conrad—no fool—was inclined to think the case was one in which the listener had heard not what was said, but what she wanted to hear, but the note pleased Mrs. Conrad very much just the same. Mrs. Conrad was often afraid to do anything for fear of doing wrong, but then when she did nothing, she reproached herself for being ineffectual. Rachel's note reassured her that she had some good effect in the world, which was a comfort to her.

When she heard Dr. Conrad's light step on the stairs, Sophronia gently slid Rachel's letter beneath her shawl.

"Oh, dear, you look so tired!" she greeted her husband. "Was your meeting very tedious?"

"No, not very," replied Dr. Conrad, sitting down at her bedside and smiling pleasantly. "Did we disturb you?"

"Oh, no," said Mrs. Conrad quickly. "Not at all."

"Do you think you could sleep?" Dr. Conrad gently lifted one of her hands to his lips, kissed it, and replaced it in Mrs. Conrad's lap. "You've been up for a long time."

"Not yet. It was Mr. Tudge who came to visit you, wasn't it?"

Dr. Conrad affirmed this, and regretted that his guest should have been so loud.

"He didn't disturb me," repeated Mrs. Conrad. "I knew it was him by his knock on the door, that's all. Did he have any news for you, dear?"

Dr. Conrad named a few of the topics the two clergymen had discussed. He did not mention Josiah.

"And—has Mr. Tudge's cousin come to town?" Talk of somebody's cousin, at least, could not be thought "too much" for her to endure.

"I don't believe he has any cousins visiting, no." Dr. Conrad shook his head. "He didn't mention any."

Sophronia weighed the situation carefully. Her husband was determined to spare her. She was determined to be informed.

Mrs. Conrad's fingers brushed Rachel's note.

"I meant the cousin who is to represent our Mr. Woodley at trial," she said boldly. "It seems strange he has not come yet to consult with his client."

Her husband shifted slightly in his chair.

"You mustn't worry about things," he said gravely.

"I'm not worried, only interested," Mrs. Conrad replied. "Will he come soon, do you think? Court day is nearly here."

Dr. Conrad put the tips of his fingers together.

"He's a young man," he acknowledged, "and perhaps thinks it's better for him not to be too closely associated with a case of—this nature. But much may be done by letter, and I assure you there is a steady correspondence ongoing between Attorney Tyrode and Mr. Woodley."

Mrs. Conrad had heard (through the medium of the disapproving Mrs. Tudge) that Mrs. Woodley also sent letters to Mr. Tyrode, and that neither of the Woodleys was entirely satisfied with the number or nature of the letters they received in return. Sophronia did not reveal to her husband that she knew this.

"I think it would be very bad if Mr. Woodley were convicted of a crime of which he was not guilty," she said instead.

Dr. Conrad replied blandly that he knew his "darling Sophy's" faith in God was too great for her to fear any such thing. "In any case, it's out of our hands," he said. "Rest now, why don't you? You look very tired."

Beneath the shawl, Mrs. Conrad fingered Rachel's letter again—for courage.

"*Is* justice out of our hands? Earthly justice, I mean."

Her husband refused to understand her. "Entirely. Sleep now, and I'll visit with you again later."

CHAPTER TWENTY-ONE

When Rachel got to the jail, she found Mr. Brown was about to be released—again. Mrs. Brown was already in her husband's cell, stripping the bedlinens for washing with a degree of energy she did not often display, meanwhile saying to Josiah, "So grateful to you, sir," with heartfelt warmth.

Josiah addressed himself to her husband, in a kindly shout. "Remember you may call upon me at any time day or night if you feel yourself falling, Philip. The sheriff has assured me that if you call up to me from the street, I will hear, and you will hear my answer."

He turned, and upon seeing Rachel, his face lit up as it always did. Feeling unable to speak openly before the Browns, Rachel was only able to answer his expectant look with a slight, despairing shake of her head. Josiah answered it with a shrug, and a resigned smile.

"Mr. Brown has found work more suited to his talents than hedging and ditching," he said. "He's a trained mechanic, you know. He's going to work for Mr. Yeardley at the gristmill."

Rachel repeated, with surprise, "Mr. Yeardley?" Mr. Yeardley was a prominent Methodist—the very denomination growing most at the expense of Josiah's own congregation.

Another shrug from Josiah. "There's a strong temperance faction among them," he explained.

The sheriff growled impatiently from below, and Mr. and Mrs. Brown hurried away, calling back their thanks as they went.

"How did you manage *that?*" asked Rachel, as she and Josiah attempted an embrace through the cell bars. "And how long will it last?"

"Well, if my prayers are worth anything to heaven, forever," said Josiah. "But I can't count on that, I suppose. How did I do it? Oh, by letter, of course. I don't get out much these days."

Rachel recognized this for a joke, and laughed.

"This may be the remaking of Mr. Brown, Rachel. I hope it will be."

"But if he's remade into a Methodist?"

"If Methodism makes Mr. Brown a steady and sober worker and a proper father to his children, I won't begrudge the Methodists his attendance at their church," Josiah said. "But let's not think about the Browns. I take it you were unsuccessful in securing any useful information from the doctor?"

"He won't testify," Rachel told him sadly, "and would put his name to nothing he had not already said at the inquest."

"Then let's not think about the doctor, either," Josiah said firmly. "We're together, we're in good accord at last, and the day is fine. Let's enjoy it as much as we can."

"How many more such days will we have to enjoy, Josiah?"

"No one knows the answer to that question." By pressing his face between the bars, he just managed to kiss his wife's hair. "Let's talk about the garden," he urged. "Tell me about the garden. There are roses there. We came too late to see them bloom last year. Will we have roses this June?"

A plaintive note in the question informed Rachel that Josiah was beginning to lose hope he would live to see them.

*

The sheriff no longer bothered to set limits to the Woodley's visits together, and it was not until Kitty came with a loaded basket that Rachel realized how much of the day had passed.

"It's rabbit today, Mr. Woodley," she told Josiah. "A friend of mine caught it, and he give it to me."

Rachel communicated to her husband by means of a wry look that the "friend" was most likely Dan Gage.

"Oh, and you got a letter, Mrs. Woodley!" continued Kitty. "You'll never guess from who. Go on, try to guess! You never will, though. Not in a month."

"You're right," said Rachel. "I can't guess."

"It's from Mrs. Conrad!"

The Woodleys exchanged surprised looks.

"And you'll never guess what it's about, neither," added Kitty, groping in the basket. "Now where is it? It would be just like me to leave it home, wouldn't it?"

"Kitty!"

"I didn't though. Here it is," the girl said, producing it at last—a little grease-stained. "It's an invitation for you to call!" Hastily, she added, "I didn't *read* it. I only know because Mrs. Conrad's girl Rebecca told me what it was when she brought it."

The Woodleys scanned the note together.

"I won't keep you," said Josiah immediately, looking at his watch. "You must go now, Rachel, or be too late. Thank your friend for the rabbit, Kitty. It's a great favorite of mine."

Almost before the sheriff had bowed them out, Rachel saw him turn eagerly toward the stairs. Rabbit was a favorite of his, too, she surmised.

"What does Mrs. Conrad want to see you for?" asked Kitty as they walked—then answered her own question. "Some church business, likely. It's funny, though. She don't usually see anyone."

"No," agreed Rachel absently.

"She *used* to visit," continued Kitty, "before she got sick. That's what Grandma told me. She used to go out all the time. She and Dr. Conrad had people to dinner, even."

"Did they?"

"And not just dinners, neither. They built that big house on purpose to have people over, Grandma says. Did you know she almost caused a scandal when she first got here?"

Calling her mind back from where it had raced on ahead of her, Rachel asked, disbelievingly, "Mrs. *Conrad?*"

Kitty looked delighted to have surprised Rachel. "It's true," she said happily. "It was at a harvest dance she and Dr. Conrad had. Being a preacher's wife, Mrs. Conrad oughtn't to have danced anyway, maybe, but she did, and she danced *so high* Grandma said you could see half her petticoat almost! The old folks in the church didn't like it, of course. They never like it when young folks have fun. But when they tried to make a scandal about it, Mrs. Conrad said as the petticoat was her nice new red flannel one, she thought it *deserved* to be seen!" Kitty added with regret, "My, how things change, don't they? Now she don't ever even go out."

"They certainly do change," agreed Rachel. She half-wondered whether Kitty's story could possibly be true. "We'll part at the corner, here, Kitty. You go on home."

Sophronia sat in her usual place near the window, watching the street below. Dr. Conrad was at the church, preaching another funeral, and she was anxious to have her interview with Mrs. Woodley before he returned. She had no clock in her room. Dr. Conrad thought the ticking of a clock might unsettle her. But she knew the approximate hour, and worried Rachel might come too late. John allowed nothing to interfere with his wife's naptimes, which he thought vital to her health.

A flash of something blue caught her eye: Mrs. Woodley had come at last. Though an invalid, Mrs. Conrad was still a woman. As Rachel knocked, Sophronia patted her hair into place and smoothed her dress.

"Come sit, dear," invited Mrs. Conrad as Rachel entered. To Rebecca, she added, "Bring tea, please." The girl could not eavesdrop if she was downstairs making tea. Knowing tea-making didn't take long on a stove kept perpetually lit, she then hurried through the ritual of establishing the present state of the weather.

"And how does your husband do?" she then asked eagerly. "How is Mr. Woodley?"

Rachel responded cautiously, to show a due regard for Mrs. Conrad's health. "He is—well."

"He does not despair, I hope?"

"Oh, no. His great faith…"

"Yes, of course. Faith is a bulwark against despair. But in his difficulties, your practical assistance must be a greater bulwark still."

Though Rachel was aware her efforts on Josiah's behalf were talked about in the town, she had not expected Mrs. Conrad, of all people, to know of—far less to allude to—them. Before Rachel could offer any excuses or apologies, Mrs. Conrad added quickly, "May I say how much I admire you for your efforts? You are very brave."

Lest "brave" be a tactful euphemism for some less-flattering characterization (at her last visit, Mrs. Tudge had, in a meaning way, pronounced her hostess "adventuresome"), Rachel did not answer this.

"I think you very brave," Mrs. Conrad repeated. "But I wonder that Mr. Woodley's advocate does not relieve you of the responsibility of interviewing witnesses by coming and doing so himself. I wonder very much at it. John tells me that legal matters are often conducted this way, but I do not like it. Do you?"

Rachel didn't answer this.

"And Mr. Tyrode's letters?" Mrs. Conrad continued. "Do they give you the sense he grasps the substance of the case and will plead it effectively?"

Before Rachel could reply, Mrs. Conrad suddenly put a finger to her lips. Rebecca was mounting the stairs.

"Two cups, Rebecca," said Mrs. Conrad sweetly, when the tea tray had been set before her.

"Two?" the girl echoed in surprise. For a moment, she looked as though she might refuse.

"Two," affirmed Mrs. Conrad, and Rebecca remembered her place. As she went down again, Mrs. Conrad explained, "I don't usually drink tea. The doctor thinks it too stimulating. But today I will." When she heard the kitchen door slam behind the annoyed Rebecca, she added, eyes bright, "You are *not* satisfied with Mr. Tyrode, are you? I can see you're not. Tell me what you have written to him, if you will, and what he replied. And tell me what you learned when you visited Mr. Cockburn. Dear Mr. Cockburn! We used to be great friends."

With such encouragement, Rachel couldn't keep her pent-up fears from pouring out. Mrs. Conrad paid rapt attention, only stopping her guest long enough for Rebecca to deliver the second teacup and be sent away again on another errand to the opposite end of the house.

"And have you spoken now to everyone who identified Mr. Woodley as the man with Miss Hale?" Mrs. Conrad asked, when Rachel stopped talking.

"I don't know. I believe I have."

"And they are united in maintaining that the fellow was tall, and dressed in the clothes of a professor?"

"And a fur hat," added Rachel. "Yes."

Mrs. Conrad considered this. "Of course, many men wear a beaver," she said. "Beaver is a very common material for a man's hat."

Rachel shook her head. "Not a beaver, ma'am," she corrected Mrs. Conrad. "A fur hat. The publican's wife suggested it might have been rabbit fur."

A brief silence gave Rachel time to remember her hostess was too frail for such exciting talk. "I should go," she said, rising.

"No, I'm well," Mrs. Conrad replied quickly. "Perfectly well. And Mr. Woodley has no such hat?"

"Does not, and never has."

"Might it have been squirrel?" asked Sophronia.

Rachel stopped to think. "Possibly. It was *not* felted beaver. I think once I'd been assured of that, I stopped listening closely."

"Of course, of course." Seeing Rachel determined to go, Mrs. Conrad added quickly, "I have so enjoyed our visit, Mrs. Woodley. Thank you for confiding in me."

Rachel smilingly assured her hostess that all the thanks due were on her side, and, on an impulse, bent to kiss the older woman's cheek.

Mrs. Conrad blushed like a girl.

"Look after your health," she advised.

*

From the window, Sophronia watched Rachel go then turned her head to watch in the opposite direction for the return of her husband.

She had met John Conrad while he was in his last months of study in the college in New Haven, when he had come to a dance given in her honor by her father. The dance was intended to acquaint Sophronia with young men whom her father considered acceptable as potential mates, for Sophronia was nearly twenty-six, and her unmarried state was beginning to be an embarrassment to him.

She had been a headstrong child, defying her parents to control, or her governesses to teach her. She climbed trees, swam with the boys in the brook, rode her pony out unchaperoned, and vowed she would never, ever submit to a husband's rule. Six years in a ladies' seminary failed to tame her, though it forced her to give up the trees, brook, and pony, of course, and afterwards she returned to her father's house. She lived up in every way to the ideal of a Woman and a Lady, but she would not, she declared, ever be either Wife or Mother.

One set of dances with John Conrad changed Sophronia's mind on the topic of marriage. She fell in love with the tall young minister at once. Whether she was equally reconciled to the idea of motherhood or not, it was understood by all that children would inevitably follow the spring wedding that was soon being planned. The fact that the bridegroom was penniless was luckily no handicap to him. Sophronia's father must have felt Mr. Conrad's handsome face, obvious good breeding, and the title of "reverend doctor" that would soon be his were wealth enough to counterbalance the considerable fortune in money that would come with his daughter.

Sophronia had a dozen pretty cousins and friends as maids-of-honor at her wedding, while the groom had but one supporter. This was a young man named Dodd, a student of the law who had been, for several years past, the sharer of John Conrad's student lodgings.

Fingering again beneath her shawl the letter of gratitude Rachel had sent her, Sophronia wondered sadly what had become of the lighthearted young girl she had been at her wedding.

*

Dr. Conrad found his wife still at the window when he came up.

"My dearest," he said—kindly, but with a hint of reproach in his voice, "should you not be napping at this hour? Don't say you're not tired. I can see you are."

"I am a little tired," Mrs. Conrad admitted. "I had a visitor today, John. Mrs. Woodley."

Her husband smiled. "So Rebecca told me," he said, beginning to open the bed for her. "And you drank tea, I heard. Is that the cause of your wakefulness now, I wonder? What is soothing to some is stimulating to you. I thought we had agreed on that point?"

"A little stimulation won't hurt me."

From his face, Mrs. Conrad could see her husband had expected a different answer from her.

"I won't do it again," she added quickly.

As he helped her from her chair onto the bed, she said gratefully, as she often did, "You are always so good to me, Doctor;" to which, equally from habit, he replied, "Oh, no. Any debt of gratitude will always be on my side."

This small ceremony complete, Mrs. Conrad began resolutely, "I am not quite satisfied with what Mrs. Woodley told me of her husband's legal advisor, Doctor. This business of preparing his defense at an arm's length can't be right, can it? I'm certain Mr. Woodley's advocate ought to come here."

"I see I must remind Mrs. Woodley of the state of your health," Dr. Conrad replied. "She is burdening you with distressing news about matters which are out of your control. Mr. Woodley's advocate is competent, Sophy; and in any case, the matter lies principally in God's hands, not ours."

"My faith in God in this matter is perfect, Dr. Conrad," said his wife. "But I sometimes wonder whether *He* is as satisfied with *our* efforts. Mr. Tyrode seems very young and inexperienced to plead so important a case. Are we doing enough for Mr. Woodley by giving him such representation?"

When her husband did not immediately answer this, Sophronia added worriedly, "Have you—have you reason to doubt Mr. Woodley's innocence?"

Though he seemed, almost, to hesitate at first, when he answered, Dr. Conrad's manner was very positive. "Not in the least, no," he said firmly.

"Then we must help him to prove it," said his wife.

Dr. Conrad smiled. "It's like you to be so thoughtful. But what more can we do?"

"We must write to Mr. Dodd."

From his slight start, it was apparent Dr. Conrad had not thought of his old friend for some time.

"Mr. Dodd?"

"I've heard he is now considered one of the best legal men in the state," said Mrs. Conrad.

Her husband smiled. "No doubt, Sophy. And I'm sure his fees are correspondingly high. Mr. Tudge has already complained of the cost to the church of Mr. Woodley's defense. If I press for still more money, I'm afraid he'll lead the Deacons in open revolt."

Mrs. Conrad had a ready answer to this.

"Then we must pay Mr. Dodd ourselves."

Dr. Conrad, his smile grown tight, rose to go. "Rest, my love," he urged.

Mrs. Conrad was as surprised as her husband to discover that though the carefree laughing girl of her youth might be dead, the headstrong stubborn one still lived within her.

With set jaw, she declared, "You mustn't blame Mrs. Woodley for telling me about Mr. Woodley. I asked her to. There was very little of it I didn't already know anyway."

"Mrs. Tudge, I suppose," said Dr. Conrad heavily. He walked to the window and lowered the blind. "Though I shouldn't say it, the woman is an incorrigible gossip. I wonder how Herbert ever came to choose her?"

"I learned some of it from Mrs. Tudge, yes. But not all. I hear things up here, John. I hear people talking on the street. I see them walk by, or hear their footsteps, and I know at sight or by the sound whether they are about their business, or only out to take the air. I believe I could identify every house on this street just by the bang of its front door. You can hardly imagine how much I learn from listening. Especially in the night. I am often wakeful in the night, you know, and I hear all the little night noises; all the dogs. Dogs are as good as people for telling me things. They bark differently for people they recognize and strangers."

"Do they?"

"I hear people going about in the night," his wife continued. "Why would anyone be out in the night, I wonder to myself? But of course, it is because they think they are hidden then. I wonder if, in the night, people sometimes do things no one who knew them would ever believe of them?"

Dr. Conrad still stood at the window, now fussing purposelessly with the shade cord.

"Of course, I don't judge such people," Sophronia added quickly. "They have their reasons for what they do."

A long silence ensued.

As Dr. Conrad, smiling blandly, turned to break it, Mrs. Conrad asked, "Did you know the man who was seen walking with Miss Hale on the night she died wore a fur hat, John? Agnes Tudge said it was a beaver, but she was wrong. The publican's wife identified it positively as fur, not felt. She identified it positively, and she will testify to it at trial. She guessed it was rabbit or squirrel. She wasn't certain which. The pelts of rabbits and squirrels are very much alike, aren't they?"

Before the minister could reply to this, his wife asked abruptly, "Do you still correspond with Mr. Dodd, John? A lovely man, though not a Godly one. I enjoyed his company. And as I mentioned, after college he became an advocate. A very *good* advocate."

Lowering the shade had made the room too dark for Dr. Conrad to be able to read his wife's face clearly, but he thought he saw something in it—a hint of something; perhaps a warning—that made him ask, "And you would you like me to write to him, Sophy? On our Mr. Woodley's account?"

Mrs. Conrad's penetrating gaze did not waver. "Of course, time is very short," she admitted. "But we were all such good friends in the old days."

"Yes. Then—if you want it, my dear, I will write him this very hour."

His wife nodded, but did not, as she usually did, instantly let the matter go. Instead, she persisted, "And—may I see the letter? Somehow I feel as though it will not be until I have seen it—and seen it go to the post—that my mind will be entirely relieved."

"I will bring it to you," Dr. Conrad agreed.

"Thank you, Dr. Conrad. You are so good to me."

Chapter Twenty-Two

The relief of heart Rachel was feeling when she left Mrs. Conrad house was instantly extinguished when she reached her front doorstep. A dead cat lay stretched across the threshold, a noose around its neck. Propped against its stiff body was a sign crudely lettered, "Rev'd. Woodly." Shocked, Rachel simply stared for a moment, then retreated a few steps. Unable to bring herself to step over the animal, she finally walked around the house and entered at the kitchen instead, where she found Kitty and Mr. Gage sitting and talking—the table, to her relief, decently between them.

One glance at Rachel's white face brought Kitty instantly to her feet.

"Now, you just come and sit down here," she said, reaching for Rachel's hand and guiding her mistress gently to the chair she had just left. "Whatever's happened? Oh, gracious, did Mrs. Conrad—?"

Rachel gestured vaguely toward the front of the house. "The porch," she whispered.

Kitty's expression hardened.

By now the stunned and sheepish Dan Gage had risen, too, and in response to a jerk of Kitty's head, he started for the back door—not to leave, as Rachel first thought, but to help.

"I'll get the shovel," he said as he went.

"Mr. Gage'll get the shovel," Kitty repeated comfortingly, pushing aside the dishes on the table to clear a space before Rachel. "He'll take care of that—mess, and you can just have some nice tea. I'll get a cup."

Rachel was about to refuse (she had just had tea at the Conrad's, after all) when it occurred to her a cup of Kitty's tea—never, despite Rachel's careful instruction, a delicate lady's brew, but always over steeped and milked-and-sugared to a ridiculous extent—was exactly what she needed. By the time she had drunk half a cup, Rachel felt more herself.

From the kitchen window she could see Dan Gage digging in a corner of the yard. It occurred to Rachel she had seen him digging there at least once before, and, tiredly, she asked, "It's not the first time, is it?"

Kitty reddened. Beginning to clear away the remains of Dan's interrupted meal, she muttered, "People's just being silly, is all."

"Silly," Rachel repeated. "Oh, Kitty."

After this exchange, the two women were silent until Dan put his head in at the door to say he was going. Rachel called her thanks to him; adding, with sudden decision, "I am going to the woodyard tomorrow, Mr. Gage. Would you have any objection to my taking Kitty with me?"

Mr. Gage had no legitimate grounds for objecting. Kitty was bound to do as her employer ordered. What Rachel intended to convey by the question was a tacit acknowledgement of Dan's position. The young couple had clearly come to an "understanding." As the man who would one day take Kitty from her father's protection and care into his own, Mr. Gage had a legitimate interest in what the young woman did.

Or so Rachel had been taught.

Whether this viewpoint was defensible or not, it was the prevailing one, and the glow the question produced on both young faces, Kitty's and Dan's, reassured Rachel she had said exactly the right thing.

*

The men at the woodyard were rushed with work, but they wished to be helpful. They did not understand at first who Rachel was or what her interest was in Mary Hale's death, and knowing no other acceptable way of dealing with the haunting memory of the dead girl's set, white face, the boys who had discovered her body were at first inclined to make crude jokes about the event. One went so far as to seize a cord and mime his own hanging, his tongue outthrust— though he put only a loop of rope and not a noose around his neck, as though he were troubled by an irrational fear the joke might end somehow in his accidentally hanging for real.

Feeling sick, Rachel closed her eyes and put a hand on his arm, murmuring, "Oh, dear, don't, please," and the young man, who had only wanted to catch Kitty's eye and impress her with his daring, looked suddenly ashamed.

"Tell me everything you remember about the morning Miss Hale was found," asked Rachel. "Omit nothing, please. Anything you tell me may be of use."

A brief silence ensued before the boy who had pretended to hang himself asked, with deep suspicion, "What do you want to know for?"

Rachel suddenly thought of the dead cat. For all she knew, one of these boys might have been the one to supply the animal, another might have lettered the accompanying sign, and the third might have placed the stiff body across the threshold of the Woodley house.

Anyone she met, Rachel abruptly realized, might be someone who believed her husband was a murderer.

"I am the Reverend Mr. Woodley's wife," she admitted, her voice shaking. "But I am—was—also the mother of a girl who might have grown up to find herself in Mary Hale's position one day. I want to see justice done—for Miss Hale, and—assuming he is not guilty of this base crime—for my husband."

Before the woodyard men could raise their eyes from where they'd fixed them on the ground, Kitty blurted out impatiently, "Where was it done, for goodness sake? Walking up I looked all over outside, and I didn't see anything anybody could hang anybody *from*."

Reanimated—even excited—by this chance to share what they knew, the three young men eagerly escorted the two women outside. The stack of logs over which the rope had been looped had diminished since the January day on which Mary had died, but Kitty's quick eye noted and pointed out to Rachel the place near the bottom where the sheriff had speculated a smallish young woman might have stepped up to tie a knot above her head.

"And that's where her pocketbook was laid," added their guide, pointing to another protrusion.

"Did anybody think to look in it for a note?" asked Kitty eagerly.

"Oh, yes. The sheriff did," the young man said, thoughtfully stroking the novice attempt at a beard on his chin. "Wasn't none found, though, nor any about."

Rachel, meanwhile, was scanning the area. "No houses nor shops nearby. What a lonely place!"

Kitty said flatly, "That's the best kind of place for the type of business Miss Hale was about. And I *don't* mean getting hung!"

"Kitty!"

"Then the sheriff called for women," one of the woodyard boys continued, stifling a smirk, "and when they came, they took the body into the shed here"—he led the way back to it—"and looked her over, I guess. Them and the doctor. The doctor come after, and didn't the women just hate to let him in! The sheriff had to say he was going to break the door down before they'd unlock."

"What did they all do to her?" Kitty asked curiously.

"We'll discuss that later," said Rachel. "And the rope and so forth. The evidence. Did the sheriff take it?"

"That's right."

"The rope was tied above her," Rachel mused. "But did she tie it herself?" Turning to the young men, she begged, "Could you show me exactly *how* the rope was tied, please?"

The oldest of the woodyard boys retrieved a coil of rope. "Well, let's see," he began, unwinding a few feet. "The part up above was tied like this, see? In a double-knot. That time of year, there was a log at the top of the stack was sticking out convenient to put it on."

Rachel nodded.

"Then around—That is, at the *other* end," he continued, "was a clove hitch. The knot had worked itself up under her ear and I could see it plain."

"Can you show me a clove hitch?" asked Rachel.

The man nodded. "Just let me get something to tie it around, first. A clove hitch won't stand by itself, like a double-knot will. It's a knot has to have something at its middle."

When the clove hitch had been made around a block of wood, Rachel took it from the woodyard boy's hand. "This is the knot by which Miss Hale was hanged?" she asked, studying it closely. "I've never seen a knot like this before."

"Oh, it ain't a knot any *woman* would know," Wispy-beard said wisely. "It's a sailor's knot."

"But a woman could tie one if she wanted. Anyone could, couldn't they? It doesn't look to me like there's anything especially difficult about making a knot like that."

The men looked at each other. "Well, maybe," one conceded. "But you don't know how *now*, do you?"

If Mary had hanged herself, she would have had to know how to tie a clove hitch. Rachel persisted, "If you taught me, I would know how. Show me!"

After seeing it done twice, Rachel was able to produce her own clove hitch.

"Not a woman's knot, eh?" she said, showing her work with satisfaction. "There's no end to the vainglory of you men."

To her surprise, the young men laughed delightedly.

Urged Rachel, "Now you, Kitty."

Kitty took longer than Rachel to learn to tie a clove hitch, though Rachel suspected she was not so much slow to catch on as simply enjoying the sensation of having a young man stand in back of her and put his arms around her to guide her fingers from behind.

"I can't seem to see how to do it from looking at it in his hands when he stands over there, because then it's the wrong way around," she explained demurely, when Rachel objected to the intimacy of the position. "This way works much better."

And then, to prove the system's efficacy, Kitty promptly produced a well-tied knot.

There's no trick to it. Any woman could learn this, Rachel thought. Aloud, she asked, "I wonder if I might have this stick and a piece of the rope?"

A woodyard boy pulled out his knife and was preparing to cut the rest of the coil of rope away from the piece knotted around the wood when one of his fellows stopped him.

"Wait now," he said. "Was it *this* rope you wanted, ma'am? Or was it the kind of rope Mary—Miss Hale, that is—hung herself with?"

"Oh, yes, please! That kind of rope," Rachel said—hiding her satisfaction that the remark suggested the woodyard boys were convinced Mary Hale had committed suicide.

The length of rope the boys now provided was a softer, whiter cord than the hempen one they had taught her to tie, and braided in another way.

"It's cotton, mostly," one explained, when Rachel asked about it. "It's made here in Milltown, of short ravelings, and whatever's left over at the mill. It's not very strong, but it's cheap to buy. We use it for light work, as bundling stakes."

As they left the woodyard, Kitty reached over and tested the new rope's texture between her finger and thumb.

"Oh, yes, that's better," she said. "That's what *I* would have used. The other rope was terrible—all scratchy and all."

"Do you think on the brink of immortality you would care about a few prickles on your neck, Kitty?"

"Oh, I think too much of God to ever hang myself," Kitty said quickly. "But if I *was* to do such a thing, I'd take the soft rope."

Rachel sighed. "Let's talk about something else."

*

As they approached the house, Kitty stopped suddenly to point out a dark figure looming in the porch shadows.

"Who's that?" she asked uneasily. "I don't know him. Do you?"

Dread in her heart (had they interrupted the delivery of another dead cat?) Rachel peered closely. "No I don't," she said. "Should we just keep walking? Keep walking, Kitty." From the corner of her eye, she continued to observe the figure closely, while trying to appear unconcerned.

The mysterious man stepped into the sunlight, and Rachel corrected herself with relief. "It's Dr. Brown," she said. "Whatever does *he* want, do you suppose?"

As they neared the steps, it was necessary, Rachel discovered, to give Kitty a little push in the direction of the back yard to make the girl recall that as the family servant, she did not enter at the front door.

"Don't bother with tea," Rachel whispered sharply as the girl went. She wanted a cup very much, but felt she would as soon die as show Dr. Brown any such courtesy. "Except for yourself," she added. At this, Kitty, who had looked chagrinned, squared her shoulders again and went off happily toward the kitchen.

Catching sight of her, the doctor came forward eagerly, his hand half-extended until he saw that Rachel did not intend to offer hers.

"Mrs. Woodley," he said, forcing an embarrassed smile. "Mrs. Woodley."

"Dr. Brown," Rachel replied, her voice frosty.

Dr. Brown groped in his pocket for a handkerchief, then wiped his upper lip with it.

The two were at the Woodley front door by now, but when Rachel made no move to invite him in, Dr. Brown began hastily, "Mrs. Woodley, I have already seen your husband to offer my thanks—my humble thanks—for what he has done, but I couldn't rest until I had thanked you, too. Your kindness is unexampled. Please allow me to—to—" Here, the doctor's fine language failed him. "To thank you," he repeated. "For your kindness."

Thanks from such a source were so unexpected that Rachel could not think of any answer to them. After a pause, she invited, "Come in, won't you?"

Dr. Brown leaped across the porch to hold the door for her.

"For what are you grateful, Dr. Brown?" Rachel asked, sitting down on the first parlor chair she came to and untying her bonnet strings. "I have done you no service I can recall."

"Not me directly," said the doctor—still standing, since Rachel had not invited him to sit. "But for my Uncle Philip and his wife. A most unexampled kindness, as I said. Uncle Philip's…struggles…have been a great concern to me, but I really did not know what to do for him. I hope—all my family hope—the opportunity your husband found for him may lead him back toward a more—ah—*respectable* style of life."

He would have gone on, but Rachel stopped him.

"Oh, *that*," she said, in a friendlier tone. "Please don't mention it. For the little I've done myself for Mr. and Mrs. Brown, you are very welcome, but the offer of the position at the gristmill was all Mr. Woodley's doing. I hope it works out well for your uncle."

Rachel rose and half turned her back on her guest to remove her shawl, hoping Dr. Brown would take the hint to go. She was pleased to know he had visited and thanked Josiah, but as for herself, her appetite for tea was considerably greater than for praise.

Instead of leaving, the doctor hurried to assist her. "I wonder whether I may in some way repay your kindness, Mrs. Woodley?" he asked as he took the shawl.

Wasting no time—or words—Rachel demanded, "Will you testify at trial on my husband's behalf?"

Dr. Brown blushed. (Rachel would never have taken him for a

blusher.) "Oh, no, no," he said quickly. "As I told you, I gave my opinion at the girl's inquest, and I have nothing further to add to it now. And anyway, I don't think my testimony would help your husband as much as you imagine."

"Why is that? And sit down, won't you?"

His hands clasped between his knees, Dr. Brown earnestly explained his position to Rachel.

"I've offered testimony in court before, as I told you," he said. "And you may believe me a physician's word doesn't count for much there. A jury, you see, is made up of twelve ordinary citizens, and in medical matters, they may easily be imposed upon. Were I to testify on the Reverend Mr. Woodley's behalf, as soon as I was done, the prosecutor would simply introduce his *own* medical expert to cast doubt upon what I had said." Added Dr. Brown uncomfortably, "He'll more than cast doubt, in fact. He'll laugh me to scorn, if he can. That's what's commonly done in these cases."

Rachel was forced to concede the doctor's position in the witness box might be unenviable. "But," she countered, "whether you testify or not, there's nothing to stop the prosecutor from finding someone— some plausible somebody—to allege Miss Hale was only three or four months…expectant. And if the jury believes that, it may be fatal to Mr. Woodley!"

"The notes I made at inquest will be entered into evidence," said Dr. Brown quickly. "And furthermore…" Here the doctor paused to draw his chair a little closer to Rachel's, his manner slightly conspiratorial. "You may not know it," he told her in a low voice, "but I was assisted in my examination of Miss Hale's body by three women."

"I did hear that. Just today, in fact."

"And did you hear that all three of those women were as convinced as I that the case was of a young woman five months gone with child who committed suicide in a fit of despair? That is the very thing you want the jury to hear, is it not?"

Rachel considered what he was saying. "I can't imagine the testimony of three *women* will count for anything in a law court," she said.

"Oh, I think it might count for a great deal!" replied Dr. Brown eagerly. "For one thing, those three women will probably be found to have brought half the members of the jury into the world in the first place!"

"They are midwives?" Rachel asked.

The doctor—holder of a diploma written in largely correct Latin—could not quite suppress his sneer. "Oh, half the crones in Milltown practice midwifery," he said. "Untrained, illiterate…" He caught himself. "Not that I wish to disparage them, of course! My point, Mrs. Woodley, is they are the very ones whose testimony you need. The prosecutor will not *dare* to make a laughingstock of *them*. It is never wise for a lawyer to humiliate on the stand a respectable lady of advanced years."

"And you say they believed Miss Hale was a suicide?"

"Oh, certainly. We agreed between us she was. The girl was small, but she was perfectly healthy and strong. If anyone had tried to harm her, she would have struggled. There wasn't a single mark on her body that suggested struggle, nor any sign of a blow to the head that might have rendered her unconscious, or passive."

Rachel considered her next move.

"If I give you a paper," she asked slowly, "will you write these ladies' names and where I may find them? But first, ring that bell, if you would. I think we should have tea. Don't you?"

CHAPTER TWENTY-THREE

Next day, before Rachel had gotten all the way in at the door of the jail, Josiah was already calling excitedly to her from above. The sheriff, though not smiling—he never smiled—seemed as near to smiling as it was possible for him to be.

"Come up, come up," Josiah called. "I have news. I think you're going to like it."

An unexpected letter from a Mr. Dodd had arrived, Josiah told Rachel as he took her hands. Mr. Dodd was a person previously unknown to him, and the letter served both to introduce him as an attorney and to announce his anticipated arrival in Milltown tomorrow.

"But why is he coming?" Rachel asked, amazed. "I've heard of Mr. Dodd, I believe. He practices in Boston. Oh, Josiah, darling, do you think my father—?"

She broke off. Informed of Josiah's situation, her disapproving father had recommended she leave her husband's house immediately. Her mother, he indicated, was "willing" for her to return to them.

Josiah's face told her the matter was nothing to do with her father. "Mr. Dodd mentions Dr. Conrad, so I suppose he has been retained by the church, like Mr. Tyrode."

Rachel refrained from saying what she was thinking—that the church had certainly taken its time about providing what looked likely to be more competent advocacy for her husband.

"The sheriff knows him, of course," added Josiah. "He thinks him the best legal man in the state."

"The best…!" said Rachel faintly. "Oh, but will it be enough?" she cried. "The opening of court is next week!"

Josiah, though joyful, was also tranquil—as he nearly always was. "Making up a case on short notice will probably not be new to such an experienced lawyer," he said. "This is an answer to many prayers, Rachel!"

*

When Rachel got home, Kitty was in the kitchen entertaining a few members of her large family.

Seeing Rachel, the girl cried, "Oh, come and meet everyone!" as blithely as though she didn't know she needed to ask permission before bringing guests into the house. "Now, three of these is cousins of mine," she went on happily, "and this one's my next-younger sister." Kitty then pronounced all the young ladies' names, but Rachel, worn out from a long session of planning Josiah's defense with him, caught none of them.

She was, however, alert enough to guess when a chubby child was thrust into her arms that it must be the baby Kitty had characterized as the "cutest, fattest love of little boy" belonging to one of her cousins.

The sight of a child, Rachel found, did not now immediately bring her to tears. She felt a stab at her heart, of course—but was still able to smile appropriately, coo and tickle the boy, and praise him as "remarkably forward for his age." Time had done for her grief what only time could do. The burden of her loss could finally be borne with composure.

The three cousins and Kitty quickly cleared a place for Rachel at the kitchen table (her kitchen table), and plied her with tea (also hers) and abundant helpings of the treats the visitors had brought with them.

"My mother's is the best," Kitty reported of every dish.

Toward evening, the young ladies at last rose to leave. Two were married and had husbands to feed.

"I don't know which is harder," the baby's mother remarked. "Working a shift at the mill or washdays. Tomorrow's my washday, and I feel like I'm tired out from it already!"

Until that moment, Rachel had forgotten Kitty had once told her that the cousin who had the "love" of a baby boy had previously worked in a mill. Now, putting a hand on the young woman's arm, she asked hopefully, "You'll think this an odd question, perhaps, but do you know the knot called a 'clove hitch?'"

"A what?"

"A clove hitch. It's a kind of knot. I thought it might be used in the mills."

"Not as I recall," Kitty's cousin said, her forehead creasing. "Unless maybe by the mechanics. You might ask one of them about it."

As Mary Hale had not been a mechanic, what knots mechanics knew or did not know could not be relevant to Josiah's case. Rachel thanked the girl, soundly kissed her little son's cheek, and let the matter go.

Once Kitty had closed the door behind her cousins, the girl's face turned somber.

"I didn't like to mention it before everybody," she said, her eyes on the floor. "But you got a letter. No, don't do none of the clearing away," she added, since Rachel had begun, almost unconsciously, to carry dishes to the sink. "That's my job. The letter's in the parlor. You just come and sit and read it."

The reason for Kitty's solicitousness became immediately apparent to Rachel when she saw the letter. It was black-bordered.

"Oh, poor Anne!" Rachel exclaimed, putting her hands over her face. "And poor Mr. Woodley! Kitty, should I go now and tell him?" It was almost the hour at which Josiah and the sheriff usually dined and talked, a high point of Josiah's day.

"Let him sleep peaceful one more night," Kitty advised. "Tomorrow's soon enough."

*

Next morning, as Rachel had known he would, Josiah took the news of his brother-in-law William's death very hard. Nothing she said could entirely convince him he had done no wrong in leaving his father's farm to be worked by a man with a bad chest.

"Do you ever think all this"—Josiah waved his hand vaguely around him—"is a judgment on me?"

Rachel replied firmly that she did not. "Will was a good man, and his reward for it was heaven," she said. "Don't begrudge him heaven."

Her husband smiled faintly. "Do you promise you won't begrudge me heaven, if it comes to that?"

Rachel was spared answering this by a bang of the jail's door and a hearty voice greeting the sheriff below.

Simultaneously, both Woodleys exclaimed, "Mr. Dodd!"

"They're up there together, are they?" said this new voice. "Excellent! I shall introduce myself at once." Though he proved a moment later to be a short, portly, red-faced man with a broad smile, the attorney's step as he ran up the jail stairs was as energetic as a boy's.

As soon he saw her, Lawyer Dodd exclaimed, "Mrs. Woodley!" as familiarly as though he already knew her. "This is indeed a pleasure!"

Rachel, remembering that Mr. Dodd was a Boston man, asked whether they had met before, perhaps?

They had not. "What I know of you I had from Sophronia Conrad," Mr. Dodd said. "She speaks very highly of you. Very highly. She's a magnificent lady, Sophronia, and always knows another."

Rachel discovered she did not mind being flattered a little.

Mr. Dodd then turned to greet Josiah, and immediately got down to business.

Indicating the black-bordered envelope on Josiah's makeshift desk, he asked, "Does that letter relate to the brother-in-law whose sick bed you set out to visit last January? It does? Then please accept my heartfelt condolences on your loss." Before Josiah could answer this, Mr. Dodd continued, "And yet this may be said to be, in some ways, a very timely occurrence. Tragic, of course—but timely. It has been a critical point against you that you left Milltown on the very day Miss Mary Hale's body was found hanging in the woodyard. This sad event—though in every other way to be regretted, of course—at least makes clear the urgency of the business that called you away."

Rachel thought this an excellent point.

When Josiah's stiff reply—which he seemed to look to her to reinforce—was "I hope my private griefs will not be made a point in my defense, sir," Rachel decided to leave immediately. The lawyer would have a better chance of carrying this or any subsequent arguments, she thought, if she were not present. After pressing her husband's hand (she was too shy to kiss him before others), she went down.

As Rachel reached the bottom of the stairs—where she found the sheriff still lurking—Mr. Dodd was saying breezily, "Oh, we need not make a 'point' of it, precisely, but we'd be fools not to take advantage of any opportunities to inspire the jurymen with compassion toward you."

"I perceive you are a cynic, sir," Josiah quietly replied.

The sheriff and Rachel flinched together.

But Mr. Dodd only answered without shame, "I am indeed! Come now, I have made a *precis* of your case, Woodley. Look at it, and tell me what you think."

Rachel murmured, "Will you ask Mr. Dodd to visit me?"

The sheriff nodded.

He did not escort her to the jailhouse door, as he usually did. He was already making himself comfortable five steps up the jail's stairs, his ear cocked toward the cell above.

CHAPTER TWENTY-FOUR

Rachel was not quite sure, at first, what to make of the chameleon Mr. Dodd. With Kitty, he was jovial and familiar; with Rachel, serious—even grave. Once seated in the Woodley parlor, he inquired earnestly, his eyes soft as a spaniel's, as to how Rachel was bearing up. When she answered him in a voice that did not break, he instantly read her (correctly) as someone not desiring sympathy, and assumed a more matter-of-fact demeanor.

"Mrs. Woodley, I have spoken at length with your husband," he said. "I believe I am now acquainted with the facts of his case, and wish you to know at once that I am confident Mr. Tyrode and I can make him a good defense."

"Mr. Tyrode?" Rachel repeated blankly. "Are you—? Are *you* not to represent Mr. Woodley, sir?"

Mr. Dodd pinched the bridge of his nose. "Mr. Tyrode arrived yesterday on the late stagecoach, and he is most anxious to assist me," he said then, allowing Rachel to guess from his expression that he suspected Mr. Tyrode of coming hot-foot to protect his fee. "One can always use assistance. In this case, Mr. Tyrode's younger legs will be of great use in rounding up witnesses to see they present themselves in good time at the courthouse."

"But you will plead the case in court?" Rachel inquired again, anxiously.

"Every word."

Her mind relieved on that score, Rachel asked, "Now that you have heard the evidence, Mr. Dodd, do you agree with me a jury can only bring a verdict of not guilty?"

The attorney did not immediately answer this.

Finally, he said, "Unfortunately, the evidence in a case is not the sole determinant of a verdict."

"What else, then? Speak frankly, please."

Mr. Dodd permitted his back to rest comfortably against his chair and folded his hands over his ample belly—an easy posture Rachel envied but decorum did not permit her to assume.

"I had a client once—we will say once. I have probably had several—who was as innocent as a babe newborn of the crime of which he was accused, but who had a threatening manner and a habit of picking fights. The jury pronounced him guilty as a means of removing a man from their midst of whom they were all afraid."

"But Josiah—!"

"You are about to say your husband, in contrast, has no enemy but Satan," Mr. Dodd finished for her. "That is true—as far as it goes. But if Miss Mary Hale was murdered and someone does not hang for it, then the good citizens of Milltown will be left with an uneasy sense there is still a murderer living among them. They may wish to be rid of Mr. Woodley on that account—to reassure themselves they are safe. I have known it to happen."

"Oh, surely not!"

The attorney shrugged. He was indeed, Rachel saw, a cynic.

"I am convinced the citizens of Milltown will turn out in great numbers for this trial," he went on. "My endeavor in the courtroom will be to supply them with another murderer they may try, convict, and consign to the hereafter, and thereby put an end to their fears."

This fantasy—it could be nothing else than a fantasy—made Rachel stare. "But—who?" she stammered. "No other name but Mr. Woodley's has ever been suggested!"

"One has," stated Mr. Dodd.

He surely could not mean Dr. Conrad, Rachel thought. But who, then?

Before she could ask, the lawyer hurried on. "Let us go over the evidence together now, shall we, Mrs. Woodley? Do you know I've never said that to a client's wife before? Sometimes I don't say it even to the client himself. By consulting the evidence alone I avoid the usual catalogue of justifications and tears. But you're different from the usual run of wives. I was told you were before I came. You're all reason and intellect, with your emotions kept well under control."

Rachel blurted nervously, "My husband permits me to—"

"I should think your husband rejoices in it," Mr. Dodd interrupted, speaking firmly. "Now, what I need to discover is whether there is a single relevant fact—anything, however small—of which you are aware, Mrs. Woodley, that I am not. I want to hear the whole matter in *your* words. Begin at the very beginning: When and from whom did you learn of Mary Hale's death?"

After a moment's surprised silence—the advocate's admiration seemed perfectly sincere—Rachel leaned forward, clasped her knees with her hands, and began the speech she had rehearsed a hundred times in her mind.

"I heard it in a shop," she said, "from Agnes Tudge…"

*

It was afternoon by the time Rachel finished her narrative, closely questioned at every point by Mr. Dodd. There were few details of Josiah's case with which the advocate was not already familiar from Dr. Conrad's letters. He expressed surprise only when she mentioned the fur hat Mary's escort was alleged to have worn.

"I don't recall John mentioning that," he said, producing his pocket-memorandum to make a note of the point. "Or I simply forgot about it. You're absolute certain Mr. Woodley has no such hat?"

"I would swear to it," Rachel said firmly.

Mr. Dodd at last prepared to go.

"You remember what Josiah wrote about the publican's wife, don't you?" Rachel asked anxiously, watching him gather his things together.

"I do, and she will testify. You may depend upon it."

"And you will inquire further into the business of the clove hitch knot?"

"I will. I must tell you I'm not hopeful we can make anything of it, but I'll see."

"I understand. And the letters… You will ask to see the letters, won't you? I am certain only the one he admitted to was written by my husband."

"I have examined the letters already, and I will examine them again tomorrow morning," Mr. Dodd promised.

The two talked a moment longer, and then, refusing tea, Mr. Dodd left.

*

Supper in the Woodley kitchen was a brief affair, for Rachel had no appetite.

"I have done all I can," she told Kitty wearily. "The matter is in

God's hands, now—as it always was, really. But have I done enough? Have *I* done enough? I hope I have."

"Oh, yes," said Kitty instantly. "You done all you could do, so it must be enough, mustn't it? Is it enough praying now, too, do you think? My knees are about wore out with praying."

"Enough praying?" repeated Rachel. "I suppose we can never pray enough. You needn't pray on your knees, though, if it hurts you."

Kitty was silent for a moment, then asked hesitantly, "Mrs. Woodley? What—what ought I to have been praying *for*?"

"Beg pardon?"

"Well, I *have* been praying for Mr. Woodley to be set *free*. But ought I to be asking for that? What if it's not God's will for him to be free? Is it wrong for me to try to tell God what to do?"

Rachel tried to smile. "Whatever prayer we say, I'm sure God already knows we want Mr. Woodley to come home a free man. He knows everything in our hearts."

"Then what're we *praying* for? If He already knows, I mean."

Josiah, Rachel thought, in sudden confusion, would have known how to answer this. She herself was at a bit of a loss. Religion was something Rachel accepted as it was handed down to her. She had been taught to pray in difficulties, so she prayed. She had never thought to examine the whys and wherefores of it. "Well," she said slowly. "I suppose it's always right for us to pray He send us the strength to endure His will. You may make that prayer, if it would make you feel better."

Kitty persisted, "But if He knows what's in our hearts and all, don't He already know we want strength to endure His will?"

Rachel considered. "Yes, of course."

"So what do we pray for?"

"Kitty dear," Rachel said, getting up quickly, "I'm so very tired. May we discuss this at another time? Just carry on praying as you have done, and leave it to God to understand you. Maybe it isn't really very important *what* we pray for, so long as we take the time to remember and honor God upon our knees. Or, as yours are sore, in some other posture. Will that answer satisfy you for now?"

"Oh, yes, Mrs. Woodley." Kitty began to clear the table. "I already know it's all right to pray sitting up, for we do that in church. But my mother says we must never wait to say prayers until we are lying in bed at night, no matter how cold the floor is, for fear we should fall asleep before the 'amen'!"

*

On the last Sunday before the court sessions opened, Rachel went as usual to church.

Since Josiah's arrest, churchgoing had become more of an ordeal than a comfort to her, as it both began and ended with the running of a gauntlet of church-members making a point of coming forward to speak kindly to her, or of turning as pointedly away. When she reached her pew at last, Rachel sat down with relief to find and mark the morning's text and try not to hear Mrs. Tudge's comments to Mrs. Birdwell concerning her dress in the pew behind her.

"Ah! A black bonnet," said Mrs. Tudge, approvingly. "So much more suitable than *straw* for a bereft mother. I did think I glimpsed her around town once or twice wearing *blue*, with a straw bonnet, but I see I was mistaken."

Mrs. Birdwell replied, in a tone that suggested she did not really care to discuss the subject, that she believed Rachel had resumed black owing to the recent death of a brother-in-law.

Mrs. Tudge had not heard the news about William. "It is not for her child, then? How strange. I'm sure I would never leave off mourning if, God forbid, I should lose a child."

"It has been a year," said Mrs. Birdwell. "A year is enough."

"Enough for some," answered Mrs. Tudge.

Mrs. Birdwell's reply to this was that she thought Rachel set a good example, by her dress, of cheerful submission to the will of God—a remark to which Mrs. Tudge fortunately seemed to have no answer.

Throughout the exchange, Rachel feigned deafness, as she had learned to do in response to the shouts that sometimes followed her in the streets. Though she and Kitty knew by now which shops they were welcome to patronize and by which routes they could most safely move through the town, they were still sometimes taken off-guard by a rude hiss in a crowd, or an insult called out from somewhere behind them. The only satisfaction to be gained in such situations, Rachel had found, was to deny her tormentors the pleasure of being certain she heard them.

Mrs. Tudge, with her smiles and affected kindly concern, was a particularly pernicious type, Rachel thought, and she was seized with a desire to thank Mrs. Birdwell for speaking out in her defense. She half-rose from her pew and turned to look behind her, as though for a friend, or to see how full the church was. Her real intention was to catch Sister Birdwell's eye, and signal, somehow, her appreciation.

Instead, when she turned she saw Mr. Cockburn. He was standing awkwardly at the back of the sanctuary, glancing about him in a way that made it clear he did not know how to proceed.

He looked like what he was, a rough laboring man who had probably not seen the inside of a house of worship for some time, but he was cleaner in person and dress than when Rachel and Kitty had met him at the ferry landing and wore a collar and an attempt at a cravat. Twisting his cap nervously in his hands, he was apparently looking for where he should go. Distracted, as Rachel saw, by the passage of every well-dressed lady, he did not observe that the balcony was the place to where members of the humbler classes were streaming. She found herself blushing for him, poor man—and for her church-fellows, so badly lacking in charity as to leave him, friendless, where he stood.

Rachel stood fully up, hoping to get his attention and point him to the stairs, but the ferry master did not see her. He seemed, in fact, to be turning to go. No one attempted to persuade him to stay. Indeed, passers-by seemed to be avoiding his eye.

Dropping her testament into the pew, Rachel started after him, hurrying more than was ladylike (she heard Mrs. Tudge's startled exclamation behind her) to intercept the ferry master before he could get out the door.

By the time Rachel was near enough to speak to him, Mr. Cockburn had been so overcome with humiliation that, intent on making a speedy escape, he did not even notice her approach. Gingerly, Rachel touched his arm.

As he turned, she said, forcing a shy smile, "Do you remember me, Mr. Cockburn? I am Mrs. Woodley."

Mr. Cockburn brightened at once, and answered the greeting with half an oath, the rest of which he just managed to keep back. Out of habit, he reached for his cap—and looked sheepish to discover it was already in his hand. Nervously, he stammered, "Well, I thought as you and the other young lady had been so kind as to invite me, da—! I mean, I thought I might come." He looked around eagerly, craning his neck, Rachel suspected, for a glimpse of Kitty. "Been forty years, da—. That is, I believe I ain't been in a church in forty years."

Rachel did not find any difficulty in accepting this statement as truth. "Do you have a seat?" she asked, adding, when he shook his head, "Oh, do come this way, then."

She meant to lead Mr. Cockburn to the balcony, and to put him by someone she knew would not mind him—Mr. Gage, perhaps. But on second thought she realized there really was no time left to do it. The hum of talk in the church was giving way to an expectant rustling, as the congregants settled themselves in their pews and turned toward the pulpit where the minister could soon be expected to appear.

Rachel hesitated, unsure what to do. Mr. Cockburn was greasy, and he was profane, and whatever small claim to the title of "lady" the Mrs. Tudges of the town still permitted to her would surely be lost by any further association with him. In fact, Mrs. Tudge herself was just turning in her pew to look back and sneer.

Ultimately, it was the sneer that decided Rachel. She must regard Mr. Cockburn as nothing less than a spiritual brother. "Come and sit with me," she said, swallowing bravely. "Since Mr. Woodley cannot be with me, there is an empty place."

Mrs. Tudge's gasp was audible through half the sanctuary.

While Rachel was settling Mr. Cockburn in the pew beside her, Mr. Dodd was across town, listening—apparently raptly—to a Methodist sermon. The lawyer was flexible in his religious observances. He attended Divine Service wherever he thought it would benefit a client for him to be seen. Leaving no stone unturned in the difficult Woodley case, he had gone earlier to a Baptist service. He knew all the hymns of both denominations and sang loudly.

Afterwards, he dined alone at his hotel, where he ordered brandy (as it was the Lord's Day, he asked for it, with a wink, by the name of French coffee), and helped himself to a liberal glassful. He was in a reminiscing mood, and his college days, when his friendship with John Conrad had been formed, were particularly in his thoughts.

In his young years, Mr. Dodd had liked very much to go hunting. At college, when his studies did not permit him sufficient leisure for hunting, he annoyed John by taking shots from the window of their shared lodgings at any small animal appearing on the lawn below. It therefore made a good joke a few years later when, on the occasion of his erstwhile roommate's marriage, the wedding gift he presented was a hat made from the skins of some of the unfortunate squirrels who had ventured a college lawn within range of his musket. Sipping his brandy now, he recalled lovely Sophronia affecting to believe the gift was for her, and clapping it on over her curls while everyone looking on laughed uproariously. The Conrad wedding had wrought, in fact, a bittersweet end for them all to the days of their youth.

He wondered—he had always wondered—whatever had possessed John Conrad, a notably worldly and doubting soul, to go into the ministry. He wondered what had become of the lively young girl poor haunted Sophronia had once been.

And—fingering the letter in an inner coat pocket, written on blue paper and asking him to come to Milltown to defend Josiah Woodley against a charge of murder—he wondered what had become of the hat.

Chapter Twenty-Five

Mr. Dodd visited again to remind Rachel the court sessions were to open on Friday. There were, of course, other cases to be tried, but Mr. Dodd thought by Friday afternoon, she should expect a jury to have been empaneled in Josiah's case.

"There's too much interest in it for the matter to be long deferred," he said. "I expect all will be over in just a day or two. Mr. Fisher, who is to prosecute, favors a short, sharp style of attack, and the jury won't dawdle in reaching a verdict. It's spring, and the farmers have work to do at home. A few days spent in town hearing a trial make a pleasant break in their routine, but once the arguments have been presented, they'll become anxious to be back in their own barnyards."

"Will there be many farmers on the jury?" asked Rachel.

"As many as I can get." Mr. Dodd nodded. "I believe I can make something of the fact that your husband is the son of a farmer himself."

It was like Mr. Dodd to be always thinking of what use any piece of information might be to him in court. He and Josiah had already clashed—to the extent the mild Josiah could ever clash with anyone—over the issue of what clothes Josiah would wear. The lawyer wanted him to appear in mourning, to remind jurors of his bereaved state.

"You are in mourning, are you not?" Mr. Dodd had demanded.

"Then why not wear the appropriate emblems of that grief? The black stock and crepe hatband I recommend are the smallest expressions allowable by our society in so near a bereavement as one's own brother. Brother-in-law, then," he amended impatiently, when Josiah corrected him. "A small difference. I'm sure it made none at all to you. You loved him as a brother, did you not?"

"I shall mourn indeed, for justice and for humanity, when I believe a melancholy aspect and three feet of crepe trailing from his hat is what is required for an innocent man to be acquitted of false charges," Josiah replied firmly.

Though Rachel—and, judging by his expression, the sheriff—thought the lawyer's recommendations sensible, they were unable to gain their point. Mild, yielding Josiah could be stubborn when he felt he had right on his side.

On Thursday, Rachel went early to the jail. It would be her last chance to see her husband by daylight until his trial was over. While it continued, when he was not in the courtroom Josiah would be confined in a cell in the basement of the courthouse, where no visitors were allowed.

On arrival, Rachel found the door of the Milltown jail locked, and the sheriff did not answer her initial timid knock, nor her second, more forceful one. When calling (most unladylike!) up to Josiah from the street still elicited no response, Rachel panicked. Hardly knowing what she was doing, she first pounded on the jail's door, then knocked at its front windows, and finally, after vainly straining to see through it, rapped sharply with her knuckles on the tiny window of the lean-to at the back of the jailhouse. Several surprised faces appeared at windows in adjacent buildings, but no one answered from the jail.

Not knowing what else to do, Rachel finally turned back toward home, eyes streaming. Her husband had been snatched from her without warning. It was a wrench almost equivalent in her heart to a death.

Fortunately, as she rounded the first corner, she met Josiah and the sheriff walking toward her. The two men were talking together so companionably that—but for the shackles Josiah wore—they might have been mistaken for a pair of old friends. Josiah had been transformed by a bath and a shave. Catching sight of her, he brightened, and called out, "Dearest!"

Where a public endearment would usually have caused Rachel to look shyly aside (and to chide Josiah for it later in private), on this occasion Rachel's response was to walk straight into her husband's arms and lay her head against his chest.

"I didn't know what to think!" she cried, tears still flowing. "I thought you'd been—" She didn't say the word "lynched," but Josiah— and the sheriff—could easily guess it. His bound hands made it impossible for Josiah to fully embrace her, but he soothed her with soft words, and kissed her hair. The sheriff, meanwhile, bashfully turned his gaze elsewhere.

After a moment, Rachel pulled away, and, straightening her bonnet, looked her husband up and down. "Dear me!" she said, husky-voiced. "You look fit for the pulpit again!"

Now that there was a decent space between the two Woodleys, the sheriff dared to look at them again. With his usual dryness, he said, "The pulpit, or honest work, either one. There was a little accident happened to that white stock you brung him for tomorrow, Mrs. Woodley. Got dropped in some mud. Might be Mr. Woodley'll have to wear the black one to court after all. I'll see Mrs. Brown gets the white one to wash, but I hear she's real busy this week." Where

Rachel and Mr. Dodd had failed by pleas and persuasions to win their point regarding mourning attire, the sheriff had prevailed by... other means.

Josiah's lawyers, Mr. Dodd ebullient as always, Mr. Tyrode grim, were waiting for them at the jail when they reached it.

"Tomorrow begins the process of your exoneration, Mr. Woodley!" Mr. Dodd said, as though exoneration were assured. "Soon you'll be a free man again."

Mr. Tyrode, lurking in the background, did not second this assertion. The young lawyer had initially hoped his association with Mr. Dodd would gain him experience and professional stature, but since the older man generally ignored his advice and permitted him no experiences beyond those of an errand-boy, Mr. Tyrode's mood had been soured by the reflection that if the Woodley case were lost, he would gain no more from it than the generous fee he had demanded.

Josiah did not want Rachel to attend the trial. "The Milltown courthouse has no gallery where ladies can sit apart," he explained. "In any case, I can't bear to imagine what you might hear in the courtroom. Mr. Dodd has warned me it will be in Mr. Fisher's best interest to paint me for the jury as a monster of depravity."

Though Rachel wasn't entirely certain what a "monster of depravity" might be, she assured Josiah she was entirely equal to the experience of hearing the term applied to him.

But Josiah was adamant, and the Woodleys parted on Thursday evening with no expectation of seeing each other again until Josiah's trial was over.

"God keep you," Josiah whispered.

"God send you home," returned Rachel. "And if He delays you to test me, or as a lesson in patience or humility or something, I must tell you plainly I think it's—"

"Unjust?" Josiah finished for her, smiling. "Oh, there's some great lesson in it, no doubt. We just haven't figured out yet what it is."

*

At home, Kitty proudly informed Rachel that Mr. Gage had given up his job at the docks.

"It's not that he don't have any use for the money," she explained. (Kitty's interest in Mr. Gage's financial well-being was by now very keen.) "He done it because his gang boss wouldn't let him have time off to go to the courthouse. Mr. Gage wants Mr. Woodley to see plenty of friendly faces there. He'll come tomorrow at the dinner break to tell us if Mr. Woodley's been acquitted yet."

Kitty then added shyly, "We were thinking September, maybe. I mean, if you can spare me by then."

Her mind on her husband, it took Rachel a moment to understand what Kitty was saying.

"Of course I can spare you to your own home, Kitty!" she cried then, smiling. "How could anyone deny you that? And autumn is a beautiful season for a wedding. I look forward to dancing at yours."

Though her smile was forced, Rachel's words and subsequent kiss were sincere.

Sensing this, Kitty returned the kiss, added a warm hug, and clung on for a minute. "I think I might be the happiest person in the world right now," she exclaimed, a sob in her throat, "if only Reverend Woodley was here too!"

It was Rachel's turn to cling and cry. "Don't put off being happy, Kitty," she murmured. "Not for Mr. Woodley or for anything at all.

When life sends you joy, be joyful." To herself she thought that if, as Josiah said, there was some "great lesson" to be learned from the preceding months of misery, maybe she had grasped it at last.

*

Friday morning was a hundred years long.

Kitty divided the time between boiling a chicken (Dan was very fond of boiled chicken) and running to the window to see if he—or better still, Dan and Mr. Woodley together—was coming up the walk yet. Instead, the midday dinner bells at the mills had rung, and the end-of-dinner bells, too, before Dan finally arrived—alone.

Having been warned that seats at the courthouse filled up quickly, he had gotten up before dawn to be sure of securing one. "Some people paid a boy to come and sit for them," he reported, "but I wasn't going to waste my money paying a boy to do what I could do myself for free."

Kitty beamed her approval of Dan's thrift.

The morning's court cases (which Dan seemed to have dozed through) concerned lesser matters, the young man reported. Mr. Woodley's trial wouldn't begin until the afternoon. Having said that much, Dan quickly fell to enjoying the boiled chicken.

Rachel, meanwhile, could eat nothing.

Dan returned again in early evening—still alone, to Kitty's surprise and disappointment. Over cold chicken and salad he broke the news that Josiah's case wouldn't be heard until Saturday at the earliest. "They've got to pick a jury first," he said.

"Oooh! Saturday!" Kitty clapped her hands happily. To Rachel, she said, "Then maybe Sunday morning, you and Reverend Woodley can walk to church together like you used to!"

Rachel pretended to like this suggestion, while secretly thinking she wasn't entirely sure she ever wanted to see the inside of the Milltown church again.

At ten o'clock on Saturday morning, a little ragged boy brought a message from Dan that Josiah's jury had been chosen. Shortly after noon, Dan himself arrived.

Rachel thought immediately that his manner seemed slightly furtive, though she didn't mention it.

"Not too much happened yet," he said, in response to Kitty's eager questions. "Mr. Woodley's statement was read out, from when he was arrested."

"His statement at arraignment," Rachel suggested.

"That's it," Dan agreed. He avoided Rachel's eye. "The clerk read it, and then asked Mr. Woodley if he wanted to change anything."

"He said 'no,' of course," Kitty put in wisely.

"Right. Then the judge asked if he wanted to change his plea from 'not' to 'guilty,' and he said no to that, too."

"And how did he sound?" Rachel asked. "Was his voice steady?"

"Oh, yes. He sounded just like he always did in church. No different at all."

"And his face?"

Dan had not seen Josiah's face. "Got his back to the courtroom," he explained.

After that, Dan continued, Mr. Fisher had made a goodish-length speech to the jury outlining his case. Dan's attitude regarding Mr. Fisher's case was sneering. Whatever was causing Dan's apparent unease, it was not the strength of Mr. Fisher's case.

"Then it was Mr. Dodd's turn," Dan said.

"And what did Mr. Dodd say?"

"What Mr. Dodd said was he wouldn't talk long, and he didn't." When Kitty started to exclaim, Dan added quickly, "He said he didn't need to, because the witnesses would tell the jury the facts, and the facts would speak for themselves."

Rachel thought this over. "I rather like that strategy," she admitted.

Dan seemed reassured. "Then a Seabury man was called up. I don't remember his name. He had to get straight back to Seabury, so the judge agreed Mr. Fisher might call him right off."

The Seabury man testified he'd once seen Josiah and Mary Hale talking alone together, Dan said.

At Rachel and Kitty's simultaneous groans, he added quickly, "But I think it's all right, because when it was Mr. Dodd's turn, Mr. Dodd pointed out that Mary and Reverend Woodley couldn't have been talking secretly if the witness fellow had seen them. When the witness fellow said, 'well, they meant to be secret,' Mr. Dodd asked him how he knew what they meant. The two of them went back and forth until the man admitted the two of them were only on the church porch. There's no scandal in two people talking on a church porch."

"People can make scandal out of anything," Rachel said bitterly. Kitty reached to squeeze her hand. "And then?"

"Then the sheriff was called. He was supposed to be first, except the man from Seabury had to go first like I said. Did you know the sheriff's first name is Virgil? *Virgil.*"

Kitty giggled.

"Who cares what his name is? What did he *say*?" Rachel demanded impatiently. Virgil?

"Just what he saw at the woodyard," Dan replied. "He didn't take long, and Mr. Fisher didn't have any other questions for him."

"And Mr. Dodd?"

"All Mr. Dodd asked was if the sheriff stood by what he'd said about Miss Hale's neck being broken, and the sheriff said he did. Then the sheriff was excused, and Dick from the woodyard was called. You know Dick, I think. Tall fellow."

Rachel remembered the oldest of the woodyard boys had been much the tallest of the three. "What did Dick say?"

"Mostly the same things as what the sheriff said. About Miss Hale's...body. Mr. Fisher asked him about the knot."

"Did Dick say it was tied in a clove hitch?"

"That's right."

"I can tie a clove hitch!" Kitty put in.

"I wish you'd been there, then," said Dan soberly. "Because after Dick, Mr. Fisher got a mill girl on the stand to say she'd never heard of a clove hitch knot before in her life."

While Kitty, sputtering, declared her willingness to go to court first thing in the morning to swear any girl could tie a clove hitch as good as a man, Rachel asked Dan what questions Mr. Dodd had put to the woodyard boy and the mill girl.

"Mr. Fisher'd made quite a lot of the business of Miss Hale's feet being on the ground when she was found, but Mr. Dodd made him say the kind of rope she was hung by was soft, and might've stretched."

It was extremely important, as all three of them knew, to establish that the fatal rope might have stretched post-mortem. Dan seemed to feel the point had been adequately made.

"And the mill girl?"

Mr. Dodd had asked no questions at all of the mill girl, Dan said.

"So she was let go," he continued, "and then the letters found in Miss Hale's hymnbook were passed around the jury."

"And—?" Rachel asked hopefully.

Dan leaned back in a thoughtful posture, hands linked behind his head. "Well, first Mr. Fisher pointed to this and that thing in them, and said they were writ all in one hand, and then Mr. Dodd pointed to this and that other thing in them and said they weren't. The judge finally just told the jury to decide for themselves who was right."

The contrasting colors of the letter paper had not been mentioned at all—to Rachel's annoyance.

"And then?"

"And then the lawyers talked some with the judge and some with each other, and then court was adjourned for the day," Dan concluded. "That's all."

Rachel stood. "I should go to the jail. Is Mr. Woodley's supper packed, Kitty?"

Wholly unexpectedly, Mr. Gage caught her arm. "No," he blurted. "Beg your pardon, Mrs. Woodley, but the sheriff said I should keep you away tonight." When Rachel stared at him, he added, shamefaced, "He said Mr. Dodd needs time to talk to Mr. Woodley alone."

Rachel saw that the young people must have had time to exchange a few private sentences before she herself had been aware that Dan was in the house, for as Dan spoke, he looked at Kitty. The girl took it upon herself to explain gently, "It's just that no one's come from the church. To the trial, I mean. And people are saying it's…peculiar. Mr. Dodd wants to talk to Mr. Woodley about it and he said it'd be better for you not to be there."

Rachel was too stunned to answer this immediately. Surely the clergy and church elders all knew what the jury might construe from their absence! Groping for her handkerchief, she whispered, "Oh, my poor darling! My poor Joe!"

Another look passed between Dan and Kitty, and jumping up from her chair, Kitty embraced Rachel and offered what comfort she could. "Don't you worry," she said, her voice shaking with indignation. "Mr. Woodley has got God on his side. That's what matters."

"No," snapped Rachel, pulling away. "What matters is that the devil appears to have got the deacons and ministers on *his*! Oh, what am I going to do? Those men will break Josiah's heart, and the sheriff will hang him!"

Kitty turned suddenly practical. "We'll have to come up with something to beat the devil, then," she said. "What beats the devil, Danny?"

"Fire and brimstone," the young man suggested.

Rachel was about to say—crossly—that she unfortunately happened to be fresh out of brimstone at the moment when a different answer occurred to her. "Armor," she said. "And the belt of armor is truth."

"Oh, the truth's good," agreed Kitty. "My mother always says, 'tell the truth and shame the devil,' so truth must work."

Truth must work, Rachel repeated silently to herself. Truth was all she had.

The next day was Sunday, but Rachel did not go to church. She dressed as though she intended to do so, but after sending Kitty home in time to attend services with her family, she went back upstairs and sat in the front bedroom like another Sophronia, secretly watching her neighbors as they streamed by on their ways to Sunday services. Like a soldier, she was preparing herself for a battle.

CHAPTER TWENTY-SIX

*A*s Dr. Conrad turned to close the parlor door behind him, he was startled to hear Rachel Woodley's voice. "Good day, Doctor," she said. Rachel had seated herself where she'd sat on her previous visit, in the chair beneath Sophronia Conrad's picture.

In a pleasant tone, but warily, Dr. Conrad returned her greeting. "We missed you at service this morning. I was afraid you might be ill."

"No, not ill," Rachel answered. "Only sickened."

The minister's face showed he didn't quite know what to make of this remark, or what to say in return. Instead of replying to it, he said, "Rebecca didn't tell me you were here."

"She doesn't know. I let myself in, at the back. I believe no one saw me come, and no one but we two need ever know that we met today."

Though clearly more and more taken aback, Dr. Conrad maintained a determined calm. "Why such secrecy?" Taking his own place at the small table, he glanced at the window blinds, which were still lowered as he had left them. "If you are afraid of scandal, why come alone, or at all? I would gladly meet you in my office at the church at any time. Shall I ask Rebecca to sit with us?"

"I don't think you should," Rachel replied. "I don't think you would like for her to hear what I have to say. No, I'm not afraid of scandal. Nor, what is more to the point, of sin. I'm a little afraid of gossip, and so should you be. There is so much of it about." Abruptly, she leaned forward. "I didn't see your fur hat on the stand, Doctor. How do you keep it in the warm months? Do you like camphor, or have you a cedar box?"

It took Dr. Conrad a little time to adjust his brain to this unceremonious change of topic—and to the sudden realization that the hallstand, where hats and coats were hung, did not lie on the way between the kitchen door at which Rachel had entered and the room in which they now sat.

"Cedar, I believe," he said guardedly. "But if it's advice on housekeeping you seek, perhaps you would like to come at another time, when Sophronia is well enough to talk to you."

"You have a fur hat, then."

Dr. Conrad laughed. "I have misunderstood you." He leaned back in his chair. "I thought the existence of the article was already established, and you only wished to know how I keep it from the moth. Yes, I have a fur hat. It's a terrible old thing, with nothing to recommend it but that it is very warm to wear. I wonder whether I need take any steps at all to preserve it at this stage. I doubt that by now the moths would think it a desirable abode."

Rachel did not answer this beyond a nod. Nor did she take her eyes from his face.

After an uneasy moment, and still attempting a light tone, Dr. Conrad said, "My friend Dodd has told me all you have done on your husband's behalf. It hasn't been easy for you, I'm sure. You have great reserve, and your exertions have obliged you to deal with so many and such various people. You must be glad to be done with it all."

"I shall be glad," agreed Rachel, "when it has proved effectual, and Josiah is free of any charge against him."

"He will have you most to thank when he is."

"He is thankful already. To me, and to God."

"Yes, of course."

They sat in silence for a moment. Then Dr. Conrad began again, in a friendly tone, "I saw Mr. Woodley yesterday. He seemed in very good spirits. But then, he usually is, isn't he? It's the effect of a quiet conscience, I suppose. There was a little despairing at the first, but it soon passed off, and his inner peace and fortitude have been an inspiration to me. And, indeed, to all of us."

Though Rachel's face burned, her voice was cold. "I am always pleased to hear Josiah's praises sung. But I find it unsettling that you, of all people, should speak of his fortitude. Is *your* conscience quiet, Doctor? While Josiah has been suffering the cold and the shame and the loneliness and the vermin, and you have slept safe in your own bed, have *you* been all at peace within?"

Dr. Conrad recoiled slightly. "I'm afraid I don't quite comprehend you. We are all most truly sympathetic to Mr. Woodley's sad situation— by which I mean, of course, that we do indeed suffer with him, though our sufferings are probably less than his own."

"Your conscience doesn't trouble you, then?"

"My heart troubles me on Mr. Woodley's behalf. But my conscience—no. Why should it?"

Her anger overcoming her, Rachel hissed, "Because Josiah never killed the poor girl who was seen on the night she died in the company of a tall clergyman with a fur hat. It struck me from the first there was more than one tall clergyman in this town. Foolishly, I imagined for some time you were neither of a character nor an age to reasonably provoke my suspicion."

Dr. Conrad sat back in his chair and studied Rachel thoughtfully.

Finally he said, "You are making a very serious accusation of which you have no proof. I understand. I know you've been under a great deal of strain. Therefore, I don't hold anything you may say against you. But I do warn you against making such an accusation publicly, where it might be heard by some who would not be as charitable as I."

"Look in your desk, and tell me what color notepaper you see there," Rachel suggested. "The notepaper on which you write letters, and with which you sometimes mark the place in your prayer book."

Dr. Conrad did not move.

"You won't look?"

"Why should I? I know what color paper I have," he said. "It's paper of a very common sort, and color."

"I haven't found it so," Rachel said. "And I've made a study of the matter. And your hat? I came on purpose to find out about that. Not five minutes ago you admitted to me you own a fur hat such as witnesses describe the man seen with Mary Hale wearing on the night of her death."

"Another common object."

"Though again, not so common that Josiah has one. And what about those witnesses? The ferryman, and the tavern keep, and the rest? When they identified Josiah, they were in want of other suspects. But if you were made to stand before them, might they not see their error? Was Mrs. Conrad aware you went out that night?"

Dr. Conrad stiffened suddenly. "Don't involve my wife," he said in a tone of clear warning. "You will find me much less indulgent of you if you attempt in any way to involve my wife."

"Your wife has enough to suffer," Rachel agreed bitterly. "Nor has anyone any need to ask her anything. Your girl Rebecca would give much better testimony."

Dr. Conrad looked past Rachel to the small portrait on the wall behind her.

After a moment, he asked, more calmly, "Why did you come to me? Why not go to the sheriff with your baseless accusations? Go and see whether he will permit you to swear out a complaint against me."

Though this suggestion in fact gave Rachel pause, she exerted herself to answer back with an appearance, at least, of confidence. "I will if I must. Tomorrow, should the verdict go against my husband, I intend to go to the sheriff—or straight before the judge, if that's what I need to do. I will present my evidence against you then and there. I'd prefer to leave you to God to deal with, but I'm not going to let Josiah be hanged for your crime."

It was John Conrad's turn to flush. "No, no," he said quickly. "I have done, and will do, everything in my power to save Mr. Woodley myself. Nevertheless, I think you are playing a dangerous game if you imagine you will vindicate your husband by turning suspicion on me instead. I've lived in this town much longer than you have and am much better known here. And then, what will be the response to your allegations if they aren't believed? That you are a woman unbalanced by grief, probably."

Rachel's tone became weary. "What matter if people think that?" she asked. "I'm certain there are many who say as much, or worse, of me now. Let me be clear, sir: I came to warn you it would be in your own interests to see to it my husband is discharged a free man. If I accuse you, whether or not anyone believes me, and however much opprobrium accrues to me for doing so, your reputation will suffer. It's the nature of these things."

Dr. Conrad leaned forward again, and said with sudden intensity, "Mrs. Woodley, I did not murder Mary. My hanging would be as much a miscarriage of justice as your husband's. I beg you to believe me in this."

Rachel looked at him with scorn. "Luckily for you, I *do* believe you. I think Mary Hale hanged herself. But you left a despairing young girl alone in a dark woodyard, and what happened after that is more your fault than hers."

The minister looked guiltily aside. "What do you want of me?" he asked then. "What can I do that will help?"

It was the question Rachel had come hoping to be asked.

"I want you there in the courtroom tomorrow," she said, her voice rising. "I want you, and I want Mr. Tudge, and I want as many of the deacons as you can get. And arrive early. I'm told the seats fill quickly, and I want you where Josiah can see you. No skulking at the back."

Dr. Conrad slightly nodded. "I will speak to the deacons, of course. Naturally, I cannot command a fellow minister."

"No, Mr. Tudge must come. I don't care how you do it. I want both of you there as well as some deacons. And I want you *seen* to be there. Not just by Mr. Woodley, but by the whole courtroom. Do I make myself clear?"

Dr. Conrad's eyes flickered.

After a long pause he remarked, in what seemed to Rachel to be an irrelevant turn of the topic, "Do you know, there are rumors about the town that someone has written to the church board in Boston undermining my authority."

Rachel rose and smoothed her skirts. "If you mean to imply it might have been me," she said coldly, "I must inform you that you are entirely mistaken. Now go and distract Rebecca from the kitchen, and I'll go out the way I came. Good day to you, Doctor. Please convey my kindest regards to your wife."

Chapter Twenty-Seven

fter leaving the Conrads' house, Rachel went straight to the jail, where it was clear from the sheriff's face he believed Saturday's testimony had *not* been a triumph for the defense.

Mr. Dodd, however, was cheerful.

"It's true that Fisher scored many points," he acknowledged. "But it was always my plan that he should. We will score our hits just before closing, so they'll be fresh in the jurymen's minds while they deliberate." In response to a muttered comment of the sheriff's, Mr. Dodd added briskly, "Yes, the exultation of the millhands at every point Mr. Fisher made was bound to have its effect on the jurors' minds,"—Rachel had not heard before of the millhands' rejoicing—"but don't forget that many of the mills' *owners* are members of the Reverend Mr. Woodley's own church. By tomorrow, I expect they will have made it plain to their employees that anyone seen at the trial rather than at the mill forfeits his employment."

Rachel's spirits rose a little. This was likely to be true, she thought, since it was exactly Mr. Gage's situation.

The attorney shook the sheriff's hand, and—when she shyly offered it—Rachel's. "I was sorry to miss hearing Mr. Tudge preach this morning," he told her, with a covert wink for the sheriff. "But duty obtruded. And now I must go. There are a few witnesses I still need to see."

When the sheriff escorted Rachel upstairs, she discovered Josiah was no longer alone there.

Men from smaller towns and hamlets around Milltown whose cases would be heard after Josiah's had been brought in from wherever they'd previously been held to await their own turns before judge and jury. The chair had been removed from the tiny single cell and replaced by a pallet on which a young man now rested uncomfortably, his hands folded behind his head and his gaze fixed on the stained ceiling above, while what Rachel continued to think of as "Mr. Brown's cell" was shared by two men.

These were presently arguing over which of them should have the narrow cot to sleep on, and which the floor. Seeing the sheriff, they appealed to him in the matter.

"Why can't we have that other cell?" one asked, indicating Josiah's. "There's room for *two* beds in that one."

Knowing Josiah as she did, Rachel was certain only absence of mind prevented his agreeing at once to the proposal.

The sheriff, on the other hand, replied to this suggestion with contempt.

"You boys only get one cot," he said, "because only one of you *deserves* a cot, see? Other one deserves the floor—or worse."

The two men looked at each other.

"Well—but which one?" one demanded. "We both done—that is, we're both *charged* with doing robbery, though I done nothing of the kind."

"Nor me!" the second man put in quickly.

"So which of us deserves the floor, then?"

The sheriff didn't bother to answer this until he had placed the chair for Rachel's convenience.

Then he said, pulling a pack of worn cards from an inside pocket, "Fellow deserves the floor is the one that loses. And see you settle it with the cards and not your knuckles. I hear any fighting up here, I'll show you both what's worse than a jailhouse floor to sleep on." He tossed the pack between the bars and turned away.

A noisy contest between the men for the privilege of "first deal" gave the sheriff a chance to say quietly to Rachel, "They'll make enough noise none of 'em will hear a thing you say. Stay as long as you want, Mrs. Woodley."

Josiah did not want to talk about the trial.

"What is there to say?" he asked wearily. "The outcome will be as God wills."

"Let's talk about what we will do after, then," Rachel suggested. "When all this is over, do you think we will stay in Milltown, or do you think the church will want to send us someplace else?"

This attempt at conversation provoked a response—though not the one Rachel might have wished for.

"Where we go may not be decided by the church at all," said Josiah grimly. "There's a rumor afoot I'm to be struck from the clergy."

Rachel had not heard this, but immediately thought of the Reverend Mr. Tudge and his wife. They were capable of conniving at such a thing.

For Josiah's sake, she pretended to find the idea preposterous. "Never! But let's imagine for a moment it did happen. It would mean we could go anywhere we liked. Where would you pick?"

"The moon?" he suggested glumly.

"Too cold." Rachel moved her chair closer and reached through the bars to take Josiah's hand. "Pick someplace pleasant."

After further urging, Josiah exerted himself to enter into the spirit of things. After rejecting—among other possibilities—Boston and Paris, France, the Woodleys decided at last upon the Illinois frontier. "You could teach in a school," Rachel said. "You'd be a good teacher."

There was not much of substance either could say on the subjects of Illinois, or of teaching. Neither had been to Illinois, and Josiah had never considered being a teacher before. But for want of other safe topics, the Woodleys—their hands clasped and their heads close— tirelessly repeated to each other the few facts either knew about frontier life and students, hoping in their hearts, meanwhile, that Monday would indeed bring them the wished-for new start. Neither noticed the sheriff's repeated visits, or the boisterous conversations and occasional squabbles of the other inmates.

"May I not come to court tomorrow?" Rachel begged—not for the first time—as she was leaving.

But Josiah would not hear of it, and Rachel had been raised to believe a husband's word must be his wife's law. She went to bed that night with no intention of disobeying him.

She rose the next morning, however, fully resolved to do so. Should the verdict be unfavorable, she told herself, Josiah must not be left to face it alone.

At breakfast, a glance at Rachel's black dress and heavy veil told Kitty immediately what she had planned.

"Oh, that's a good thing to wear," Kitty said approvingly. "Nobody would dare bother a lady in mourning. Remember to leave something on your chair, like a handkerchief or such, when you come back to dinner. That will keep your seat for you."

Though the sun was scarcely up, when Rachel got to the courtroom, the first four rows of chairs were already full, mostly occupied by boys and old men who had not come to view the trial themselves, but been hired to hold places for others. Rachel managed to secure a good seat in the sixth row by fixing her eye on a still-empty chair and heading determinedly toward it. Two men advancing on the same spot immediately backed away. Kitty had been right that no one would want to be seen contending with a woman in deep mourning.

When Rachel looked around, she was surprised to see how casually the gathering spectators in the courtroom mingled. The rich rubbed elbows with the poor, the professional and tradesman with the farmer and factory hand. This was a sight she had never witnessed in town meetings or in church. She supposed it was because they were all men. Only women, it seemed, could be tainted by association with the "wrong" sort of person. Mr. Dodd was circulating, chatting cordially with all, his thumbs looped like a bumpkin's through the armholes of his waistcoat. As Rachel knew from Dan Gage, in his opening statement Mr. Fisher had characterized the defense counsel as "a pair of city-born fellows unfamiliar with our country usages." Mr. Dodd's present affability, Rachel suspected, was intended to counteract the remark.

Mr. Tyrode, on the other hand, sat stony-faced at the defense table and spoke to no one.

Rachel had sat for a quarter hour, trying not to notice how she was stared at from all sides, when the attention of everyone was suddenly drawn to the doors at the back of the courtroom by the tramp of many feet. A moment later she watched, astonished, as the Reverend Dr. Conrad, followed by a dozen black-coated deacons, streamed up the center aisle.

Through sudden tears, Rachel counted them. Not a single deacon was missing. Mr. Tudge came last—glowering, but duly present. By what means, Rachel wondered, had Dr. Conrad gotten him there? When she had denied being the "someone" attempting to undermine him, had Dr. Conrad concluded Mr. Tudge must be the guilty party? Had he *blackmailed* the younger minister into coming?

Rachel discovered she no longer found such a thing as blackmail among the clergy impossible to believe.

Meanwhile Mr. Dodd, while appearing to look idly around the room, managed to catch her eye and touch one finger to his forehead in salute.

When the courtroom was completely full, every chair occupied and late comers standing shoulder-to-shoulder in a double row around the back and sides, the bailiff called the spectators to order as a door behind the judge's bench opened, and Josiah at last appeared.

He was not, as Rachel had feared to see him, loaded with chains. In fact, aside from being a little pale, her husband looked as he always did. He saw her and smiled slightly—a smile that appeared rueful, but not at all surprised.

An instant later, his gaze fell on the black-clad row of clergy and deacons.

Rachel had never seen Josiah more joyful—not even on their wedding day, when she'd started toward him on her father's arm. His face shone as though he'd caught nothing less than a glimpse of heaven's glory. Deacon Birdwell caught his eye and pressed his palms together to indicate Josiah was prayed for, and Dr. Conrad (Rachel could forgive him much for it) smiled and bowed. Josiah was too happy to notice when Mr. Tyrode placed a beaver hat trailing a long crêpe "weeper" from its brim before him on the defense table.

Some court business was dealt with, and then the first witness of the day, the tavern keeper's wife, was called to take the stand.

Her testimony was exactly what she had told Rachel: Between ten and eleven o'clock on the night Mary Hale was killed, a tall clergyman had stepped into her tavern and asked for food. When informed none was available, he left. The exchange had taken, the woman thought, less than five minutes, and the tall man had been a stranger to her. She stated first that she did not remember his face, but when instructed to, she studied Josiah's and agreed it was like.

"Dark eyes, anyway," she said. "And no beard."

"And is it usual for you to have much custom late at night?" Mr. Fisher asked.

The woman said it was not.

"Do you think this man was out because he had some *business* being out?"

Before Mr. Dodd could finish objecting to this question as leading, the publican's wife answered it.

"Not honest business. Not at that hour."

Mr. Dodd, when it was his turn, merely reminded the witness of what she had said—that she did not know the man who came to her tavern on the night Mary Hale died. (He always spoke of Mary Hale as having died, Rachel noticed. He never used the descriptors "murdered," or "killed.") He made her repeat that the man had been tall, then asked what kind of hat he wore.

"Fur," said the tavern keeper's wife.

"Like that one?" Mr. Dodd asked, pointing at the felted beaver top hat before Josiah.

"No. Fur, I said."

"Fur like—oh, say…the pelt of a rabbit?"

"Yes, like that."

Mr. Dodd fixed the jurymen with a look. "The Reverend Mr. Woodley has stated he has no such hat."

Mr. Fisher—predictably—rose from his seat to counter that the court had only Mr. Woodley's word on the subject.

"Produce the hat, and I will withdraw my statement," replied Mr. Dodd, and a ripple of laughter—quickly suppressed—ran through the jury box.

"You say the man was tall," continued Mr. Dodd, musingly. "Might his apparent height only have been the effect of his long coat and fur hat?"

The witness glanced at Mr. Fisher before answering, but then said she supposed it might.

Mr. Dodd excused her without further questions. He dare not ask any, Rachel thought bitterly, for fear the answers to some of them might cast suspicion on a certain old friend of his.

Mr. Fisher summoned a few more witnesses to the stand, but these were questioned only briefly and dismissed without, Rachel felt, doing perceptible damage to Josiah's defense.

With a smile Rachel found intolerably smug, Mr. Fisher then announced his final witness. She did not know the name he called, but it was prefixed with the alarming title of "professor." Thwarted, like Mr. Dodd, in his efforts to make Dr. Brown testify, for his last witness Mr. Fisher had summoned an expert.

Unnerved, Rachel was about to reach for her handkerchief to fan her heated face when it occurred to her that many in the courtroom, including some of the jurymen, must by now have recognized her as the defendant's wife. The least demonstration of fear on her part might be interpreted by them as anxiety that evidence damaging to Josiah's case was about to be exposed. By an effort of will, she managed to assume a serene expression, and in defiance of convention, she turned back her veil to show it to the world.

The learned professor—the words "learned" and "professor," Rachel had always understood, were inseparable—was a thin man, nearly outweighed by the two large leather-bound books he carried. These, he explained before anyone had time to ask him, were medical volumes containing depictions of the gravid female anatomy *so unflinching* the courtroom would have to be cleared before the jurors could be allowed to view them. Not a man on the jury knew the meaning of the word "gravid" (Rachel didn't either), but "female anatomy" was clear enough, and the jurymen sat up with interest.

The judge did not like to be told when his courtroom needed to be cleared.

"Professor Smithson," he growled, "before you speak further, please be sworn."

The swearing-in was accomplished, but the judge, still annoyed, refused to order the spectators to leave. Over Mr. Fisher's startled protests—the advocate had clearly been certain the point would carry—the judge instead advised the professor merely to be "discreet" in how he showed his pictures.

"And mind your language," he added. "Speak as you would if ladies were present."

The "if" made it clear he felt any woman spectating in a courtroom was not a lady.

Mr. Fisher began, "You are a professor of anatomy at the college in New Haven, are you not, sir?"

Professor Smithson, it immediately developed, was a man eager to share all he knew. No further questions were necessary to prompt him to speak at length of his early life, his education, various accolades and awards he had won, and—eventually—to explain how, by means of comparing the plates in his books with the notes about Mary Hale's unborn child's development Dr. Brown had made at her inquest, he had incontrovertibly determined Miss Hale was no more than three and a half months pregnant at the time of her death. As everyone in the courtroom understood—though the professor left it to Mr. Fisher to remind them—a three-months' child was one Josiah Woodley could have fathered.

Mr. Dodd challenged this assertion—though only perfunctorily, Rachel thought. "You were not a witness to the inquiry yourself, were you, Professor Smithson?"

The professor, visibly nettled at the inference, brandished his books.

"Ah, yes… Those books." Mr. Dodd, the possessor of a cherished and over-stuffed bookroom, flicked his hand in a gesture dismissive of books. "Let's move on to those, shall we?"

At Mr. Fisher's recommendation, the anatomist came out of the witness box and stationed himself directly facing the jurors before beginning his testimony.

Initially avid, the jurymen appeared to quickly lose their taste for the "unflinching" pictures the professor displayed, but his confident manner and scholarly vocabulary clearly impressed them. Though most of the twelve only glanced—and a few would not look at all—where he pointed on his books' large colored plates, when Dr. Smithson announced, "I'm certain now that you are able to observe for yourselves the differences between a three month's fetus and a five month's fetus, you will agree I am perfectly right in what I say," the juror's heads—and, to Rachel's despair, many others in the courtroom—nodded agreement.

Mr. Dodd, when it was his turn, asked the professor no questions beyond obliging him to reiterate he had never seen Miss Mary Hale either alive or dead, and afterward dismissed him with another airy wave of his hand.

Mr. Fisher then rested his case, and a short recess was called. Rachel spent it wondering despairingly whether Mr. Dodd would now—finally—actually begin defending her husband.

The recess over, a Mrs. Wallace was called to the stand.

A moment's thought was necessary for Rachel to remember Mrs. Wallace was one of the ladies Dr. Brown had listed as among the midwives who had examined Mary Hale's body—a list she had then passed on to Mr. Dodd.

Mrs. Wallace had a thrusting chin, a decided manner—and evidently a touch of vanity, too. Once sworn and in the witness box, she took time to straighten her bonnet and arrange her shawl before replying to the bailiff's invitation to state her name and business.

"Midwife. Fifty years."

"And what is your connection with the case before this court?"

"I done the girl's inquest."

Before she could say more, Mr. Fisher sprang to his feet to remind the court it was, in fact, a certain *Dr. Brown* who had performed the inquest upon Mary Hale's body. Naturally, he did not miss the opportunity to repeat the news that Dr. Brown himself had declined to testify in the case.

"Oh, the doctor came all right—in his own good time," Mrs. Wallace agreed, smoothing her gloves. "Not that there was any need of him hurrying. What happened to the girl was perfectly clear."

"And what happened to her?" Mr. Dodd asked.

"The same as has happened to many like her," pronounced Mrs.

Wallace. "Being five months gone with a shame-child, she'd put a rope around her neck and jumped off a log pile to end things. Dr. Brown agreed with me about it and signed the papers saying so."

Mr. Fisher did not like this statement, and quickly rose again.

"Dr. Brown 'agreed' with you?" he demanded, eyebrows raised. "Surely it was for you, as only a midwife, to agree with a *trained medical man*?"

Mr. Dodd interrupted, "Your Honor, Prosecutor Fisher is out of order, isn't he? His opportunity to cross-question comes later."

He sounded amused, and the jurymen dutifully laughed.

Mr. Fisher conceded the point and even apologized. Mrs. Wallace was not entirely placated.

"Been midwifing fifty years, I said," she sternly reminded the attorney. "How long you been lawyering, son?"

Despite his objection of only a moment before, Mr. Dodd indicated to Mr. Fisher he was welcome to answer this question, if he liked.

Mr. Fisher apparently did *not* like. Sitting back down, he only muttered, flushing, "You trained with a woman, Mrs. Wallace."

"I trained with my mother, and yes, my mother was a woman," retorted the midwife. "And since you don't seem to know it already, I make bold to tell you *your* mother was a woman, too!" She swept the jury box—the whole courtroom—with a disdainful eye. "All you men come from women, and don't you forget it!"

At this, the crowd hooted with laughter—stifled when the judge reached for his gavel.

Mr. Fisher repeated the words "trained medical man" feebly, and subsided.

"Proceed, Mr. Dodd," the judge ordered.

Given license by Mr. Dodd to explain in her own words and time by what means she and the other midwives in attendance at Mary Hale's inquest had concluded the girl was fully five months advanced in pregnancy, Mrs. Wallace gave precise and minute testimony. In her description of the appearance of Mary's unborn child's fingers and toes, eyes, ears, and nose, Mrs. Wallace used words the jurymen were familiar with, and displayed no disturbing colored images.

"Would have been a little girl," she declared.

"You observed these things with your own eyes, of course," Mr. Dodd said, reminding the jurors with a look that Professor Smithson had never seen Mary. "Were there any marks of violence on Miss Hale's body?"

Mrs. Wallace said there were not.

It appeared to Rachel the midwife did a good deal of damage to the testimony of Mr. Fisher's expert—provided the jury did not discount it because it came from a woman.

When it was his turn to question the witness, the prosecutor quickly discovered that he could not, by any reasonable means, persuade Mrs. Wallace to retreat a single inch from any point she had made. Mary Hale's pregnancy was five months advanced, the midwife maintained, and she put no stock in indecent books that indicated otherwise.

"Medical books," contradicted Mr. Fisher.

Mrs. Wallace, lips primly pursed, repeated that the books were indecent. "What other kind of books but indecent can't be shown openly in a courthouse?" she wanted to know.

Several jurors nodded agreement with this. Rachel allowed herself to begin to hope again.

Mr. Cockburn was next called to the stand.

As long as Mr. Cockburn was in Mr. Dodd's hands, the only oath the ferryman had an opportunity to swear was the one to tell the truth. Such routine details as his name and occupation were supplied to the court by the lawyer himself, with the ferryman required to do no more than to affirm their accuracy.

"Been running the ferry ten years, da—!" he said in conclusion, successfully biting back a curse.

"Now, sir," continued Lawyer Dodd, "a story seems to have gotten around this town that you said you saw Miss Mary Hale and the defendant, the Reverend Josiah Woodley, walking together on the night of Miss Hale's murder. But this story is not accurate, is it? What you attested to the sheriff was only that on the night of Miss Hale's murder you saw a tall man in a long coat walking with a young lady with dark hair. Is that correct, Mr. Cockburn? Or did you in fact identify the tall man as Mr. Woodley, and the young lady as Miss Hale?"

Questions tightly strung together required only a single answer for all, which Mr. Cockburn gave. "No," he said.

"The witness must answer one question at a time," Mr. Fisher objected.

Mr. Dodd begged pardon, and tried again. "You attested you saw a couple walking, but you did not identify the couple as Mr. Woodley and Miss Hale, did you?"

The ferry master considered this. "That's right." He added, irrelevantly, "Pretty young lady she was, d—! I mean, she was pretty."

"At the time you made your attestation," Mr. Dodd continued, "you were not in a position to identify either Mr. Woodley or Miss Hale, because you had never seen either one of them before. Is that also correct?"

"Aye."

"And yet you are an observant man, are you not, Mr. Cockburn?

That is, you *would* have been able to identify them if you had seen them before, wouldn't you? Mr. Woodley crossed the river with you at a later date, and you not only remembered his face, but the fact that he carried a dog-skin valise."

"I did, aye."

"It stands to reason, then, that you would have recalled him as the man who, only a few days before, passed the ferry landing with a young lady *if he had been that man*."

Mr. Cockburn considered this. "Likely so," he agreed.

Looking at the jury, Mr. Dodd finished, "You did *not* recall that it was the Reverend Mr. Woodley because it was not the Reverend Mr. Woodley you saw walking with Miss Hale on the night she was killed. It was another tall man—and possibly, another dark-haired young lady."

Risking a few extra words, Mr. Cockburn agreed the tall man might have been Jehoshaphat for all he knew. "Tall man," he said, positively.

Mr. Fisher began his cross-examination as Rachel had already anticipated he would, by attempting to discredit Mr. Cockburn's testimony by discrediting Mr. Cockburn himself. He repeated some of Mr. Dodd's questions and demanded longer answers to them, though before more than two half "damns" and a complete, but indistinct, "bugger" had escaped the witness, Mr. Dodd put an end to this game.

Trying a new way to provoke an outburst, Mr. Fisher suggested meaningly, "You have long been a friend of the defense counsel, haven't you, Mr. Cockburn? A good enough friend to wish to help him where you can?"

Mr. Cockburn prided himself on his integrity, and was duly nettled by this remark. He contained himself, however, only repeating what he had already said, that he had never sworn the tall man who passed the ferry landing on the night of Mary's death was a clergyman.

"You would not help a friend?" Mr. Fisher pressed.

Mr. Dodd started to his feet, but Mr. Cockburn did not wait to be helped.

"Dammit," he said angrily, "I never said the fellow I seen walking with the lady was a parson, damn you! If he'd been a parson, damn him, I'd have known him, see? I'd have known him from my ferry, because where's the damn parson can afford to keep a damn carriage to cross by the bridge?"

The Conrads kept a carriage. The state of Mrs. Conrad's health required it, and the amount of her fortune made one possible. Mr. Dodd must have known this as well as Rachel did—but of course he did not mention it.

Mr. Cockburn refused to say more on the subject of what he would or would not do for a friend, and after being mildly rebuked by the judge for his language, he was permitted to leave the witness box.

Before the bailiff could call another name, the sheriff suddenly appeared at a side door, a young woman behind him. Rachel recognized the girl as Polly, Mary Hale's former roommate, and she was carrying a cloth-wrapped bundle Mr. Tyrode hurried to the door to take from her. Having laid the bundle across the table without unwrapping it, he sat back down looking, Rachel thought, much less gloomy than he had all the preceding week.

Mr. Fisher had apparently also observed the change in Mr. Tyrode's demeanor, for when at the judge's summons he joined Mr. Dodd in approaching the bench, the prosecutor wore a look of deep suspicion. A discussion with the judge, brief but intense, ensued.

"I will allow it," Rachel heard Mr. Fisher say finally. The bailiff called the court back into session.

In response to the name the bailiff now bawled out, another young woman—not Polly—hurried forward to take the witness chair. This girl was one who had been called to testify on the first day of the trial, Rachel discovered.

The judge required some moments to make it clear to the witness she would not be re-sworn, but should consider her earlier oath to tell the truth still in force. Once she had been reassured that this oath would expire when a verdict was announced in the case, the young lady—who agreed honesty was a good and virtuous thing but who did not want to find herself under any legal obligation to tell the whole truth and nothing but for the rest of her life—sat down.

After a few preliminary remarks, Mr. Dodd asked the young lady whether she remembered the name of the knot by which the woodyard boy had specified Miss Hale had been hanged. "He called it a clove hitch. Do you remember that?"

"Oh, yes. A clove hitch," the mill girl agreed eagerly.

"And you said you did not know it," Mr. Dodd reminded her. "Is that right? You cannot tie a clove hitch."

"No, sir."

"Do your friends at Number Four Mill know how to tie a clove hitch knot?"

Mr. Fisher rose to remind the court the point had been established earlier.

Mr. Dodd cheerfully conceded. "None of the young ladies said they knew the name of 'clove hitch.'"

He then retrieved the cloth-wrapped bundle from the defense table and opened it. Within was a wooden contraption, which he displayed to the jury.

"Now, miss," he said. "Can you tell me what this is called?"

The young spinner looked relieved to be asked a question she was well-qualified to answer. "Oh, yes," she said promptly. "It's a part of a spinning machine."

"A spinning machine such as you use in your work?"

"That's right. That there's what we call the yoke."

"Let me see," mused Mr. Dodd. "The threads, I suppose, must pass through this part here, mustn't they? And then what? Where do they go from there?"

"Why, to the spindles, of course."

"To the spindles. Thank you. And how many of these 'yokes' do you manage? You yourself. Do you attend only one?"

"Oh no," the girl answered, seeming slightly offended by the question. "I manage four spinning machines generally, and each one has a yoke, so that's four yokes. I can do as many as six, if I'm needed to—but not all day long."

"Six! Why, what a wonder you are, miss! Six machines at once! Now tell us, is this yoke the kind of yoke the spinning machine Miss Mary Hale worked had?"

"Yes. We only have one kind of machine in Number Four. Some of the other mills has got other kinds, but that's ours." She added several more details concerning the style of the spinning machines in the Number Four mill.

Rachel observed that Mr. Fisher, who had previously shown himself a restless man, was now sitting quite still.

"I see that this piece," Mr. Dodd continued, indicating with his hand the piece he meant, "is secured to this other part by leathern straps. Have I got that right?"

"Oh, yes."

"Leathern," Mr. Dodd repeated, looking at the jury. "And because they are leathern, do these straps ever break?"

"They do sometimes."

"And when they break, do the mechanics repair them for you? Do they repair or replace the leathern straps so you can continue to work?"

This question elicited a torrent of speech from the mill girl.

The mechanics, she complained, were too few and too busy. The proceeds from the output of four machines were necessary to her to meet her expenses, but it sometimes took hours, or even until the next day, for a broken machine to be serviced. "Not but what the mechanics aren't doing the best they can," she acknowledged, so abruptly Rachel wondered if she had spotted Number Four Mill's owner—her employer—in the courtroom somewhere.

"And if the mechanics are delayed," Mr. Dodd asked, "do you ladies sometimes take matters into your own hands?"

"Well, sometimes we have to," the mill girl said. "Sometimes we just have to up and fix it ourselves, the best we can."

Mr. Fisher raised one hand slightly, as though he were about to object, then let it fall back onto the table before him.

"And how do you do that?" Mr. Dodd continued meanwhile, one eye on Mr. Fisher. "How do you secure this piece to the rest of the 'yoke' if the leathern straps fail?"

"Well, what we do is we tie it up."

"Tie these two pieces of the yoke together?"

"That's right. We keep a bit of rope handy to do it with. I always have mine in my work apron pocket."

"Can you show the court?" asked Mr. Dodd. "I have no rope, but perhaps this cord will do." He retrieved a length of cord from his pocket as he said this—a piece identical to the kind found around Mary Hale's neck. "I'll unbuckle the strap, and you come here and show us how, if it were broken, you would mend it."

Mr. Fisher objected, on obscure grounds, and was overruled.

The mill girl left the witness box to do as she'd been asked, informing the court as she did so the trick only worked if just one strap had broken. "If it's more than one, only a mechanic can fix it," she explained. "And not even all of them."

Judging by the speed with which the girl performed the repair, Rachel guessed she must have tied up a yoke a hundred times before. "It's not good as new," the mill girl said, stepping back to show her work. "But it usually serves."

Mr. Fisher leaned back in his chair and folded his arms.

"Very clever!" exclaimed Mr. Dodd, looking closely at the cord. "But—what is this knot you used? Does it have a name?"

"That?" The girl looked blank. "Why, that's a yoke knot, I guess. I think that's what it's called. The other girls taught it me when I first went in the mill."

"Sheriff?" Mr. Dodd asked, turning.

Rachel had not noticed the sheriff was still present. He rose from a place some rows back in the courtroom and said as though he had expected to be asked, "I'd call it a clove hitch."

Mr. Dodd repeated portentously, "A clove hitch," but no one heard him. His voice was drowned by the sound of two hundred throats all gasping at once, followed by two hundred murmuring voices asking each other if the sheriff had really identified the knot the girl—the mill girl—had tied as a *clove hitch*.

Josiah managed a quick glance back at his wife, his expression as surprised as any in the courtroom.

"There's others call that knot a double hitch," the sheriff added, when the hubbub had died down. "I never heard it was a 'yoke knot' before, but it's the same knot any way you name it."

"Clove hitch; double hitch; 'yoke knot,'" said Mr. Dodd musingly. "This is a knot of many names, it seems." Raising his voice, he asked the sheriff, "By whatever name, it's the knot that was tied in the rope around Miss Mary Hale's neck, too, isn't it, sheriff?"

"Aye. That's the one."

"A knot this young lady—a spinner, like the late Miss Hale—has tied so many times, she could probably tie it in the dark. Could you do that, miss? Could you tie this knot in the dark?"

Mr. Fisher objected to this question—and was sustained, but Rachel didn't care. The jurymen were talking among themselves and for the first time looking openly—not sidelong—at Josiah.

From elation, Rachel was instantly gripped by cold fury when Mr. Dodd immediately announced that his case was closed. What had become of his pledge to supply the mill workers with someone other than Josiah to blame for Mary Hale's death?

She had no opportunity to demand an explanation. Though it was one o'clock, instead of adjourning to midday dinner, the judge called for closing arguments to be commenced at once.

Mr. Fisher spoke at length, revisiting every point of his case including the fur hat Mary's escort had worn, though it had never been convincingly linked to Josiah. In reference to Mary's pregnancy, he pronounced the words "three months" so many times Rachel thought she would never hear either word again without feeling a heave at her stomach. He made much of the victim's feet having rested on the ground when she was found, and referred to Josiah as a "seducer," a "debaucher," and a "calculating and base murderer." His medical witness was "the very learned doctor," while Mrs. Wallace, in contrast, was a "mere midwife," and "an ignorant female."

Rachel squirmed in her chair and struggled to read the jurors' faces.

Finally, it was Mr. Dodd's turn to speak. Rachel sat up straighter, and willed him to be very forceful.

Instead, the attorney was mild.

"Mr. Fisher's prosecution of this case was skilled and honest," he began. "But it was a case that should never have been brought. There is no murderer. The evidence clearly shows that in a fit of despair and using a knot known to probably every girl in every mill in Milltown, Miss Mary Hale went to a deserted place, tied a rope around her own neck, and after first climbing up, jumped down from a log stack to end her life."

With an eye, no doubt, on the mill workers, he went on to say, his voice as full and mellow as a pipe organ, "Miss Hale will one day face judgment before a higher tribunal than ours. Perhaps she has faced it already. And if she deserves mercy, mercy will be granted her there. Let us not second-guess that tribunal. Let the body of Mary Hale, as well as that of as her innocent child, continue to rest peacefully in consecrated ground."

Then, with his head bowed as though almost overcome by grief, Mr. Dodd sat down and stared at the table before him. He had spoken for no more than ten minutes.

It had been an affecting performance, Rachel conceded to herself, judging by how many masculine eyes in the courtroom required to be discreetly wiped. Whether it was enough to sway the jury now being instructed by the judge to deliberate the *facts* of Josiah's case, she did not know.

At half past two o'clock, and without time for more than one brief glance back at his wife, Josiah was led away, and the jury sent out.

Chapter Twenty-Eight

As soon as the jury was gone, there was a general stampede of spectators toward the courthouse doors. So great was the press of people that Rachel, wishing to go in the other direction, toward the defense table, could hardly advance a step.

The sheriff was aided by his authority, no doubt. Though he started from a place behind her, he reached Mr. Dodd before Rachel did, and as she approached, she heard Mr. Dodd saying to him, "When do the shifts at the mills let out? Should we expect trouble, do you think?"

Rachel stopped where she was to listen.

The sheriff, in a low voice, admitted that trouble was possible. "You better have somebody standing by to take you away. I have spoke to that Conrad fellow. He sent a boy to hire a carriage—closed—to get Reverend Woodley clear."

The absence of any honorific before the name of "Conrad" caught Rachel's attention—and Mr. Dodd's.

The lawyer said, with a shrewd look, "You have your own idea about things, do you, Sheriff?"

The sheriff stared stonily away and did not answer.

"God, I could do with a dram!" sighed Mr. Dodd.

Mr. Tyrode caught sight of Rachel then, standing far enough off (she hoped) to pretend she had heard nothing, and whispered in the senior attorney's ear.

Mr. Dodd turned. "Ah, Mrs. Woodley!" he exclaimed when he saw her. "My dear lady, you must go home to dinner. No, no, I will hear no argument on the matter. Go home, rest, and eat. You are tired, and there's no knowing how long the jury will be out—until tomorrow, perhaps."

Mr. Tyrode raised his eyebrows at this remark.

"Oh, you know farmers," Mr. Dodd said quickly. "They'll discuss crops and the weather for an hour before they move on to settling the case. Go home, Mrs. Woodley," he repeated. "Mr. Tyrode will see you safely to your door. I'll send for you in plenty of time to hear the verdict."

Dan came up just then—to Rachel's relief, since she had no wish to walk with Mr. Tyrode—and at the sheriff's direction, she and Dan left the courthouse by a side door.

*

At home, Kitty fussed, "Well, I did think you'd be home for dinner two hours ago, and you'd for sure bring Mr. Woodley with you. I made boiled beef—see?—and now it's near ruined."

"We'll turn it into soup and have it for supper," Rachel replied absently. "Mr. Gage, why did the sheriff say there might be trouble? What kind of trouble? What did he mean?"

Dan cast a longing eye at the beef. "He meant if the verdict doesn't go the way the millhands want it to. Once the mills start letting out, there's nothing to stop them coming down to the courthouse if they want."

"They don't want Mr. Woodley to be let go," grumbled Kitty. "Do you know I don't think they care much whether Mr. Woodley's guilty or not? They just want to see somebody punished for what happened to Mary."

Rachel silently agreed with this. "Is that why the judge called for closing arguments before the dinner break, and Mr. Dodd was so quick in summation? To get a verdict before the mills let out?"

Mr. Gage said it was. "Even if they're happy with what the verdict is, the millhands not want to wait for—." He didn't finish.

"Have some beef, Mr. Gage," Rachel said, walking out of the kitchen. "Have all you want. You've earned it."

*

Rachel sat alone with her thoughts.

The clock in the parlor continued to tick, its pendulum swinging back and forth as usual behind its painted glass panel. And yet, unaccountably, its hands did not seem to advance. Even after Rachel had drunk the broth Kitty silently set beside her; repeated all the prayers she knew; recited her time's tables to the twelves and all her favorite Bible verses, the clock stubbornly maintained that no more than an hour had gone by. Rachel walked to the window and stared out.

Not until the clock admitted to the passage of two hours did Rachel permit herself to return to the kitchen.

She found Kitty sitting alone there.

"Where is Mr. Gage? Did Mr. Dodd send for me?"

"Nobody sent," Kitty replied, getting hurriedly up from her chair. "Danny just went back to the courthouse to check on things is all. He'll come back for you when the time comes. Come near the fire. You look cold."

Rachel shook her head. "I believe I won't wait for Mr. Gage," she said decidedly. "If I can go to the courthouse at all, I can certainly go by myself."

"Yes, but not now you can't!" Kitty protested. "The mills will be getting out!"

Rachel ignored this. "Where did I leave my gloves? Have you seen them?"

Kitty looked like she intended to argue the point, but before either woman could speak, Dan burst into the room. He had entered the house at the front door—a liberty he had never before permitted himself, and a sure sign he had important news.

"They're back!" he cried. "The jury! They've got a verdict!"

"Gloves, Kitty," ordered Rachel faintly. Without arguing, Kitty thrust them into her hand. Dan offered his arm, and Rachel took it. "Can we run, do you think?" she begged as they crossed the parlor. "Do you think we can make it in time if we run?"

Petticoats precluded running, and when Dan and Rachel arrived at the courthouse, it was to find trial spectators already streaming out. They seemed in no great hurry, since judgment had already been pronounced. Though Rachel looked eagerly into every face that passed, she could not guess from them whether Josiah had been acquitted or not. All were equally sober; no one either wept or exulted. To Rachel's astonishment, the murmured snatches of conversation she caught in passing suggested the attention of most of the men had already turned to the next case to be heard, or to home matters.

Only when, as she came through the courthouse door, she saw Deacon Birdwell vault the rail dividing the onlookers from the court proper to shake Josiah's hand did Rachel know for certain her husband was a free man. She stood still, transfixed with joy, until Dan, who still held her arm, nudged her gently forward. Remaining courtroom observers, recognizing her, drew aside to let her pass.

The men gathered around the defense table did not see her.

Mr. Dodd was saying with his usual cheer, "Come along, Woodley. Come out and breathe the free air, why don't you?" He indicated the way toward the courthouse's back door.

"Come on, Reverend," the sheriff added, seizing Josiah's right arm as though were still his jailer. "You don't want to keep Mrs. Woodley waiting."

Rachel suddenly realized neither he nor Mr. Dodd had ever intended to summon her back to the courthouse.

"It's time we were gone, sir!" cried Mr. Tyrode, grasping Josiah's left arm. "Come this way—no, *this* way! We'll avoid the crowd."

Josiah caught sight of his wife, and throwing off both the sheriff and Mr. Tyrode, he reached for her.

"You did not doubt?" he whispered as he embraced her, to which Rachel replied untruthfully, "Not for a moment!" The preceding anxious months had taught her the value of a comforting lie.

The sheriff stirred restively. "I don't like what I'm hearing from outside. Come on, now, Reverend. Let's see if that coach has come up yet."

He took Josiah's arm again and attempted to lead him toward the door behind the judge's bench. Mr. Tyrode was going that way already, his face anxious; Mr. Dodd was donning his hat.

Rachel herself was agreeable to the idea of a closed carriage. It was Josiah who proved obstinate.

"I'm going this way," he announced, pointing toward the double front doors of the courthouse. Outside was Milltown's principal square. "I'm a free man. I'm going home by the door free men enter and leave by."

"Home is exactly where you're *not* going," contradicted Mr. Dodd. "We've got things all arranged. You're going to your sister's for a while, Woodley. You have wanted to see your sister, haven't you? A visit with her will be a pleasant thing for you and Mrs. Woodley, and when you come back, the mood of the town will be calmer."

"I'm a free man," repeated Josiah.

How had she ever imagined her husband was spiritless, Rachel wondered?

"Take my arm, darling," she said, offering it. "We'll walk home together."

The sheriff and Mr. Dodd exchanged looks. "Well, see you walk *fast* then," the sheriff reluctantly agreed, glancing around uneasily. "Once we get out the door, don't stop for nothing at all." To Dan he added aside, "You go out the back and get in that coach yourself. Pull down the shades and tell the man on the box to drive to the ferry like he was told. With any luck, there'll be those who see it and follow, maybe. I'll look after the Woodleys."

As they emerged from the courthouse, Rachel on Josiah's arm, Mr. Dodd (smiling genially) and the sheriff (glowering) behind, the lingering remnants of the crowd turned to stare. Someone, somewhere, pronounced the word "murderer."

Hearing it, Josiah drew Rachel protectively to him.

The sheriff had heard, too. "Now, Reverend," he muttered, eyeing the crowd warily, "why couldn't you just take the coach? What do you want to make so much trouble for?"

"I don't want to make trouble," Josiah said. "I just want to go home." He added politely to a man who deliberately blocked his way, "Excuse me, please. May I go by?"

Someone near the edge of the crowd shouted it, now: "Murderer!"

The sheriff, sighing deeply, pushed aside his coat to permit the crowd to observe the pistol in his waistband.

Mr. Dodd remarked, in his full, courtroom voice, "My, isn't it warm for the time of year?"

Some in the crowd, initially scattered about the square and surrounding streets, began to draw more purposefully together. One young man was—despite the sheriff's pistol—bold enough to run up and shove Josiah from behind.

Rachel, steadying her husband on his feet, swallowed nervously. What good would a single pistol be against a mob?

"To think I once characterized you as inclined to be too compliant, Woodley," commented Mr. Dodd, deftly diverting another reaching hand from Josiah's shoulder. "I think I would know better, now." He began, loudly, to sing a hymn.

"Oh, Lord," muttered the sheriff. It was not a prayer.

The decent people in the square were hurrying away, leaving Josiah's determined ill-wishers behind. Despite his obvious exhaustion, Josiah continued walking steadily in the direction of home, but his weary progress was slow, and they had still many blocks to go.

Between verses, Mr. Dodd asked Josiah with grim humor, "Explain again to me, if you would, why we are making this little stroll?" He warned off with a look another attempt at a disrespectful jostle.

"I want to go home," Josiah said stubbornly.

"But not in style, or you'd have allowed yourself to be driven there."

"I didn't entirely trust you to take me. Anyway, I might as well let it be known at once that as I have been acquitted of wrongdoing, I intend to conduct myself in future exactly as I did before I was accused. I live here. I'm an innocent man. I won't grin and cower like a beaten dog."

"Apparently not," Mr. Dodd agreed wryly.

There were further shouts of "murderer," and a "shame, shame" or two—but not too nearby.

"You're right to face them down, my love." Rachel squeezed his arm. Over her shoulder, she called back, "Josiah and I are going to Illinois, Mr. Dodd. Josiah's going to be a teacher."

"Leave this minute, and I'll send your things on to you personal," offered the sheriff dryly. "You, there! Stand aside unless you want to find yourself brung up on a charge of obstructing the public roadway!"

Mr. Dodd began another verse of his hymn.

The crowd parted to allow someone through. The sheriff's hand moved casually toward his waist.

The intruder proved to be only Mrs. Brown, carrying her youngest child in her arms and with her five older children and her husband following after. Mr. Brown, Rachel noted with relief, appeared sober. At a word from their mother, the little Browns recited in ragged chorus, "Good-evening-Reverend-and-Missus-Woodley!"

Glaring at the surrounding crowd, Mrs. Brown said loudly, "We just wanted to come to thank you both again for your help."

Josiah returned the well-wishes, and while Mr. Dodd distributed pennies to the children, the sheriff, seeing an opportunity, propelled Josiah forward again. The Browns followed, depriving pursuers of further chances to jostle Josiah from behind. By this means, the group gained another easy quarter-mile.

The angry millhands began to drop away. It was suppertime, they were hungry, and outrage was poor food. Seeing them going, the Browns also turned for their home, the children with a chorus of goodbyes. After a sharp look around, the sheriff allowed his coat to cover his pistol again.

Another block, and the four at last found themselves alone in the street, the Woodley house in view.

"I'll take my leave, if you don't mind," said Mr. Dodd, stopping. "It's been a pleasure; a positive pleasure. I hope the next time we meet, it will be under happier circumstances." He bowed over Rachel's hand.

The sheriff walked a short way in company with the lawyer, then turned back again to follow the Woodleys home. Josiah's arm was around his wife's waist now, and she rested her cheek against his shoulder. Both were unaware of the sheriff's presence five yards behind them. Entirely engrossed in each other, even when, at the porch steps, the two stopped to look back at the moon, they seemed to see only each other.

"It's like we're beginning our marriage all over, Joe," Rachel said in a low voice. "I think this time we'll get on better than we did before."

After a moment, Josiah asked hesitantly, "This new marriage of ours... Do you think it will it bring us children?"

Rachel realized suddenly she wanted children very much. She wanted children, and everything having children implied. Eyes shining, she whispered, "I don't see why not."

Alone in the dark, the sheriff made a slow tour of the Woodley yard, even looking under the porch and behind the woodpile to be sure no one was lurking in those places. When he was satisfied all was well, he sat down on the stump where the firewood was split, set the axe close at hand, and folded his arms. His job was to keep the peace, and he would watch all night to see that no one broke it.

By The Same Author

The *Antlands* series:
Book 1: Antlands
Book 2: Annasland
Book 3: Farlands

Other writing:
The Complete Raffles (Annotated & Illustrated)

Available now via your local Amazon store

About The Author

Genevieve Morrissey is a passionate student of British and American social history, but through one of those strange little quirks of fate she spends most of her days talking with scientists.

Marriage And Hanging is her first work of historical fiction.

She enjoys reading obscure books, travel, good cooking, and solitude.

Stay up to date with Genevieve and her writing via her web site:

antlands.com

Printed in Great Britain
by Amazon

42195685R00172